PRAISE FOR DAVID MARKSON

GOING DOWN

"Beautifully constructed. One of the most important books published in America in years." —Frederick Exley

"Breathes a low fire that sears the reader . . . an achievement of a rare kind." —*Louisville Courier-Journal*

"Reading it is like running barefoot over shards of beautiful broken glass." —*Women's Wear Daily*

VANISHING POINT

"With a deeply philosophical core, this novel proves once more that Markson deserves his accolades and then some . . . He has become a minor master." —*Publishers Weekly*, starred review

"Keeps up his near single-handed effort to keep American prose significant, deep, and subtle . . . Breathtakingly seamless perfection . . . brilliant, high, fine, masterful, deep." —*Kirkus Reviews*, starred review

"David Markson's books are stunningly true and wildly inventive. They are unsettling and consoling. They are full of strange echoes, paradoxes, and hilarious stories, and in their accumulations they are great homages to great art, celebrating the work of the imagination and at the same time reminding us of swift time and the fragility of cultural memory." —Joanna Scott

THIS IS NOT A NOVEL

"From the erudite and extraordinary Markson . . . subtle, inventive, ineffably moving." —*Kirkus Reviews*

"Magnificent . . . it's almost impossible to stop turning pages . . . my soul was humming." —Sven Birkerts, *New York Observer*

"Reads as addictively as an airport thriller . . . masterful." —*Bookforum*

"No, it's not a novel, but it is a masterwork." —*Publishers Weekly*

GOING
DOWN

A NOVEL

david markson

COUNTERPOINT
BERKELEY

Library of Congress Cataloging-in-Publication Data is available.
ISBN: 978-1-59376-064-9

Cover design by Gopa & Ted2

Printed in the United States of America

COUNTERPOINT
2560 Ninth Street Suite 318
Berkeley, CA 94710
counterpointpress.com

To Elaine, my wife

And to the memory of
Malcolm Lowry, a friend

The battle was fierce and the fighting intense. It was a memorable sight to view us all streaming with blood and covered with wounds; and some of us were slain. It pleased Our Lord that we should achieve the place where the image of Our Lady used to stand, but we did not find it there.

—Bernal Diaz del Castillo
True History of the Conquest of New Spain

GOING
DOWN

ONE

Accept the illusion. Night. Mexico. The immense, rife stillness of a village in the Mictlán hills . . . There are two cemeteries. This one, with its gutted chapel, has been long abandoned. Only the dark's fecund whisperings of pine and frond belie its destitution here at the roadside.

Yet there is a grave here that the girl knows. She will not think of it now, however, not yet, any more than she will question that she has ceased to run. Poised, as if thoughtful, now she is even calm.

But accept the girl too, where she enters amid the tumbled wood crosses and the sunken mounds, a girl quite lovely, and fair, whose left hand is deformed. A withered fist, it hovers abeyant without the heavy wool sarape that clothes her.

It is in that hand that the girl clutches the machete. Yet her face, her eyes, are vacant, without expression.

Or does she perhaps understand where she is, to what

part of the town she has fled? The whole of it is small, clustered about the precipitous hillsides of the lakeshore. Well beyond the central zócalo, she has emerged out of a labyrinth of plunging, irreconciled walled passages like scars upon earth. Perhaps too she is conscious of chill, of the sharp still clear mountain air.

Languishing and remote, the light that draws her now may be that of a solitary candle, deep within the ancient chapel. The building is stone, its ruined bulk spanned with high dark beams, windowless and forlorn. Within, it is desolate save for a massive stone altar at its rear. There is a stench of violation, of decay.

Between the great shattered doors the girl halts. Almost consumed, the candle burns fitfully upon the defiled floor at the altar's base, though there is no sign of another's presence. Later, the girl will remember this, will ask herself what deluded soul, venturing out of the bereavement of the Mexican night, had found solace in very abandonment to fix his poor glimmering offering here. Now, still, she asks nothing, thinks nothing at all.

Atop the altar, stark where such Christ as once it bore has been long since lifted bodily down, an enormous stone cross looms, one of its beveled arms smashed asunder. In the uncertain light it seems to list above her, and on the chapel's rear wall its misshapen shadow flickers and reaches, flickers and falls.

But there is a painting also, the girl perceives now, contrived upon the surface of the stone itself. Approaching, she finds it a pietà, though archaic and crude, and faded there, worn by time. Where they kneel with their burden of sorrow the several women are dim, shadowy, anonymous, despoiled. Yet this holds her, her gaze is fast.

Then, as at some abrupt sound behind her in the

outer darkness, the girl starts. There is a constant, un-diminishing hum of locust. "Is someone here?" she says. "Quién es?"

Her lips are pursed, and again her look might appear thoughtful. After a moment she steps around, making a complete turning about the altar. Where she halts, the distorted shadow is full upon her.

"Well, now who do I think I am talking to in this place?" she says.

So it is coming back now after all, or beginning to, if not quite clearly, not quite yet. Rather her eyes dart and flash, they confront again the mutilated Christ abject and streaming. And then movement, a sense of movement. Is there a dog? Is this now? Here? A dog gaunt and terrier-like, yet baleful, with pale, wet eyes that glitter and fade? Or was this earlier, amid ochered adobe walls in some rutted callejón, some tortured lane? Where?

There is no dog, though something scuttles into shadow near the great doors and is gone, perhaps a tarantula. "Dog?" the girl says. "When did I see a dog?" Now her expression, her voice, is almost plaintive. "Well, now what do I think I am doing in this place?" she asks.

Her hand is at her lips. When her other hand rises also, when she discovers the machete at last, she possesses the rest of it then, this simply, even the dreadful re-membered monody of her own cry, and yet it is without terror now—now there is only a slow, sick burgeoning of pain. "Oh, my dear Jesus," she whispers. "Oh, my dear God."

The sarape drops from her shoulders. Grasping the machete in both hands, slowly she goes to her knees amid the blanket's gathering folds. Only when she has set the blade at the base of the altar does her head lift, do her eyes close. A sob racks her naked body.

For a long moment then, where she kneels as if in terrible obeisance, her hands tremble above her thighs. Then her head falls, her hair spills golden and bright upon her breasts. "Lee," she says. "Oh, Lee—"

Silently, huddled, the girl weeps.

Yet she is somehow almost calm, almost composed, when she arises suddenly at the footfalls. Collecting the sarape about herself she does not even hurry. She has not quite concealed her nakedness when the man appears.

It is someone she knows, though not well. Already upon the threshold, between the askew doors, he has halted, and she understands that he will be here by chance alone. She says, "Doctor, hello—"

Her voice is steady, though her chest rises. As he stares, she says, "Hello, yes. Buenas noches." She is adjusting the blanket. "Excuse me. I seem to be undressed—"

Scowling, bewildered, the man stands. "Well, I've been running," the girl says. "Doesn't everybody run with their clothes off? I mean wouldn't they, rather?"

"Yes," the man says. "Running. I see."

"Now, damn it. All right, yes, I was sick. In fact, I suspect I came close to . . . but that would be just shock, wouldn't it? Because I think I screamed, too. And I've been chasing around town ever since, evidently—"

Again her eyes close, and she swallows deeply. Despairing, she thinks: Dear heaven, forgive me, but will he please see it now? Perhaps it is only vanquishment, only fatigue, but a queerly uncontrollable sensation of laughter takes her too, then. Or is it merely the abused cross, at which she has laughed in the past, its shattered arm? Thinking: Poor maimed fool, yet still laughing soundlessly, almost at once she thinks: And while you're at it, do forgive the inadvertent disrobing also. But then your place of worship ain't in such hot shape neither. "Listen," she says finally, "has anybody told you . . . but someone must have, surely? There's an American poet buried here. He's quite good, too. I suppose most people don't read poetry. But you should. Really—"

"Yes," the doctor says. "Someone let me borrow the book." But he is approaching her at last, scowling still, though with concern now, in solicitude. "Tell me, why not? Do. But why don't I take you home first, Miss . . . Winters? Fern—?"

"Home? Why, certainly, that sounds appetizing. Your place or mine, did you mean?" She is not looking at him again, however, hardly conscious of her words either, because she is gesturing finally, has lifted even the deformed hand to do so. The hand falls away, she knows it exhaustion now in fact. Yet she sees him see the machete at last, sees the dark startled eyes as they leap back to her own.

A cock crows, hideous and prolonged. As it ceases, a breeze takes the candle, and with it there comes a faint, cruel scent of orchid.

She sobs once in the darkness. Then she says, "I'm sorry. Sometimes it takes me a while, to make my point. But it is a weapon. And it has been made use of, I'm afraid."

TWO

"As if a few scattered clinics like this might counteract the indifference of centuries," the doctor said. "Because even after they do learn to trust me a little, still, what good? Take Mexico City itself, do you know anything about the hospitals? Patients in the wards carrying sticks to beat off the rats, or dying after simplest surgery when some semiliterate mestizo nurse forgets the most elemental detail of postoperative procedure—"

Talking, although probably not aware of it himself: ceaselessly, indefatigably, a drone. Yet by the end of his first week in the town, before the other had occurred, before enough had happened to make him forget his work, or his lack of it, entirely, at least the pattern would have become obvious, there would have been only two patients in the five days. So even when the several younger Americans began to make of the clinic a gathering place, the best he might have anticipated was a kind of tolerable boredom.

Then he met the girl, met Fern.

This was that Tuesday, only the second afternoon, and already he had been pacing, though in fact the first of the two had appeared not an hour before. He had done the best he could with the woman, an Indian, simplifying, being forcefully reiterant. The child would die without further attention, he had insisted, speaking deliberately in the Spanish she would possess as a second language, choosing words she could not fail to follow. "In Toluca," he said. "In the hospital." He told her the address, gave directions and then caught himself up. "No, wait," he said, "here, I will write it," commencing to do so and not realizing until he had finished, but then without needing to glance up, that of course she would not read. She did not say so. She said nothing at all now, a woman perhaps thirty or perhaps forty-five, her nutcolored face seamed about the eyes, the texture of beaten leather. She wore rags, was shoeless. Standing before the desk in the consulting vestibule, the somnolent, wasted child dressed again and drowsing in her arms, she was scarcely more mobile herself. She made no move to accept the paper either. "Just show it to someone," the doctor said. "A police officer, the driver of the bus. They will treat the boy at the hospital. My name is written here also. There will be no cost." At last he literally pressed the prescription sheet into the woman's hand. "The bus," he repeated. "Today. It is urgent." Then he realized something else. "Oh," he said. "Oh, yes. Here." He fumbled in a pocket. The money was not out of clinic funds. "Twenty pesos," he said. "It will be more than sufficient. For the trip, for food. Everything else will be without charge. It is the government that pays—"

† 7 †

That was the first. The clinic fronted on a street adjacent to the zócalo, the main square, two doors removed from it, a reconverted butcher shop in actuality, with beneath the fresh whitewash of its facade a gratuitous CARNE still faintly discernible. From the wide, arched front entrance the doctor watched the woman, the encephalitic child bound into her rebozo now, riding her hip, as she crossed into the leafy walks. The Toluca bus stop was in a street which entered the square from its opposite corner. It was hot. From the doorway he watched the woman cross, passing through the shadows of fan palms and rubber trees and the several tall fresnos, toward the ornate central bandstand. He heard his coffee behind him, the water for it, boiling noisily in the sterilizer. When he returned to the doorway the woman was gone from sight.

So he anticipated boredom. Nor would it have been otherwise had he learned that same afternoon instead of weeks thereafter that the woman had not sought out the bus. He would understand why, perhaps even now already suspected it. *Because she will not know what a hospital is, has no concept.* So when he did learn, it would augment his general frustration only, no more. He would be occupied with filling out inconsequential forms when she returned, when he glanced up to find her in the doorway, again submissive, expressionless, having no idea how long she had been waiting there beforehand either but sensing that she would have remained indefinitely without a word until he became aware of her. And then he would sense the rest before he noticed the money too, hardly the same bill now but others, lesser denominations, crumpled in her fist. "Fourteen," she would say. "When my husband gains employment I will give back the remaining. But since the government offered it for such a thing as a journey—"

"For a coffin," he would repeat. "Because naturally she walked out of the office and went right back to one of the local shamans, a folk healer. Came expecting some sort of ready miracle and instead got only some words about a bus to Toluca, an awesome metropolis of fifty thousand souls and not two hours away, but to which she has probably ventured one terrified excursion in her lifetime. The shaman sold her a dried snakeskin. To be wrapped around the child's head—"

But that would be later, in weeks, when the other was over, had become disjointed recollection of something never fully apprehended at its passing nor solved in unintermitted talk thereafter, though pervasive still, spectral, even when again there was only the tedium, the idleness and the remaining Americans. The one he had become friendly with most immediately was a sallow, red-bearded, seemingly otiose man named Talltrees, who claimed to be a writer. Then it was Talltrees who told him about Fern Winters.

This was on that same evening, some hours after the Indian woman had come and gone, after the girl herself had appeared at the clinic. It was not business, she was simply passing. Nor did she even enter at once, pausing casually in the doorway long enough to smoke one cigarette rather, the bright shimmering autumn glare behind her in the cobblestoned street, so that he did not see her well either, not then, not really. He missed her name, too. "Normally I'm not sure I'd have trusted my Spanish," she said. "But since Harry Talltrees says you studied at Rutgers—"

"In fact I grew up there," the doctor said. "My mother is American. But I did my medical work in the city, at the National University." He did not explain that this was not by choice, that none of the American schools to which he had applied would have him. All his life he would refuse to believe it a result of failure on his own part anyway, though his credentials, his grades, had been less than impressive. Twenty years later he would still think it: If I had a name like Cohen or Goldberg they would have taken me quick enough. "This is the last of it," he said, "six months out here instead of the second half of a full internship. It's a new notion, a way to get physicians into backwater towns where most of the natives are still waiting to hear about Cortes—"

Now and then the sun caught random threads of her hair where she stood. She did not stay long, nor would he recall much of what was said. Yet it would never strike him to blame this on himself either, if even he realized it. So probably it was the idea of her presence alone, there, a girl so attractive, her face as he finally perceived it somehow innocently curious and yet bemused too, older than her twenty-two or twenty-three years. He had already several times had to avert his eyes from the deformity, the hand, held in abeyance slightly, that elbow raised and the arm drawn back, the hand poised as if about to enter some imaginary pocket into which she could not be certain she had deposited anything. Or was it precisely the opposite, even unconsciously deliberate, a way of getting it over with? The doctor could not have cared less.

She was at the office no more than ten minutes, perhaps only five. Yet he knew when it became irrevocable, that at least. It was after she told him that she painted. "Ah, like Quigley, then," he said. Quigley was another of the Americans, a pale, nervous youth he had already seen at work several times, sketching, about the zócalo. But when he mentioned the name the girl smiled. "Not like Joe," she said. "He has nothing to compensate for." Not following, the doctor scowled. So then she displayed it after all, lifted the withered hand to grimace with a look of bleak irony, obviously feigned, yet beautiful and touching and amused at once. "A little magic in the other one," she said, "since this one is such a dud." In that first instant the doctor thought: It is because I am an MD, she could not do that with anyone else. Yet she laughed too, briefly. Nor was it forced. When she said something about an errand the doctor found himself taking her arm. "Let me show you the rest of the facilities," he insisted, though it was ridiculous, there was only one large inner room. Screened, at a corner, there was a single bed. "Mostly I'll just give inoculations," he said. "Or do minor first aid that any qualified nurse could handle. It's really only a sort of transfer point, for when something critical comes up." The girl had followed, but only to that doorway, from where he indicated the high, sheeted examination table, cabinets, assorted equipment. Then they were at the entrance once more, that quickly, she was leaving. And again the doctor did not immediately understand. "Raw meat?" he said. She was in the street, laughing, that impossibly lovely face lifted now, her chin tilted upward. "Oh," he said at last—"the old sign. Yes, I suppose it isn't remarkably appropriate at that. It hadn't occurred to me—"

So it was more than improbable, it was absurd. "Or for that matter she will probably be married," he said to Talltrees. "A girl like that. Indeed, and simply cannot wear a ring on that hand. Or perhaps wore one on the other and I did not think to notice. But my God, how beautiful. Even with that disfigurement—"

"With, or because of?" Talltrees asked him.

"I beg your pardon—?"

But he had decided he did not like Talltrees even before this. Already in two days the man had appeared at the clinic a dozen times, friendly enough, even gratuitously informative about the town, the rest of the Americans, but with something irritating in the very profligacy of his idleness, an attitude less ingenuous or pleasant than privately entertained, as if at something withheld after all, some joke the doctor had not only not unraveled but which he had not even quite yet realized was being told. He would not remember that he had endured something of the same sensation with the girl herself, not at once. And then he realized that he was not listening when Talltrees told him.

"What?" the doctor said. "Three? Some house on a hill? No, I don't know it, haven't yet seen . . . but are you trying to tell me that she, and two men, are—?"

"Who?" Talltrees said. Behind the coarse red beard the smile still seemed superior, a little smug. "Did I say that? Three, I said, yes. But it's he, Chance, who comes out ahead. He and the two girls—"

The doctor stared at him. Possibly it was still only misunderstanding. "Listen, are we talking about the same person?" he said. "The one I met this afternoon? She, and some other woman, and one man, are living together in some . . . sharing a—?"

"Sharing," Talltrees said, "an innocuous enough word." Now he might have been thoughtful, unpremeditative. "Maybe," he decided. "Except that the house is just about the smallest in town respectable enough to be offered for rent to Americans. Not counting the kitchen and the bath, there are two rooms without even a door between, only an open archway. And with only one bed in the place too, that and a cot—"

"But the second girl must simply be visiting," the doctor insisted. "Surely, now. Or broke. Particularly if you say she hasn't been here all the while—?"

"Corpses and guests," Talltrees said. "Isn't the adage Mexican—both begin to stink after three days? This is three months. The two of them came a year or so ago, yes, the one you met, Fern, and this Chance—and no, not married either, though not that it would matter to anyone—living up there. And then Lee arrived. Lee Suffridge, last summer. And stayed." Now the shrug might have been genuinely indifferent also. "All right, look, think what you will. If they were any sort of reasonably communicative human beings, they could pass it off as just what you want to call it yourself. But when they walk around not giving a fractured damn what anybody thinks or says—or him, really, he's the one I'm talking about— who would probably not take the trouble to listen to anything you did accuse him of—"

"Chance?" the doctor said. "Where does somebody get a name like Chance—?"

"An old-time baseball player, wasn't there?" Talltrees said. It was late. They were in the zócalo, on a stone bench upon the elevated central mall. The square was all but deserted, its numerous beer kiosks shut down, corrugated iron jalousies locked into place across the storefronts. On the doctor's own corner, beneath a streetlamp, Indians squatted, peasants in their white cotton evidently already awaiting a dawn bus around the lake. About them the night, its tone, possessed a quality almost unnaturally still, the distant lamps leafy, filtered, tentative. The doctor was smoking, a pipe, using English tobacco he could obtain only in Mexico City, there only in particular shops. It had turned cold enough for a sweater. "One of my medical-school roommates used to spend every Sunday night in the Tanampa Square brothels," he said finally. "Three years, and never the same woman twice."

Talltrees laughed, gesturing with an exceptionally bony hand. "And what you mean is, none of that has anything to do with real life. All right," he said. "Anyway, who am I to discuss it? Especially since I've only been here since long before he appeared, which means I've been granted the questionable privilege of speaking to the man about three times—"

"But good Christ, a town of this size, with so few of you—?"

"So that you'd expect intimacy almost to a point of incest. Which there is, believe me. Flee the encroachment of middle-class civilization, escape to untrammeled Mexico . . . except that the ten or a dozen fellow expatriates I happen to have fallen into proximity with are in my hair so much I'm ready to explode. My God, I know Joe Quigley so well that I could probably walk in on his wife in the shower and hold a conversation with neither of us giving it a thought. But with Chance, nothing. Wandering around like some brooding, disinherited prince . . . and never offering an invitation any more than they ever accepted one either, incidentally, even before the second girl came. Talk about arrogance, self-sufficiency, whatever—"

The doctor decided it was being exaggerated, surely so. Yet he saw the house, that same night. He was not thinking about the man, Chance. Nor would it be the girl either, he believed, not now. *Because even forgetting the rest, after all, if she, they, have been living together for a year—* But he walked up. He had an excuse, since exercise had always been a ritual in his life. Talltrees had situated it for him before they separated, merely in passing, pointing out a street that led from the zócalo in the direction of the lake, though which climbed sharply. He did not indicate that he was going, probably he had not expected it himself. There was one streetlamp, and then mounting the pitted callejón he found himself in almost total blackness. He had no flashlight, nor was there a moon. Then when he crested the hill there was, though the road itself disappeared.

The structure was as unimposing as Talltrees had suggested, and almost forbiddingly isolated, boxlike though walled. Achieving it the doctor understood himself upon a tongue of land that would overlook the water, with the town behind him to the left. The walls extended to the bluff's edge itself, farther out than he felt it safe to walk. Rather than the lake he discerned only the far dark hills beyond. There was a breeze. He did not venture near the gate.

"But two?" he heard himself saying. "She, and yet another?"

Nor could he dismiss it, the town was far too small. He saw her again the next morning. It was eleven o'clock, and hot again. He had strolled to the zócalo, leaving the clinic open though keeping its entrance well in sight, and he was drinking bottled soda at one of the tin kiosks, seated upon a crate beneath an awning. At his side a burro was tethered, snorting beneath a massive load of firewood. She emerged from a street perpendicular to his own, crossing that side of the square past cluttered one-room shops, in white, and amid intermittent blinkings of shadow and sun she appeared even more enticing than he remembered, than he wanted to believe. Immediately, the doctor arose, and she noticed him at once too, but waved and did not stop, gesturing to indicate an imaginary wristwatch.

Dismally, the doctor managed an awkward nod of acknowledgment. A hurry, he thought. Here, in Mictlán.

Then it was compounded, the sense of repudiation rendered even more acute, when she did pause after all, to talk to someone else. It was a moment before the doctor was able to rationalize, to convince himself it would be business of some sort. Then he thought he even recognized the man, an Indian, but of better than peon class, wearing heavy laborer's shoes and a gaudy sports shirt, whom he had noticed about the square more than once. In fact he had several times sensed the man staring, he was sure, with a lidded cast of mistrust over his dark, chiseled face that the doctor had been able to disregard only because he was fully aware of the clinic's novelty, his own intrusion. Yet there was something more now, something else. The girl was about to move on, but as she stepped aside she drew back an arm to strike playfully at the other's shoulder, the gesture as intimate as seemed the laughter that followed. Astonished, the doctor thought: But with an Indian? When even someone like myself can never get through to any of them, let alone some transient American? He continued to stare until she had disappeared into the street leading toward the house.

So Talltrees explained that too, that afternoon. "Manolo Ortega, it would have to be," he said. "And he is one preciously choleric, truculent hombre also, insofar as any of those people have readable personalities to begin with. Trying to reach an Indian, indeed. Yet he is Chance's friend. In the cantinas together. Or more, in Ortega's shack, even. Listen, yes, is it three years I've been here now? And yet I have never taken one step into one of those hovels, still have no more than the vaguest notion how they really live. But Ortega's place is up near Chance's, on the far side of that slope, a typical adobe hut with a tin roof and no floor . . . well, you know, surely. And there will be Chance. Talking to the Indian, mind you, when he hasn't nine consecutive words to spare for any of us. Or never mind that aspect of it anyway, but damn it, Americans just do not do that, are not seen squatting against a wall guzzling cheap pulque out of a gourd, and with the chickens and the pigs underfoot half the time too. Granted, Ortega's wife works for them now and then, the washing at least, but nonetheless. Not that a part-time maid would cost much more than cigarette money either, but that is another thing, by the way. Since the interest seems to be developing, you might just try to find out what they live on. The three of them, up there. Precisely what is that preoccupied, impolite son of a bitch supposed to *do*—?"

Still he tried to forget it. Quigley, the young painter, had told him a confused, ostensibly comic story about an ancient horse Talltrees had owned, which either he or his wife, whom the doctor had not yet met, had apparently ridden to some disastrous end in the zócalo. The doctor had seen nothing funny in it, though it had verified what he was already thinking: What did any of them want with Mexico to start with, if they were not going to work? When he was alone he tried to read, a book Talltrees had given him, though not something he himself had written. It was poetry, by an American named Chazen whom the doctor understood had died in the town years before. He had no way to judge its quality, nor could he follow a lot of it. He meant to ask if the man were widely known or if the interest were local only, though when he saw Talltrees again he did not. Perhaps he was honest enough to tell himself, "It is because I intend to ask her, am saving it to have something to talk about." But he did not run into her that morning. That was Thursday. Then he did see the second girl, Lee Suffridge. Like Fern she simply appeared, though with the difference that she was able to say Fern had mentioned meeting him. She could not have been less self-conscious, made no pretense about it. Then the doctor wondered why she should. Because Talltrees was an ass, he decided, the whole thing was puerile.

He was more positive of it as he considered her. The girl was tall, athletic-looking, almost collegiate though she would be older than Fern or the doctor himself, close to thirty. She wore khaki pants and a man's shirt with its sleeves rolled that might well have been one of the doctor's own, too large for her, and her thick dark hair was chopped fiercely short. Her features were ascetic, and sharply etched, though the bones of her face were delicate, the planes hollow.

Yet there was nothing unfeminine about her, rather it was a kind of physical indifference, or even unawareness. Standing with her hands in her pockets, her weight on one foot and with the toe of the other lifted very like some child's about to scrawl something into sand, she was almost too casual. Or did he sense tension after all, something latent, feline, for all that grace? The girl would have to be conscious of the gossip, all three of them would. So why didn't they say something, contrive some banality even, whatever, to cover the situation, get it dismissed? ("She would be the last one to do it," Talltrees would say later. "I'm surprised she showed up, since she says less to people than even Chance does, normally.") When he finally became aware that it might be none of this, that the girl had a severe cold, perhaps fever, the doctor had to think, had to tell himself, "Well, damn him anyway, now he has even fixed it so that the last thought that crosses my mind is the professional one."

She indicated at once that she had no training. "The sight of blood never bothered me, though, if that's a help?" Her smile was wan, quite drawn. "I don't guess it would be conspicuously legal either, would it? Still, I just thought, in any sort of real emergency—?"

"God, yes," the doctor said. "Theoretically, I can call nurses from across the lake, in Chignahuapán, which shouldn't be half an hour. But if you make allowances for the usual telephone breakdown, plus the rest of the characteristic response to such things . . . well, you know Mexico—"

Before she left the office it started to rain. It was unseasonal and abrupt, unpresaged, and it would not last. Watching it, the girl stood deeply enough in the doorway so that her tennis shoes began to darken. "You shouldn't do that, with that cold," the doctor said. For a moment she gazed at him speculatively. "Don't you like it?" "What?" the doctor said—"rain? Well, yes, I suppose so—" Perhaps she was smiling again, though she had already stepped back, was bending to roll her pants.

Then the doctor had an extraordinary insight. If she had been more wet than this she would have removed the pants altogether, the shirt as well. He scarcely meant there, in the doorway. He told himself, "But she would do it in my rooms. And it would not be for any reason except because she was wet." Then he knew that was not what he meant either. *I mean she walks around that house that way, half-dressed or undressed and not conscious of it at all.* "Oh, damn it, stop," he told himself. "Stop, now."

But it would not, even as she departed some few moments later, as he stood in the doorway watching her cross into the square with that graceful, almost indolent stride, and heading there even then, probably, up that hill. *So that even if it was nothing in the beginning, that very proximity, those two small rooms.* The rain had cooled the stones, the zócalo gleamed fresh in the returning sun, it took her dark hair. Then, passing beneath a dwarfed palm, not quite breaking stride she reached upward as if to pluck a leaf, failing to achieve it but with her body arching, supple, the attitude much like that of a tennis serve. Or a swimmer, he thought—sometime in her life she would have been magnificent in the water. She had been tanned, Fern was also, though less so. *But even on the lawn, then, behind those walls, in their garden. Taking the sun. And because they have to dress, undress. And if there is not even a door between rooms—*

So Talltrees had convinced him after all, it appeared,

even if he understood something else now too. Nor would it have to occur to him that he had not really seen this one either, could not have characterized her before an outsider any more perceptively than he might the other. "Because obviously it isn't Fern now anyhow," he said. "So maybe it is just women, since this one is just as—" He went back to the desk, searching out his pipe. Then he stood gazing into the empty doorway, the street. "And Jesus, I will give him that, then," he said finally. "Whatever else Talltrees thinks. There is surely no way on this earth that you can fault the man's taste."

That was Thursday. The next evening, a little before nine, he was called to the clinic from the town's one acceptable restaurant. They were Indians, though not from Mictlán itself. "It is more than a week," one of them told him. "Yet it appeared no solemn difficulty, in that he did not bleed after the first day. It is only today that he became unconscious."

The doctor could smell the gangrene. The injured man lay head downward across the back of his burro, his left leg bound in contaminated rags. Apparently they had been hours on the road alone. He had never heard of their village.

For some seconds, before the clinic entrance, he stared dully. There was plasma, and he thought of Lee Suffridge. But the irony did not escape him either. *Surely. So I finally do get an emergency of the sort I am out here for, only the man is moribund when they bring him in.*

A crowd had gathered, evidently having followed the burro when it was led through the square, and was still enlarging silent and impassive around them. The doctor selected a boy at random, the nearest at hand. "The house of the gringos on the hill above the Calle de los Muertos," he said. "Inform them the doctor has urgent need of the

Señorita Lee. Can you remember that?" He pressed a coin, a fifty-centavo piece, into the boy's hand. The boy was unwashed, shoeless, perhaps ten. Importantly he fled. Voicing brief instructions the doctor unlocked the twin doors, and the two who had accompanied the patient prepared to lift him. "A stone," one of them had explained. "We were removing a stone. In a field of maize. A stone of monumental proportions, and it crashed upon him." Fixing the bright lights above the examination table, almost irrelevantly the doctor thought: Moving a stone. Trying to clear their fifty square centimeters of parched earth to grow corn on, for a family which probably in all of its recollected existence has never been adequately fed whether it removed stones or not. "Onto here," he said. "Be delicate with the wounded portion." He was already at the plasma. The man was old, his expression slack, placid, almost kindly in repose. "Hold this," the doctor said. The nearer Indian gazed at him vacantly. Adjusting the inverted canister at a hook above the table he waved them both away. The man's limp arm accepted the blunt needle readily.

Alone then, he scissored away the clotted rags, grimacing at the rising stench, aware of the need for anesthesia too, though there was slight chance that the man would regain consciousness. The swelling was monstrous, the discoloration acute. Already he had presumed the femoral artery severed, making it impossible to have restored circulation from the start. Yet for a moment, the laceration gaping now, he simply stared. Then he was gazing toward the vestibule. Salazar, hadn't it been? And Carlos Tejada? The last time he had assisted in Juárez General—the three of them, and he himself only manipulating the clamps?

The doctor found himself at the outer doorway, searching faces in the crowd. There were twelve or fifteen Indians, all men, unresponsive each, seeming even incurious. While doubtless he looked the prime fool himself, the doctor thought. To his right the zócalo was almost completely dark, murky shadows obscured it. Five more minutes, could she be here that soon? But that cold, perhaps she was in bed? Then it was even annoyance, as he recognized the error he had already committed. *Obviously. I should have told the boy he would not get his tip until he came back.*

But damn them anyway, who wanted this? An ordinary residence, why the hell had they started withholding certification for this? Almost enraged, he was about to return within when at last he spotted his quarry, some distance beyond the others still, only then emerging from behind a parked van. The doctor's English came instinctively, though he had time to observe no more than the tweed jacket, the white shirt. "You, please," he called. "Listen, I've sent for a nurse, but there is no time. If you could help—?"

Nor did he wait, once the man had glanced toward him. "Please," he repeated only, already turning then but thinking too: Slow down, now. Rush, but slow down. "Here," he called behind himself, "inside. No, wait. Close that outer door—"

He was scrubbing hastily, aware that he should have accomplished this earlier also, as the other entered after him. Rolling his sleeves, the jacket already discarded, the man paused to contemplate the Indian, darkhaired, appearing slight. At the automatic sterilizer now, heaping instruments onto the tray, the doctor heard him say, quietly, "Isn't he just about done?"

"Of course," the doctor said. "Of course he is. Over a week, they said, which means certainly two, at the least. Dear Christ, you'd think the stink alone would have told them. And the blood he must have lost at the start—" Hurrying, the tray wheeled into place, he busied himself with the anesthesia. But he had time to realize that he was going to talk, would not stop talking. He said, "Look, now, I appreciate this, and it's no crime to get sick. But if it troubles you, please step clear—to the sink if you can, but anyway not where I'll be slipping in it. Otherwise please try to do what I ask as rapidly as you're able. I will have to tell you to get in there with me—it can be a mess, and I will be reaching for instruments—"

"Just tell me exactly," the other said.

"Well, of course I'll be exact. You aren't trained, are you? Don't you imagine I'd have sense enough for that—?" The doctor cut himself off, glancing up, about to apologize. Then he had to fight the temptation to look a second time. It was not swagger. Yet it was not detachment either. So I am nervous at that, he thought. Because not under circumstances like this—not called in suddenly off a dark street to assist in an emergency amputation in some half-assed foreign village like this. The doctor told himself: "No. No one could have mirth in his eyes."

So he halted even as he was about to begin. He did not look at the other again but waited, already poised above the table, the first scalpel already in hand, and inhaled deeply, deliberately, containing it for a long moment. He did it a second time. Then he said, "All right, yes, even a doctor. But with inadequate facilities, no staff. You could perform eight a day in a properly equipped hospital. That towel, please, it will have to serve. If you will bunch it under his thigh—"

He commenced the severance. He was not deft. Rather he worked with a methodical, grave concentration, knowing it no better than that, perhaps, and conscious of the sound of his own voice as he had anticipated also, talking constantly, a dull, uninterrupted, sometimes hardly coherent monologue with the other not speaking once, offering no response other than physical reaction to com-

mand throughout the more than thirty minutes, the ceaseless incision and binding off, until, only moments before the
last cord would have been separated, the last inspissated
flow stanched, he said, in Spanish, "You might as well
quit, no?" The doctor had realized it an instant earlier, he
would have sworn to that. Yet he was not actually thinking about the Indian, the dead man, at all. *Because no one
does, no one could.* Or had the man been laughing at him?

The mirth was long gone now, however, the eyes were
quite empty. The man's hands and wrists, his shirtfront,
glistened with wet black blood. He was less tall than
the doctor, which was common, though a first glance had
been deceptive, neither was he slight. The doctor had
found his wrists sinewed, now there appeared a muscular
litheness in his posture as well. The man's face was weathered, unconscionably tanned, and he would not have been
thirty. "Pretty superfluous," he said tonelessly.

"Yes," the doctor said. "But I suppose I had no way to
avoid the gesture either." With a rapid, almost brutal
sequence of incisions he completed the operation. He discarded the blade.

The man had crossed to the basin. Falling into shadowed
profile his face presented a surprising angularity, appearing
almost haggard. The doctor said, "There's a girl, another
American, living here. She offered to be on call. I sent
a boy."

"Lee, you mean." The man did not look back. "She
would have been in bed. She's been running a temperature
all day."

"Oh," the doctor said. "Oh—that cold. Yes, I saw—"
For the instant he felt only stupid, even as he realized it
predictable, understood it would have had to occur this
way. Nonetheless he thought, told himself, "Well, but
anyway, I was far too busy, under the circumstances can
scarcely have been expected to stop and think—" Across

from him the man ran a wet hand through his uncut black hair, not combing it, then reached down paper towels from the dispenser. Nor was he handsome, something else for which the doctor did not possess the word, perhaps, but not that. As he stared it struck him that the man himself might well have been recently ill. Or the reverse, did he mean, not recuperating but fighting off, whatever it might be, disdaining? The face, the scowl, seemed curiously lifeless, strained. Or was it the doctor himself, simply trying too hard now, overcompensating? Aloud, at last, he said, "You will be Chance, then. Some of the others, Talltrees, Quigley, I've just been meeting them—"

The man said nothing, though he may have nodded. He had not removed his shirt. The doctor was equally bloodied, more so, though still he had made no move toward the sink. Then he felt a fool utterly. "Oh, good heavens," he said. He himself wore hospital whites. "A gown. Forgive me—"

Still the man seemed not to look at him. Near the cadaver an insect buzzed, startlingly audible. The doctor said, "I imagine I ought to tell them. The two who brought him in—"

"In some cantina by now, if they've got a spare peso between them—"

"Yes, probably. And they'll use the same burro to carry him back, won't they? I suppose I'll have to donate a sheet. Or will that make him look even more like a side of beef? Dear Jesus, this country. I suppose they'll lash him into place, too?" Finally he crossed to the basin. But talking again, why was he still talking? In spite of himself, he said, "And I didn't ask, but someone did considerably more than just bind up that leg originally, or tried to. It would be a shaman, of course. Unclean, and probably packing herbs into it, or some such. They have even been known to use dung. Which only proves the point about clinics like this, that they are not about to achieve very much without education beforehand. A man scarcely dies from an everyday amputation if it is executed before he goes into terminal shock—"

"I'll send them in," the other said. He had flung the jacket across his shoulder, hooked over a thumb above the drenched, bloody shirt. Hair spilled across his forehead, the knotted brow.

"Would you? It would help. Then I can clean this one up a little. I'll have to get some kind of name too, actually, for the record—"

From the vestibule the man was gazing back toward the examination table, where the lights still blazed. The intimation of convalescence remained, some deep lysis. "Gaona," he said. "Miguel, I think—"

"*What—?*" The doctor started. "*Who? This—?*" His eyes shot to the corpse, came back. "*You knew the—?*"

"It's . . . nothing." The other's expression may have been abstracted, no more. And his voice was without inflection. "I didn't see it at once. Maybe because he was in shock. Anyway, faces, time, the change—"

"*You—?*"

But he had started out, bloodied from waist to throat had opened the outer doors before the doctor halted him, caught his arm. "Wait," the doctor said. "I mean, thank you. For getting the others, for helping—" His hand rose and fell, the gesture without definition. He could not have said what he had in mind. In the street there were more of them now, some twenty, waiting without expression, seemingly without interest. As if in extrication, not thinking at all now, the doctor said, "Indians. The way they stand and stare. So that they actually look sinister, half the time—"

The mirth was there again, faintly resurgent. This time

the doctor knew it called for. "You only think they're thinking," the other said, stepping down.

By eleven the body had been removed and the clinic cleaned, though it seemed later. The doctor had showered. He lived in two large rooms behind the clinic itself, with a separate entrance through a walled garden shared by other contiguous dwellings that formed an open square, one house originally but subdivided now. For some reason he had returned to the office.

For a time he stood in the doorway, where light flooded from behind him into the cobblestoned street. Such light as existed elsewhere seemed to be contained within the foliage that screened it, in rusted halos. Save for the outcast dogs that he already knew he would hear all night long, the town was silent.

The Indians had departed with their grisly portage, bound into place with rope as he had anticipated, their faces grave though displaying little else. They had been drinking, in fact they carried a bottle of tequila. They had taken the leg also, which he had thought to dispose of himself. Remembering it now the doctor laughed grimly. Was it Santa Anna's he was thinking of, buried with solemn military honors after he lost it, and then exhumed when the man fell out of favor? Eventually he tried to read, the poetry again, since the book was in the desk here rather than in his rooms. He gave up on it fairly soon. He made coffee.

He was more tired than he had thought, but he decided upon his walk. He took a flashlight, though there was a moon. He did not believe he had any particular direction in mind.

Then he understood that he did, if not at once. He climbed a narrow lane which diverged from one of the streets that spilled into the zócalo, inland from the lakeshore and toward a high road with an unobstructed view. The town's better houses were up here, some few rented by Americans. The others, closed at the moment or in the custody of servants, were the property of wealthy Mexicans who lived elsewhere, vacation residences only.

There is a woman who lives in one of the former. She is in her forties, bird-faced and fleshy, though not yet fat. Her name is Tinkle, and she is a widow. She keeps tropical fish. Several times now she has appeared at the clinic, so gregarious that the doctor believes her paradoxically shy, even timid. Talltrees has told him that she gives parties frequently, though her house is quiet tonight. She has already invited the doctor to dinner, and he has had to appear, though he did not stay long.

Only when he is in the paved road before her gate itself does he admit that he has been coming here. There is a single streetlamp, some distance away, and he needs the flash to locate the bell. Then he does not ring, since he understands why he is here also, what has brought him. "Damn it, now," he says. There will be a dog somewhere on the grounds, but he does not hear it. "Damn it, now, I do not need this."

But he does not leave. This high above the lake there is a breeze. He remembers one stronger, a wind, a few nights previous on the other slope, outside the other house. And probably it is cooler there in the daytime than anywhere else, he thinks. Almost aloud, he says, "But to have known the man? An old woodcutter, from somewhere in the hills?"

He has turned off the flash, but he can see the bell now, or believes he can. His jaws are clamped, his expression is almost sullen. "Now, damn it," he says again. Then, when he does ring, it is almost savagely.

He is admitted, but only after the appearance of an incredibly powerful flash, after cautious interrogation from behind it. She is in nightdress, her hair in curlers, the sparrow's face pasty without cosmetics. Nor is she quite coherent immediately either, commencing at once to describe what has evidently been a housebreaking of sorts, or an attempt at theft, of whatever it is she possesses that might be lost. He does not listen, will not, though there is a prodigious shotgun involved somehow also, which she retrieves suddenly from somewhere in baffling demonstration. "Christ! Christ! All right!" he shouts at last. "Tell me about it later. Afterward. Look, what do you think I came for anyway?" So then it is she who is confused, but not remarkably, and not for long. "Why, Doctor," she says. Within minutes he is in her bed, amid the sheets already warmed by her unaccosted flesh. Within minutes more it is accomplished, less in urgency or even self-indulgence than out of a kind of debilitating, raw frustration. So it is not until later that he becomes truly cognizant of the leanness of what he has plundered either, in that deadly aftermath when he confronts the flaccid collapse of bosom and stomach and thigh, that sag. In her bathroom, snatching at the first misapprehended cloth in sight, only after he has rid himself of his own vitrescent excess does he discover it no towel but a sweater. "Darling?" she inquires remotely. "Surely you're not embarrassed by being too excited on our very first night?" But he is gone by then, fleeing even as he understands there will be no escape, that he is doomed now, ensnared for the entire six months. Because where can he hide? In the street, catching his breath, he says, "That son of a bitch." It is Talltrees he means. Because why in God's name did the man have to suggest it? "The pair of them?" he says. "Both?"

When he starts walking again, again this time it is without direction, though with decided purpose now, the exertion itself a kind of abrogation, or denial. Because he goes quite swiftly too, and without the flash either, so that he must attend to the ruts and potholes, the treacherously displaced stones. He is forcing himself not to think, descending along several twisting callejones he has not taken before, most of them overhung with jacaranda, though he senses that they are leading him away from the zócalo. Then he is in a level street that may be the continuation of one perpendicular to his own, roughly parallel to the lakeshore, though he cannot make out the zócalo when he looks back. Past the last of the streetlamps the way declines and then rises again, and the cobblestones cease. But the earth is packed solidly enough so that he believes he is right. The street has become the road around the lake, the bus route.

Then he believes he knows where he has arrived also, though it surprises him that the chapel should be lighted. With the flash he picks his way past the dismantled iron gate into what will be the abandoned cemetery. Then for a moment, longer, he does not move, though he has thought to snap off the flash at once. He has already discarded the notion of hallucination, as well. There actually is, deep within the ancient vault, in candlelight evidently and upon her knees, a naked woman.

THREE

It would be ten o'clock, a little past ten. She did not
wear a watch, yet she had always possessed a curiously unerring instinct for time, for the hour.
She sat in a threadbare armchair in the corner of
the room most distant from the fire. There was a floorlamp
at her shoulder. A square of cardboard, long since discolored and slightly curled, lay across the upper rim of
the lamp's dark shade so that its glow was cast downward
only, in a hazy, smoke-defined cone across the chair. She
had built the fire herself with the coming of dark, but it
had refused to draw properly. Now the logs merely
flickered and smoked above the coals.

Seated within the cone of thin, still smoke she was
not reading, though a book lay open on the arm of the
chair. Next to the book stood a small, rose-tinted glass.
A window was lifted in the kitchen beyond the doorway
near her, and from without there were nightsounds, faint
rustlings along the adobe wall beneath the window itself

that would be lizards in the bougainvillea, and now and then, remote, windborne there above the town, a cry of dogs, or of fowl. Fern sat in the cone of light hearing the fire, hearing the night, watching the girl called Lee Suffridge.

The cot stood at the wall to her left, extending along it toward the archway to the second room. It was narrow and low, set upon building bricks, draped with a coarse gray sarape. Lee lay upon the sarape, her head near the archway, her arms enfolding a crushed pillow. She lay face downward but with her right hip lifted slightly and her legs drawn up, settled as if to invite the fullest thrust of the hearth. Her hands, ringless, reaching as if in supplication, extended palm upward beyond the pillow.

Across from the fire, less than four strides from the grate, she was not covered, although she wore a bulky short furlined jacket, a man's, unzippered and fallen aside at her raised hip where her thin underpants were visible. A pair of khaki pants lay discarded upon the reed mat below the cot, two mudstained desert boots also. About her ankles white wool socks were bunched loosely, too large for her feet.

Fern sat and watched her. And the shoes his also, she thought. Not to mention the jacket. As if wearing them were becoming almost homeopathic, like some exotic ritual.

Lee did not move, her breathing hardly perceptible now, though she had been coughing moments before. Fern herself wore a robe only, of a faded material quite rough, loosely belted and with its sleeves rolled. Watching the ill, unmoving girl, she thought: But me too. So the remarkable thing is that he has anything left to wear himself, then.

She did not smile. She sat, watching, pensive, conscious of her long hair about her shoulders where the light played upon random misplaced strands like gold threads.

Across the way the unsuccessful fire wavered and smoked. The room was much longer than it was wide. Beyond the archway the shadow of her easel bulked upward unsteadily, and deeper shadows cloaked that entire corner, the clutter of her paint table, the trunk below. The smoke was actually a haze now. Sloping downward toward the fireplace and over the front door at its left, the darkly stained ceiling beams quaked and wavered.

"Lee?" Fern said.

The other stirred, a shoulder lifting.

"I just had a notion. If you stuck either one of us with a pin, would it be he who felt it?"

"Unnn?"

"I mean like voodoo, or something?"

Now there was neither reply nor movement. After a moment, Fern arose.

The hearth was constructed perhaps a foot above the glazed, worn tiles of the floor, and there was fuel heaped before it. Kneeling, selecting sticks of kindling wood individually, yet without attention, she placed them amid the coals below the charred logs. Then she stood again, tossing hair from her eyes. A machete lay on the mantelpiece, before a lopsided straw Don Quixote. Utilizing the long flat blade as a poker, she forced the wood deeper into the bed.

Waiting for it to flare she heard him then, or rather she heard the outer gate, its familiar scrape against the uneven concrete base. It scraped a second time, closing. Poised, still holding the machete, she thought: And that the only way we would ever know, no other indication until he is at the door itself. In those tennis shoes, not even a whisper on the patio. "Damn it," she said. It was not anger, though she thought: And not ever. Because yes, already in these three months I have come to recognize Lee's fully, footfalls, movements in a second room beyond sight. But forgetting even New York it is nonetheless more than a year now with him down here and still there is no single sound with which I can be completely sure, would know unequivocally as his own when I did not anticipate it.

So it might have been anyone behind the heavy door near her now, inserting the key. The door was not locked, although, having made no move toward it, she heard it become so. The tumblers fell again as the key was reversed.

The fresh wood caught then, the combustion simultaneous across the full bed, just as the door opened, bursting furiously and flooding the room into sudden stark relief so that for the instant, frozen in the glare, he might have materialized out of the very flaring itself, a kind of apparition. Laughing, thinking *Good Lord, so now it is as if we even invoke him too*, she said, "Enter Faustus, amid hellfire!" Then, the illusion enhanced yet obliterated at once as she confronted the shirt, as she commenced to scowl at what appeared blood, she said, "Steve! My God, what—?"

Scowling himself, though perhaps merely startled, he stood with his jacket trailing in one hand, the key still uplifted in the other.

"Your shirt. What did you—?"

"My—?" Gazing downward, for the instant he seemed confused. Then he said, "Oh. This. It's . . . nothing—"

"But—"

"That new doctor, an emergency—"

But she had grasped his arm, not understanding, drawing him about. "But I still don't see—"

"No," he said finally. "Jesus, it's not me, mine . . . you thought—"

"Not—"

She released him. Her heart was pounding, even as he laughed, his eyes bright in the glare. "But how—?"

"I forgot about it. Walking up, thinking about something. He had an amputation, an old Indian I once . . . I was passing, and he asked me to help."

She was actually trembling. "Forgot? Walking in here like . . . dear God, Steve, you scared me half to death—"

"I'm sorry." Flinging aside the jacket he turned to the fire. Fern inhaled deeply, it was almost a sob.

"He told me he sent someone. For Lee."

"Yes. I mean, no. You . . . how in God's name can someone . . . what did you say? Help at an operation, and then in the space of half a dozen blocks forget that he is drenched with blood—?"

"What?"

"Nothing." She shook her head. "I mean nobody came. I was just sitting, I would have heard." She was still distraught. "Not that she could have gone anyway—"

"I told him." He glanced toward the cot, a hand at the second button of his shirt, the stains still wet enough to be gleaming dully. His face was drawn, as if from fatigue. "Is she all right?"

"Better," Fern said. Drained, she watched as he went across, grimacing to discover the shirt stained at its side also, where it was bloused loosely and wrinkled at his waist, that arm raised out of her vision where still he apparently worked the button.

Sap hissed and flared in a log as he halted, and above the cot his shadow flung upon the wall was enormous, folded back into distortion among the beams of the ceiling. Beneath it, again, he appeared weary as he leaned to touch the other at the temple, at the short thick dark hair Fern knew to have been sweated earlier. His hand remained there, poised, while in shadow his arm jerked and fell.

Evidently Lee now slept. "The fever was breaking, I think," Fern said quietly.

Turning back he nodded. Then, opening his shirt,

though not yet removing it, he stood indecisively. Already the renewed fire was dwindling, though with its tan his skin appeared almost black in the glow, a native's. Not quite questioningly he looked toward her.

Realizing, at last she smiled. "Oh, hell. I'm not positive, but I think I'd take the bet that there isn't a clean one in the house. Not with Lee wearing them half the time, too—"

"Didn't Petra wash?"

Fern cocked her head. "This week? When she is very likely having that baby tonight, even? I'll admit Indians are pretty hearty, chum, but I certainly wasn't going to let her work in these last few days—"

"I forgot."

"Steve, Steve, Steve. Sometimes for all your—"

He had crossed to take the fire. "My what—?"

"Like an unlettered Indian yourself, sometimes. Seeing her up here all this time now, three days a week and not having any idea when she's . . . with that belly, as if it's got to be twins, at least." She turned, speculative: Or had that been a shirt on the back of the bathroom door? "Which is all your boozy pal Manolo needs," she said, crossing. "I mean two or so at once—" Reaching within, she did not need the light. There was a brassiere on the nail, hers or Lee's she did not know, nothing more. "But you must have something else to wear," she said. "Even a . . . Steve?"

She had been seconds only. For a moment, still at the bathroom door, she did not move. He was inside, of course, checking to see if she had been right, searching out some other garment—whatever it was, a drawer would have to be opened and she did not hear even that. Again it was something other than annoyance. All right, then. But why after all this time did it still startle her?

The machete lay where she had discarded it. Returning,

she paused to set it back upon the mantelpiece. She went to the archway.

He had not turned on a lamp. Through the entrance the diminishing fire achieved a corner of the bed, the low table at its side, the straw rug beneath. She could discern its dim reflection in the high window on the rear wall also. "That damned thing is smoking again," she said. "Would it be the chimney like the last time, leaves or something—?"

Still there was a moment. And this too: to have been alone with him in darkness, knowing it only he and she together and that he could not be more than steps away, inches, and yet to have started at his touch. She said, "Old demon Steve—?"

Soundlessly, he emerged into the light. He was placing something into his pocket—it seemed money—and he wore the same shirt. "I'll tell Manolo," he said.

"Oh, swell. With Petra expecting at any hour. So if he isn't drunk in anticipation of his fatherhood he'll be drunk in celebration. It will be a week at best, Steve, since it takes him three days to get around to anything under ordinary circumstances—"

"It isn't that cold, Fern—"

Passing her he crossed to the deep chair in which she had been sitting earlier, though beyond it, to turn again half within the faintly smoke-tinted cone of light and half without, his trunk severed into shadow. "Is this rum?" he asked. As if disembodied, his arm shattered the symmetry when he lifted her glass.

"Finish it."

She remained at the archway, leaning there as she watched him drink, barely visible in the gloom beyond the lamp. Between them Lee had shifted position, on her side now and with the jacket flung open in discomfort, the crush of one breast exposed. Outside, beyond the open kitchen window, a rooster crowed.

"Why is it I always thought they only did that in the morning?" Fern said after a moment. "I thought so before Mexico, anyway."

"Why who what?"

"Roosters, cocks—whatever that difference that I never learned either. But they go on all night, don't they?"

Now he did not reply. Discarding the glass he had lifted the book instead, one of his own that had been there when she herself sat, then stood tilting it downward into the light, his face still beyond the lamp's confined sphere. He would have to be squinting. Or peering, she thought, ridiculously, like some beleaguered anchorite at his bleak cell's window in the last precious glimmerings of twilight. As if tallow were scarce, or forbidden. Then she laughed to herself. *But my God, now when I even see him I practically do not.* "Roosters," she said again. " 'The bird of dawning singeth all night long'—is that the line?"

But the book seemed to hang suspended almost of itself now, just within the glow, his hand obscured beneath it wholly. Taking a cigarette, she said, "That idiotic lamp. Caravaggio could cope with that sort of chiaroscuro, I suppose—if he didn't go blind trying." And yet he did hear anyway, she knew. Because a week from now would tell her something improbable about roosters. Or in no apparent context would quote the *Hamlet* properly, too. Whereupon witless Fern would be the one to wonder what on earth had brought that up.

But he had closed the book at last, replacing it. Not looking toward her he crossed to the window that opened on their walled garden, the lawn before the house. "Ain't nothing out there but crickets, hombre," she said, but not aloud. She shook her head, a little forlornly. And what did he see, what stare at, so often in the night? Deep into that darkness peering. *Or as when he would perhaps mutter some single word. Like: Ananias. What, Steve? Who?* She mouthed the name, if name it were: "Ananias." There was no sound from the fire now, very little glow. Yet it should not have been the logs, not in November with the rains a month or more past. Long I stood there, wondering, fearing. "I was listening there before," she said, actually did speak again now, though softly, over the sleeping girl, "not at that window but the other. It was silly, I guess, as if I might hear it from down the hill. Petra and Manolo's baby, I mean, the first cry. Not that it really has to come today, but everything carries so well at night. Is that ironic? Me, here, being sentimental about a poor, illiterate Indian girl who works for us now and then and is about to have a child? Yet that shack, golly, and the animals—like Bethlehem, almost. And so lovely, dear God, that unbelievable Aztec face, and those innocent, thousand-year-old eyes . . . I almost told her to come up, Steve, do you know? Before Lee got sick. I thought, here, with both of us to help—"

But he had taken up another book now, had opened it at obvious random and could not have been deciphering it even, not holding it to the light this time. She recognized it from its place on the window ledge, his Eric Chazen poems. Closing her eyes she inhaled heavily on the cigarette, finding it harsh, one of his own that had been in the robe and too strong for her. Four pennies American, his cheap slow suicide. She crossed to the fire to discard it. Then she said, "Listen. Caravaggio once committed murder, did you know? Do you think it might have been because no one ever answered him when he talked?"

"What?"

"Nothing. I was just wondering if I get partial credit in the course for dusting that Saint Anselm you left on the chair again, even if I know I'll never read it?"

"There will be women there, Fern. A midwife. And she has an aunt in town."

She did not quite smile, though she thought: All right, you did. So what about the roosters, then? She had moved toward a table, not sitting but leaning there now too, her thighs against its edge and her arms braced behind her, yet not at ease. And eternally, why was the voice in her head so different from the voice she heard when she spoke? One of her sketchbooks lay open at her side, folded to a page upon which there appeared a solitary, leafless tree, from one branch of which, in aborting it, she had slashed a gross, directionless line: it might have been a hangman's noose. Yet she had caught Petra, did have that face, had gotten it down. He set the poems aside. Gazing at him, she said, "Then again it would have been an eccentric sort of gesture anyway, wouldn't it? Petra, I mean. What with the extraordinary surfeit of beds we don't happen to have around here—"

He turned, something might have flashed in his eyes. For a moment they confronted each other in the diffuse haze.

"Shouldn't she be inside?" he said finally.

"Not alone." Her voice was flat, without emphasis. "The fire never really warms it in there. You know that."

He nodded. "When it dies, then."

Fern said nothing. He was looking beyond her, possibly at the hearth. Not needing to ask, she knew: And now he is going out again. She was no longer facing him either. She sensed rather than heard him enter the kitchen.

He did not pull the light cord. "What do you want, Steve? We do hold meals around here, Lee and I, anyway, with some moderate degree of regularity—"

"Nothing."

"But you haven't eaten all day—"

"Maybe later."

Emerging, he retrieved his jacket. "Steve, good heavens, you aren't going to keep on wearing that shirt—?"

He shrugged indifferently. The blood was stiffening, a burnt umber now, though fierce in the firelight. And at play about that haunted, Raskolnikov face of his, those hollows, it would be hard to capture. There was no point in asking, she knew, even as he paused to take down the machete and poke at the coals: Where? Still at the table, still leaning there, she watched him kneel. Where, in these alien Mexican nights, and what specters fleeing?

"Christ, but you do build an admirable sort of fire, lady."

"Forgive me. I'm just that clumsy crippled girl."

"Mistress at *Withering Heights*—"

Turning, he was grinning at her, though she said nothing, was considering him merely. Before him there was new life on the grate, though not much. At last he arose.

"Fern—?"

She turned aside. There was a moment, more, in which she was conscious of him watching her.

She did not move when he touched her. Her robe had come loose, and she wore nothing beneath it. Gently, so imperceptibly that she had to think *He does not know he is doing that at all*, his knuckles traced across the flesh of her stomach, downward into the hollow of her thigh. At last her eyes lifted. His own were fixed upon her face, his cheeks might have been hot in the new flickering from the hearth. "What, Fern?"

Beyond him, over the cot's side, one of Lee's arms extended limply, as if having surrendered in some effort of reaching. The sleeping and the dead. "Nothing, Steve," she said. She continued to look past him. "I suppose I ought to understand the conditions of my existence here. Lee's too, by now—"

"Fern, there have never been any . . . conditions—"

"All right, Steve—"

The hand had fallen away, though the eyes still held her own. "Anyway, it's . . . you are a fool. Even before she came. That . . . hand or not, anyone you'd want, while I—"

She sighed, again looking away.

"One of these days you'll go," he told her.

A knot snapped in the fire. "I might," she said finally. The smile was quite private, and again it was forlorn. "We've gotten so damned humorless around here lately, I just might."

She felt the tension ebb then, sensed it slacken in him almost physically, though his own smile was grim. Only then, about to let it end, as he seemed to contemplate his shirt anew did she realize that she had not asked. "Was it something bad, Steve? An Indian, you said—?"

For a moment his response appeared only thoughtful. Then he shook his head. "Dead as Osiris. We hacked the body into great bleeding chunks and tossed them into the Nile."

"What—?" Fern winced, thinking him actually indifferent, even amused. Then she sensed the attitude strange, however, an unfamiliar speculation lurked behind it, even as she saw that he still held the machete also, was scowling at it. "Jesus, yes," he decided. "I wonder if something like that might . . . solve it up here, too?" He glanced toward the cot, back. "The sacrificial rites, by way of . . . renewal, would it be? Though we scarcely need the Egyptians, do we, with all the local gore that goes back to . . . where, Tenochtitlán? The Hill of the Star? Kindling the fires of the new solar year in the pulsating, open breast of the victim herself, in feathered serpents' robes, or—"

It should have been mischief. Yet even as the blade lifted toward her, flicking across her unbelted bathrobe, she knew it too intense, peculiarly abstracted. It became a chant. "In the name of Xipe, the flayed one—of Tlaltechli, the monster who consumes the sun—"

Instinctively she drew back. The blade jerked, followed, pressed at flesh. Laughing and fierce for the instant his eyes glittered, held fast.

"Stop it, Steve—"

Lee may have stirred also, though it did cease then, that quickly he had abandoned the machete and was at the door.

"Of all the childish, imbecilic—"

Then it was she who halted, at the look which, even as she perceived it, she found even less familiar than the other, a constrained and knotted bafflement. Startled, she waited. Then even his voice was hesitant. "Jesus, is it . . . fifteen years? When I was down here before, as a kid. I got lost once, out hunting for Toltec ruins. An Indian took me in for the night. Talk about . . . circling back, the eternal *retour* . . . to be called in by that damned fool intern tonight, and find the same old man dying on the—"

"Steve—?"

But the door closed, was drawn silently after him. For a long moment she stood quite still. Then, when she turned, it was to find Lee awake now in fact, upon her back, though with her head turned, watching. The room was darkening, the last of the fire accentuating the delicate plane of her cheek, the beautifully articulated curve of one lifted calf. They gazed at each other.

"From the ridiculous to the sublimated," Lee said at last, quietly.

"Yes," Fern said. She smiled, though worn, grave. "I think I would pay money for the privilege of having a consistent reaction to him for twenty consecutive minutes, sometime. Do you want anything, Lee? How do you feel?"

"Shitty. A blanket, maybe. Would you?"

"He left an encyclical. You're supposed to go inside."

"I heard. Fuck him."

Finally laughing, Fern started toward the bedroom. At the archway she stopped again. Only half-seriously, she said, "Three months ago you wouldn't have said that word, do you know? I'm not sure you would have said it three or four weeks ago, even."

The other's head lifted, was cocked momentarily at the difficult angle. Then she lowered it, her expression ironic or wistful, Fern could not tell. "On the Day of Judgment I'm going to borrow one of your brushes and paint it on my forehead," she said finally.

She had changed position yet again, on her stomach once more, when Fern emerged, and her breath came irregularly. Covering her, Fern did not speak.

For a time then, she stared into what remained of the fire. She was smoking again. When she threw the cigarette into the hearth, she thought only: And now it will be eleven, close to eleven. Only the hooded lamp, that corner, contained light now. At the other end of the room past the front door her easel might have been something threatening, some ominous giant weapon.

She found herself gazing at it, and again for several moments, at the hearth still, conscious of the last of its warmth, she did not move. But it was not the easel either. She knew what it was. Disturbed, she thought: Yet why now, why should I think of it now, after all this time? When she crossed to kneel at the chest below her work table, her face was quite tense, quite set.

The carton lay just within, beneath a roll of uncut canvas. Lifting it, almost surreptitiously she glanced toward Lee, barely able to see her now, shadow athwart shadow: with her dark hair, that jacket, it might have been he lying there. Briefly, though with the chest already closed, again she may have hesitated. Then she arose, she crossed beneath the arch into the bedroom.

The carton was bound with string, but loosely. Alone in the darkness, seated upon the unmade bed, she removed the cover. Then she drew out the child's doll, the Raggedy Ann.

"——Because why can't I stay home and play by my-self?" she says.

Sullen now, a frail child small for her age, she stands near the chair over which her mother has folded the dress. Beyond a window snow lies in patches upon a deep, tree-bordered yard, and on the ledge, against the frosted glass, a doll is propped. There is nothing petulant in her tone yet. "I don't want to go," she says.

"Fern," her mother says. She sighs once, the attitude already ingrained, of despair, of vanquishment. Yet she is not severe. "You have an hour," she says. "You can dress yourself here in the kitchen, where it is warmer. I'll bring down your party shoes."

Still there is only reasonableness in the child's tone. "I don't want to," she says. Past the window snow falls lightly, swirling.

"Fern, now you know it's Susan's birthday. You said you wanted a new dress and we bought you one. Is it the dress? Don't you like it?"

Lightly, at the doll, at Raggedy Ann, her hand hovers.

"Or what then, darling? There'll be no one there you don't know. They're only the girls from the kinder-garten—"

Still the child does not answer, but she can feel it beginning then. She is not thinking about her hand, already at five the reaction is instinctive, beyond necessity of predication. Yet her eyes mist.

"Fern," her mother says, "now, Fern. It's only Susan.

Susan, and Carol, and Joanie Ross . . . why, I'd bet they don't even notice anymore, they're so used to you—"

The tears come. They are not deliberate, not refuge, though she does not struggle against them either. Clasping the limp, tattered doll against herself, she sobs, "I don't want to. I want to stay home and play with Raggedy Annie."

Over the crying her mother's voice is pained but firm. "Fern, I want you to be ready when Mrs. Ross blows the horn."

Desolate, she waits as the handkerchief appears, suffering her nose to be wiped.

"Now do, darling. I have to go upstairs."

Then she is alone. Still clutching the doll, she gazes at the dress. She does not think: I hate them. She does not think: Because Joanie Ross calls me Funny Hand, and Susan laughs, since this too is already part of consciousness, unnecessary of recall. Deliberately, yet somehow almost as if without premeditation, so that if distracted she might not even remember to continue, she picks up the starched yellow garment and crosses the room. The room is inordinately large, and in addition to an electric stove there is another, an antique iron hulk still used on occasion for heating. There is fire in it now. The dress is in her right hand. She must change hands before she lifts down the quilted potholder fixed to the wall and opens the heavy door of the stove.

She does not close the door again, although she is already back at the window, seated on the floor and not watching the flames, when she hears her mother on the stairs. She has not been conscious of the smoke either, has not left the door open out of any motive. "Fern, are you all right? Is something burning—?"

She does not cry this time. Even after she has been forcibly washed and changed, she has not cried again.

Her face is set, puckered, where she waits in her overshoes now and completely dressed for out-of-doors, waits hearing her mother at the telephone in the adjacent room, the voice despairing, pained, abject. "No," her mother says, "not the furnace, not the cellar. The old stove in the kitchen. Of course ruined, Adam, I was up in the bedroom." In pauses even from beyond the half-closed door she can hear the hum and static of her father's voice also, though no words, not listening anyway, still thinking nothing except: I'm not. I won't go. She has retrieved her doll. Her mother says, "Adam, Adam, we've sheltered her so much as it is, she has to learn to face them." She stands, not listening, yet hearing: "Yes, another dress, it's perfectly adequate. I only bought the new one because I thought it might help—" Then again not listening she is thinking: Funny Hand. Because I was born. Because Mrs. Ross heard her and said Fern was born that way she cannot help it you must not laugh. Spanking her. Because Joanie said: Fern is funny, I don't want to play with Fern. And I cried. And ran. Clasping her doll against the snowsuit, she thinks: But when Freddy Ross broke his arm and the big bandage. And Joanie said: Will it be like Fern's when the bandage is off? And Freddy said: Nobody is like Fern's. And everybody said: Poor Freddy, Freddy broke his arm. But didn't laugh, didn't say: Funny Arm.

Because it would be better and be the same, two the same.

Because Freddy fell. Because an accident, and not born with.

Nor born.

She is already outside now, the door closing noiselessly behind her, sealing from hearing the quiet, pained, unattenuated voice. The door to the cellar, set into what might appear a woodshed, or a storage bin, is not locked. Entering, she cannot reach the cord, but there is light from the windows at ground level, not fully blocked by the drifted snow without. But the light is refracted, misty, unreal. She thinks: Like church. Like church when Daddy takes me in the afternoon and there is nobody, only Baby Jesus and Daddy and Fern. In the snowsuit, clutching her doll, she is not cold. Standing at the lowest of the broad plank steps, she thinks: Because Freddy had an accident and not like Fern's. Because not born.

And Baby Jesus, alone in the churchy light.

There is nothing with which to lift the handle here, though insulated it is not hot. Holding the doll in her left hand she tests it, concentrating now, quite intent. The door is far heavier than the other, set firmly, and for a moment it will not give. Using both hands then, the doll discarded, she finds the required leverage. She sucks in her breath at the immense, shimmering blast of heat.

Still she is not crying again, although her thin lips quiver. Standing in the zippered snowsuit she begins to perspire, not knowing it that, simply conscious of the enveloping heat. Then the sensation turns strange, she seems not to be standing there at all. Standing and sweating before the raw coals she seems to be watching herself at the same time, as if from above, from beyond, perhaps on the stairway. Can a person be here and be on the stairway at the same time? And the fire, how funny, because like it is burning and not. Because the coal is all red, but it is still coal. She can see their shapes.

Then she stops thinking. Not even thinking: Because born with, and nobody laughed at Freddy because an accident and not born with. Standing as if aside, above, as if watching herself, she does not even think: *So if Fern had an accident nobody would laugh at her too.* Feeling the heat, she hears the door also, hears her mother at the entry above and behind her. She hears, "Fern Ellen Winters, you come out of there this instant. Because I suspect my patience is just about at an end, now—"

Or perhaps she hears nothing at all, really, no sound of voice or footsteps, and perhaps not even the mounting whisper of flame either, the hiss and spit of singed wool, watching from that distance and not truly there, not even quite credulous at the stark, unimaginably shocking wrench of pain itself, until her mother begins to scream——

It has not been a dream. Yet when it ceases, when she jerks upright suddenly, it is as if in awakening. The agony is old, familiar, inescapable. Nonetheless she is startled to find herself in the bed, undressed, alone in the bed. She thinks: After he came. And went again. And with the blood, that shirt. Turning, she sees that nothing remains of the fire except a dim, faintly perceptible cluster of embers beyond the archway, in a haze of smoke beyond the archway.

Fern lay back, sweating. For a time, the recollection had possessed her completely. Or had it begun in dream after all, at some border of consciousness between wakefulness and dream? Watching herself, like some effigy of the child Fern. As if it were not she herself whom she remembered, but some doll she observed.

Doll?

Oh, dear Jesus. Oh, dear, sweet, dispiteous, raggedy Jesus . . .

She lay quite still now, her arms at her sides, her face to the ceiling. She recalled sitting, holding it, and then with it cradled finally too, in her crippled arm. And singing, even? Had she even at last begun to sing? As through all the years, through all of her life, whenever she had had anything to flee from?

Yet she had stopped, she remembered now, had caught herself up. How long it had been she did not know. But at last, snatching up doll and carton both, she had fled through the archway and flung them into the fire, had remained there until both had ignited. Nor had Lee seen.

No, because she had watched Lee too, her shadow where it leaped beyond the cot in that new terrible glare.

And then had slept herself. For some moments, had evidently slept.

More calmly now, Fern turned her head, again saw the barely glimmering embers, the dense smoring of smoke. From something in the doll, very likely, whatever its composition, probably it had not burned fully. In flame like herself and not burning, smoking only. Poor Annie, you deserved better than my shabby neurosis had to offer. She could actually smell it now, though it was piny, as if the logs too had burned again for a time. Beyond the bed on the rear wall she could scarcely make out the high rear window. I ought to open them, she thought. Thinking: And I have lost track of time, have no idea.

She breathed deeply, without a cover save for the twisted fold of sarape at her loins. She realized that the sheets were damp where she had been sweating. As in the snowsuit, so real the memory. It did not seem chilly, however. Yet it would be close to midnight now, she decided, would have to be that, at least. And the fire was practically dead. Yet she was not cold.

Mexico, she thought. To live at five thousand feet, a mile. And so the nights.

She lay desolately. Dear God, must she remember that forever? Yet it was fading now, now it was tonight instead, the doll, that oppressed her. Maybe if she were to paint it, like some sort of perverse therapy? Good heavens, could you? She did not smile. To get out and beyond, but truly, *really* to watch, to see? And the anxiety, could even a Van Gogh, who had found agony in commonest gardens? Because how would you get the singing in?

Yet she had stopped, did stop herself. Thirty-seven pesos, and she had thrown it into the fire. She did laugh now, without sound. So perhaps she was growing up. Had bought it a few days after Lee appeared but then forgot, until tonight forgot. And then threw it out. So perhaps in another ten or twenty years would not even have to buy them.

For some reason she was still sweating. Or had the chimney backed up completely now? There seemed a moon, yet she could not even be sure of that. When normally it would flood the bed. Really, she should open some. But still she was drained.

Then she saw that the window was open after all, was drawn inward an inch or two at its base. In the gloom, momentarily unreal, it appeared to waver, to lift and then withdraw. Or was it the room itself that drifted, illusory? Well, dear God, after all that. Smiling, she said, "Fern Ellen Winters, her two-peso version of the abyss."

Still she had not moved. And her counterfeit little ordeal of fire as well: at the age of five, trying to transmute it into something that to a five-year-old's logic might appear to obliterate the stigma. *Because an accident, and not born with.* Almost aloud, she said, "And poor Marion. Poor Mother."

She heard the sound then, wafted from some distance at first but then drawing near, dissonant where it rose and fell. It did not seem Spanish, seemed some Indian dialect until she understood it drunkenness that slurred the words. Then it came clearly, mournful and sweet. A serenade. Under her window in the depths, what benighted troubadour plucked his infernal lute beneath her window in the depths? She might have been able to see, since there was no wall about the house at that corner, rather the house itself overhung a bluff, but she could visualize him anyway, an anonymous peasant in the bleached cotton clothing of the hills, sombrero downslanted across half-shut eyes, his burro rather than the man seeking out the route toward home. The voice died on a funereal note as the singer departed down the slope and away.

"There is a city of miracles," she had been able to

translate, "and it is called Veracruz." In the renewed silence she thought: Vera Cruz. The True Cross. And yet how strange, why should she sense that she should have wanted to go there sometime in this year, should have been anxious to visit Veracruz? She could not remember. Or was she mixed up—what was she thinking of now? As if there were some picture she had meant to paint but never had, of a kind of vaulted silence, and a misted, refractory light . . . it came back: And my hand in my father's, she thought, alone in the vaulted silence of a church on an afternoon without sun.

But: Veracruz? And softly voiced, how beautiful the word . . .

She did not stir when she heard the door. Nor did she speak, though with the breeze, with the lifting air, eventually she drew the sarape about herself. She realized that she was exhausted, aware only obtusely that she had not heard the gate. Remembering the dead fire, remembering Lee, she thought: And I told him I would. She decided: Get sore, then. I've got my own disheveled psyche to cope with tonight, amigo. Then she was cold, that suddenly. Or did he still have the door open, out there?

She huddled more deeply within the sarape, hearing him move then also, incredibly, far less silent than usual. She heard the match strike too, although she barely perceived its flickering at the wall she faced now, the haze blued for less than an instant. She thought: So the power must be off again, the current dead all over town. Like her own. Dear backward Mictlán, we have something in common. Yet it was true, all of a sudden she was washed out. As if she were the one getting over something, not Lee. Shivering once, hearing him yet again, she thought: Or have I caught it from her? Do I have fever now, too? Abruptly, the sensation of hearing had become acute to an extreme, someway occult, so that sounds she would ordinarily never hear him make seemed to crash upon her consciousness like drumbeats. Dear God, did she even hear him breathing? Him, old demon? Could he have been running, was he carrying something heavy, lifting something? Was this absurd?

Fern lay perfectly still. Now it reached her like muffled conflict, or like a fury of great beating wings. Then she was sitting, stiffly, tensed. What was happening to her? Was she sick after all? Was she really sick? She said, aloud but hoarsely, "Steve?" And when she would never hear him at all, no sound until the bed took his weight?

So then her ears were filled with an uncanny rush of silence, it was tremendous. Insanely, apropos of nothing, she remembered wanting to hear Petra's baby. "Steve?" she said again. "Listen, don't tell me you can bump into something like an ordinary mortal for a change? Does that mean you're not just a figment of my imagination after all?"

It remained unbroken, idiotic. Then, facing that way, through the archway she saw the last tenacious glow of the coals suddenly surrender. It did not fade, did not begin to diminish, but suddenly, inexorably, disappeared. Then it came alive again. *So he was standing there. Had to be standing between me and the fire.* At last she laughed. "Are you drunk?" she said. "Is that it? I hope you realize you were standing in my sunlight?"

She had been right about the door, though only when it closed at last, when it thudded shut, did she realize that she had been hearing locust. She had not moved again, and she understood that she was waiting for the gate. Finally she said, "Now what the devil are you doing outside again?"

But he was never drunk either, she knew, could drink endlessly and was never. She arose then, wrapping the sarape about herself. Even standing at the bed, only steps away, she could hardly discern the contours of the arch. Striding beneath it rapidly, through the smoke that had drifted only, she went to the door. Near it her hand fumbled toward a light switch and then dropped again as she thought: All night: if the current is off now it will be off all night, probably. It was common. Opening the door, though not widely, she peered into the yard. It was deep, unwalled at its farther end above the treacherous drop, at the cliff above the lake. She could not see the lake from where she stood, but the mountains beyond were vivid, shadow heaped upon shadow. In moonlight just within the gate chrome and glass glinted on both cars, his, and the one in which Lee had arrived three months before. Threateningly silhouetted against the blanched adobe of the right-hand wall were maguey, and something that may have been a dead bird, or a simple stone, lay beneath a partially collapsed straw chair on the patio. The gate seemed closed.

She had not called his name again. Closing the door, leaning at it, she scowled almost defiantly into the polluted inner darkness. After the moonlight it was even more impenetrable now, though on the cot Lee did not appear to have moved. For the moment more irritated than distracted, Fern crossed to the kitchen. The window above the sink was open as she had left it earlier, and she forced it upward to its extremity now, horizontal against its rusted side pivots. Beyond the shadow of an unused servant's room constructed against that side of the house Indian laurel was interwoven amid the bougainvillea, but she could smell nothing. *Because all this smoke, the least he could have done was.* Still not attempting the lights she made her way back to the bedroom. She had to move a chair to achieve that window.

Climbing down after it was opened fully, she stopped, her brows knitting. Beyond a native hovel some meters away, in the rutted alley which a block below became a callejón leading down into the town, toward the zócalo, a streetlamp had been burning. Or was she going crazy? Yes, maybe that was it. Particularly since she had seemed to exhibit the proclivity as early as the age of five. "Damn it," she said. She was gazing upward, but she could tell nothing from below. She did not climb back onto the chair. But either the current was on, or the current was off. What was she acting like this for, anyway?

The lamp at the bed table went on, if weakly, barely illuminating the table itself and the floor beneath, a splash of whitewashed brick wall. Her robe, his, lay where she had discarded it earlier. Pensive now, her lips pursed, she gazed at a slip of paper inserted beneath the lamp's ceramic base, there for some days, the letters of the single word it bore blackened over and over by blunt pencil until his handwriting was almost unrecognizable: *Imposibilidad.* She was holding the sarape at her throat. "Or am I?" she said softly.

And yet damn her, now, she had heard him, she did. And people did not hear noises in the night when there weren't noises. Even people who at twenty-three hummed lullabies to rag dolls and then threw them into fireplaces. And anyway, why a match when the lights were working? Indeed. So she was but nuts north-northwest. And when the wind was southerly she knew a hawk from a handsaw. Thank you. Swiftly, she crossed to the door again. Then she stopped, turned. She said, "Intrepid Fern. So where did I leave that machete?"

The light from the bedroom did not achieve the hearth. Not trying the switch near her, not quite asking why she found herself reluctant to turn on another light, she fumbled about the mantelpiece. She felt cigarettes, a book, the straw Don Quixote. But Steve had used it also, she remembered then. That first time, when he had really been there. "Now where did he—?"

When he had really been there. Or was he ever, was he even real? As if materializing in and out of darkness, or disappearing before her very eyes . . . and that shirt, blessed Jesus, wrist deep in it, and all that talk of ritual sacrifice, chopping off people's legs . . . or were the lot of them unhinged, maybe, maybe not just she alone? Dear heaven, yes, and in this land of sun where we seem to exist forever in shadow, can any of it approach reality at all? Standing at the dead fire, distracted, disturbed, not quite with irrelevance she thought: And yet I used to wonder the same thing a year ago, more. As when Marion would call, out of simplest concern, and I would think: Can I say I am going crazy, Mother, am going slowly, undeviatingly, irretrievably mad? But only a joke then, my trivial, sad, desponding joke. In New York, before Steve. Imposibilidad. Aloud now, loudly, she said, "Lee? Are you awake? Listen, do me a modest favor and tell me the bastard was just here again, will you? Tell me somebody was?"

Now she did turn on the light. Through the smoke the room appeared perfectly ordered, although the machete was nowhere near the fireplace. Musing, for the moment in the reassuring glow almost annoyed with herself, she thought: Now what did I want the darned thing for anyway? Thinking: Good Lord, it was just the doll, just being asinine. It would have left anybody dopey. She turned to the cot. Balanced there, though as if about to fall, the blade glinted dully beside Lee's downflung arm. Still quite calm, quite rational, even as she looked to Lee herself now, she thought only: Now isn't that ridiculous? Why would she go and change into that bloody shirt of his, for heaven's sake?

Then she was not seeing Lee at all. Rather she might have been watching, observing from afar, herself and Lee both, so that when she heard the scream neither did this seem her own but may have been part of memory, even, a cry of her mother's long past, long gone. It is a sound like wailing, pitiful and quintessential, a dreadful monody like a Munch woodcut sprung to life. She actually thinks this, has a sensible moment in which she decides: Yes, the Munch, the woman on that bridge I had on my wall in New York. Yet she will not recall when the thought comes. Perhaps she is still in the house, perhaps in the gouged and anguished lanes of the sleeping town. Only in the ancient chapel is it real again, is she part of it once more. Then, speaking it finally, huddled in moonlight with that mysterious candle extinguished behind her, the enormous shattered crucifix lost to darkness and the doctor's shocked, uncomprehending face above her own, then, hideously, can she see again the hacked and mutilated white neck, the spattered, berserk, still-seeping blood upon the pillow. "Lee?" the doctor cries. "That machete? You are telling me that someone used it to—?"

Then she lost it again, though still she was calm, composed. "I don't know," she said. "I think so. But you'd better go, better look. Because I might be mad. It would not be the first time. Yet I hope so. God forgive me, I do. Otherwise—"

"What? What? You hope she—?"

She begins to weep then, in the dark of the moon, at the sick, sweet taste of orchid. There is jasmine on the breeze also. "Otherwise I am," she says. "Otherwise the joke is over, and I truly am."

FOUR

Her little joke. Her weary, stale, flat, unfunny joke, that she allowed herself to voice aloud but once, one night when Marion called. Whatever night it was, whichever of the eight hundred and some nights before Steve. Hearing: "No special reason, Fern, your father and I were just thinking you might like to come out this weekend," and she said, "Marion, what do you want?" Saying, "What do you want from me, Mother?"

Fern what are you doing with your life what doing I never heard of such a thing just painting not for a girl of twenty-two not even a job to occupy your time we are less than an hour away from New York you hardly spend three weekends a year out here there is always the club they are nice people Fern the people who make the world go round has anyone ever said your paintings are any good and that dingy apartment your father would gladly pay for something better gladly send more money aren't you even thinking of marriage Fern what are you doing what doing with your life—?

Saying: "I am going out of my mind, Marion, is what I am doing, am going slowly, irrevocably, undeniably, out of my—" Before Steve. No Marion I am not serious. No Marion nothing is wrong. Nothing is any different today than it was yesterday or last week or last month or. Yes I am eating properly. Yes, soon, I will come out. Yes I know you don't understand. Good-bye Marion good-bye Mother my love to Adam yes.

Her little joke. When her mother finally hung up she stood at the telephone stand for a moment and tried to decide what day it would be. She knew the hour, knew it a little after nine. She decided it was a Wednesday. Then she decided it was the middle of August, perhaps even the fifteenth exactly. So that would make it eight hundred, then. Would it? Thinking: Because I came to New York the day after graduation, a ninth of June, and so the two years to this June ninth would be seven hundred and thirty days. And two more months plus six or seven days would make it approximately eight hundred. If she were right and it was the middle of August.

Thinking: So I have lived a solitary, immutable night that has been eight hundred days long. Eight hundred days, my barren, immutable night without stay.

Ass, precious ass.

All right. But why wasn't she painting, then?

She was not painting. She had only one light on, the neon above the easel. She had closed two of the three front windows, all of them filthy and little more than translucent, trying to shut out the heat, and in a corner at floor level a fan was going. But it was still hot. Wearing a brassiere and pants, sweating just a little. With the tubes squeezed out since before six o'clock on the jagged shard of glass she used as a palette, the brushes cleaned and aligned, and she was not painting.

The rest of the room was dark. About her where she sat on the tall stool before the easel the shadows were profound, suggesting reaches that did not exist. She had spilled Scotch into a glass and was drinking it with water, and now and then the ice would tinkle against the glass with a sound like faint bells. Like bells at sea, distant bells. Sitting and drinking in the hot room. Probably there were trucks on the street but after two years she did not hear them. After eight hundred days. Thinking: And after twenty-two years, his bones beneath the sea, his bones picked clean by whispers beneath the sea. Yet why tonight, why again, was she going to start thinking of that again? There was nothing on the canvas but some grays and off-whites, shapes that did not mean anything yet, like piling cumulus. She had not touched the canvas for a week, but she knew what would happen. As soon as she started, it would happen again.

She had done four of them. For most of the two years her work had been turning more and more abstract, and she had liked what she believed she was finding. There had been less and less line, finally form alone, and she believed the forms had depth. But then these had begun to dissolve also and it had taken her months to understand what was happening, that she was denying color too now, as if any contrast at all even bleeding into the most cautious *sfumato* contrived line whether she intended line or not. Working darker and darker then, so that at last although a suggestion of form remained it was scarcely perceptible, less than penumbral. Because I am afraid to commit myself, she thought, to circumscribe anything. After the first three she removed the blacks from the paint chest and deposited them on a high shelf in the kitchen and started another, but it happened nonetheless. Before she was into it she knew she would need the blacks again if she were going to work at all.

So she was not painting. She told herself she would put another coat of gesso on the canvas, over the grays. Or perhaps the only answer was to try something representational, get up one fine morning bright and early and do some student exercise even, a cityscape in sunlight. Surely, she thought. Or some apples then, traditional and safe and red as my cochineal lips. She was drinking, smiling, thinking: But it is still weird, almost too blatantly symbolic to mean what anyone would think it meant. What are you painting these days, Fern? Oh, I am painting the darkness within, the gloomy, irrecusable heart and core of darkness within. No shit, I really am. She took down the canvas and leaned it against the cord of stacked dry work in the corner beyond the easel, face inward, and then stood drinking. Cezapples. Across the room the fan whirred but the hot air only drifted, was no cooler. And now it would be ten o'clock, at least ten o'clock.

She was going out. She had not been thinking about it, not consciously, no more than not thinking about sleep she knew she would eventually sleep. In the gloom she crossed over and stared at her three shelves of books. Scraps of paper marked her places in several of them, one of the volumes of her Vasari, the Nijinski diary, the Hermann Hesse. What had she been looking up in the Vasari? She took down the Hesse and held it, standing there, and then she put it back. Standing with her drink she gazed at the books. Then she was gazing at the telephone. And Fern those strange faces you have been sketching lately, those strange, tormented faces. No, I am sorry, Mrs. Winters is not in the card room, if you will hold on I can check the pool. She put the drink on the telephone stand and then crossed to the studio couch and sat. Was it a Wednesday in the middle of August? Could she even prove it was 1959? Sitting, she could see the paints on the glass below the easel. With the heat, the oils and pigments would separate, the vermillion was beginning to. She was almost out of turpentine. She stood again and crossed the room and lifted the can, hearing the faint sloshing of what remained. She went to the desk near the righthand front window and sat there. On a sheet of paper she wrote "turp." Someone was talking on the street, one floor below, sounds only, not words. Within a minute, sitting and not listening, gazing out at the dark facade of the warehouse across the way, she felt her thighs beginning to sweat against the chair. When she returned to her drink the last of the ice had melted and it had gone flat. The bottle was in the kitchen. She stood by the bookshelves holding the glass, not going into the kitchen. And it was eight hundred days, the night was eight hundred days long. She put down the drink again, straightening the Hesse in its place. Between *Ulysses* and Edgar Allan Poe. Touching the spine of a life of Van Gogh. She went back to the studio couch.

Across the room under the blued cast of neon she could see clumps of dust at the baseboards and under the radiator. On the punchboard fixed to that wall odds and ends of sketches hung askew. One corner of a Van Eyck reproduction clipped from a magazine was drooping forward. Seated near the fan now she could feel a slight breeze on her calves, but the floor was warm under her bare feet. And why no rug Fern if you must live in such a place such a slum you could at least buy? Because outside of the kitchen and the bath Marion there is only the one room, I work in it as well as live and with my paints it would get. She had been wearing frayed tennis shoes with the tongues cut out and no laces, and below the easel the sole of one of them was turned toward her, the other standing upright behind it. Gazing at them she did a free sketch in her head, thinking she could manage it with a single uninterrupted line, but they were in conflict and she was forced to double back. It was ten-thirty, just about. In the Hesse the early chapter where her place was marked was called "For Madmen Only." Van Gogh could borrow it when she was finished. Unless Nijinski wanted it first. She stood up, smiling, facing the fan for a moment. Then she went to the desk, not sitting this time, and wrote "rose madder" under the other reminder. If Nijinski was mad, was rose madder? Then she stopped, thinking a minute, and after that she wrote "lead, half gal." Because maybe she was neurotic enough for that too. Because she had never wasted paint, so maybe if she confronted herself with that much white it just might solve the problem. Or wouldn't it? Her eyes smarted from the turpentine and she rubbed her fingers against her buttocks, just below her thin pants, standing at the desk. Still it could make her cry. Going around the easel she set another pushpin into the reproduction. *Johannes de Eyck fuit hic*, it said. Was here, did it mean? Made this? She glanced at her own sketches. But those torn faces Fern, such loneliness. She unpinned the detail from the Masaccio, the *Expulsion*, tilting it toward the light. The anatomy was not right, today any beginner could get it righter than that. So why wasn't she better than Masaccio, then? She lay the reproduction aside, not seeing the others, knowing them without seeing: Murillo, Cosimo, Modigliani, her Pollocks, Bellini, Le Nain. Also the Giacometti, whom she had never been able to under-stand. And the photograph of that bullfighter with the ravaged expression, named what? She could buy every-thing on Greenwich Avenue in the afternoon, since she had to go to the bank tomorrow anyway. If she got up in time to go to the bank. Or would Adam stop by, had Marion said it was Thursday he might be in town? No Adam I just happened to be out late last night, usually I get up by.

And far beneath the sea, his bones washed clean by whispers, under sea.

Fern Adam Winters is not your.

Thinking: Except it would have had to be different on the phone tonight then too. If it were true. Not saying Fern your father and I.

She thought: But that means I am going to start again after all, doesn't it? My senseless, unremitting fantasy. And yet how persistent, and how absolute too, sometimes, for all that it is only in my mind. Holmes, she thought, Raymond Holmes, and when did I decide that that should be his name anyway, my spurious, adopted, unreal, and supposedly illegitimate plus tragically dead father? Or couldn't I even change it now if I tried?

Full fathom five thy father lies . . .

Idiot. Lippi, had it been Lippi, in the Vasari?

Manolete? Who was Manolete?

Drawing the tennis shoes from beneath the stool she stepped into them, then pressed the switch for the neon and went to the dresser near the studio couch. A shunted glow from the streetlamp below the lefthand window was reflected from the ceiling, it was not fully dark. Ineluctable modality of the streetlamp. Or something. And Filippino Lippi's mother was a nun. She withdrew fresh pants and another brassiere. As someone said: hardly of her Greenwich Village streetlamp however. Crossing into the kitchen she pulled the string for the overhead bulb. And would James Joyce have known that, about Filippino Lippi? Would she, if she hadn't been looking in the Vasari? She left the brassiere and the pants across the back of one of the two kitchen chairs, then turned on the shower. A current under sea. When she undressed she dropped the sweated brassiere and pants onto the floor in the bathroom. The water was warm but not hot. Clasping her hair in both hands she held it away from the spray with her arms raised. Yes Adam I'd love lunch I'll just take a quick. Mother, tell me, does Adam know? Fern God help me I could not, did not, the one indiscretion and. When she was finished she did not dry herself but stood allowing the water to drip while she combed her hair. Would have, Fern, would have had to, bearing you, but when Holmes died so quickly thereafter I. Then she did dry herself, remembering a sentence she had underlined in the Nijinski: "I am the one who dies when he is not loved." She put on the fresh brassiere and the pants. Fern, forgive me, I have been a good wife since. But the one night, only the one, before Holmes sailed for Spain. She withdrew her raincoat from the closet between the kitchen and the living room, depositing that over the second chair, thinking: But that too, that war, why do I always make it Spain? Because if there had really been a Raymond Holmes I would know all about it by now, probably, would surely have read a lot more than that one novel by Hemingway. Or no, I started that Malraux thing once too. Yet always, off Cádiz, the ship bombed and sunk, did not run the blockade. When I am not even certain where Cádiz is, let alone whose side it might have been on. Thinking: When fetal Fern was few weeks formed. Fern, Adam Winters is not your. Thoughts of a soggy brain in a hot season. She removed a five-dollar bill from her pocketbook and placed it into the lefthand pocket of the raincoat. Then she put in her keys. Mad Nijinski, dancing and mad. She stepped into her newer tennis shoes, knowing her soles would have blackened again even in minutes. Because Marion it is clean enough for the place I work in anyhow there are too many warehouses this far west in Manhattan it is filthy ten minutes after I. The athletic coach where I was teaching leaving for Mexico only a day or two later to embark with some Loyalist group had never said a word about his feelings before that and your father *Adam* traveling so much in those days. Thinking: No Marion I am only joking, my silly joke. Turpentine, rose madder, white lead. My father isn't my daddy, and my fantasy daddy is dead. Or was she out of Flemish siccative too? She pulled on the raincoat over the brassiere and pants, jerking her head to free her hair, and then she buttoned each of the buttons of the coat. Then she took a clean glass from the shelf above the sink and spilled in more Scotch, only a taste and not adding water this time, sipping it standing. She was holding the Scotch in her right hand. With her lamed hand she touched the outside of the coat, feeling the bill and the keys. Then, perhaps aware that she was speaking aloud, she said, "But I do not mean to joke either, Marion. Not about that, not after what you and Adam must both have gone through." She said, "Because anyway it is only this, is now, this shoddy life of mine that you do not understand at all." When she finished the whiskey she set the glass on the drainboard, already sweating again. Going into the living room she found the first glass and came back and placed it next to the other. Then she went back again and opened the two closed windows. She did not turn off the fan. She crossed to the desk, touching her money and the keys, and moved the shopping reminder under the edge of the pencil jar. "Holmes is where the heart is," she said. Had she said that aloud also? *Neu-ro-ses.* She turned out the lights in the kitchen and in the bathroom, and then she stood by the door. Veracruz, would he have sailed from? Tampico? Her left hand was in the pocket of the coat, riding there lightly, its weight upon the wrist.

Veracruz, let it be. Her other hand was already at the doorknob. Then she went back yet again through the darkness to the dresser. She removed her diaphragm and the tube of jelly from the top drawer and dropped them into her lefthand pocket, changing the money and keys to the right. She closed the drawer. Setting the lock she stepped out and tried the door. Then she went down the single airless flight and through the vestibule and into the heat, the hot night.

I am the one who dies when he is not loved.

And then stops thinking. Telling herself: Do not think now. She goes to a tavern, a crowded bohemian enclave. There are people here whom she knows, though not many, none well. "Fern," someone says—"a fern is a pteridophytic seedless plant that reproduces asexually. Through spores." He is standing at the door, lean, ill-shaven, somewhat drunk. "If you know that, what's wrong with the air-conditioning then?" she asks. The man turns, discarding a glass. "Christ, yes. Why don't we go somewhere else?" Confronting the crowd, the noise, she nods. Thinking as they depart, as it is sealed behind them: Because why wait, why bother to wait? Conscious of her tennis shoes scuffing against the concrete while they stroll as if without direction, not thinking, not hearing when the man talks. It is something about films, a book. Thinking: Eddie? Would it be Eddie? They do not walk far. At a nondescript apartment building there is invitation, idle, imprecise, and in a dismal peeling hall they climb two flights, in mustiness and gloom, in the heat. The room they enter is bleak, cloacal, ill-furnished, less large by half than her own. Not really seeing the room, forms impinging only, color, a naked radiator, stains of rust. Thinking: Anyway they are all the same, all one room. Not really thinking but telling herself: Yet I should paint this one day. Except how do you paint this? Because how do you get the not seeing in? The man opens beer, still talking, though she is still not hearing. Thinking or hearing instead: But why must you choose such a disreputable neighborhood Fern, and why alone like this? Alone. Seated, telling herself, "Stop. Just wait now, eventually he will finish that beer." Watching the sallow, ill-shaven face, and then on a torn envelope near her reading *Edward R. Goslin*, thinking: But I knew the Eddie part at least. Didn't I? Thinking *Eddie do you know I am not here, am not in this room at all?* and aware of the hand at her coat finally, coarse fingers at the buttons of the coat, his breath, the face *faceless* sweated at her neck and her own voice then, hearing: "All right, Eddie, I've succumbed once or twice in my life before, with all this humidity we can leave out the seduction part, I guess." And then is truly not there, is observer merely, as from a distance, as from above. Asexually, through spores. It is rote, the very motions mechanical, destitute of prelude, of expectation, not even forlorn. What are you doing Fern, what doing with your? In the stale confinement, in the dead stale air. Telling herself as she responds, as she pretends response, "Stop now," thinking: A place to be, a thing to do, without meaning or thought, to eliminate the need for thought. Telling herself, "Jesus, though, I could even charge money for it, would I feel any different if I charged money?" Thinking: Because I am even disconnected from it physically now too, so bloodless is it, my juiceless epithalamia. The man is spent quickly, she is scarcely aware of climax, conscious only of cessation, of withdrawal: *Edward Goslin fuit hic.* Seeping, however, sensing seepage. The cry of gulls, and the deep sea swell. Where the fish gnaw her father's bones, and the sand creeps through his sockets in the sea off Cádiz. Thinking: But maybe it is because I do not talk, not to anybody, damn it I would like to talk, would like once to be able to talk. If only about that, even, that tawdry, pinchbeck, desperate fantasy wherewith I affix poor romance to the cracked dark looking-glass of my life. My sea change, into something sick and strange. Restless and unappeased, she does not expect to sleep, not here, not now. Then she does not believe she has slept long. Yet it is dawn. For a time, gravely, she watches it, the day renewed, the sere unregenerating flawed gray beyond the window, the rusted shade. She decides: But I am still not here anyway. Thinking: Because even these awakenings do not really exist, the one solitary night without cessation or change, these awakenings to strangers behind tattered merciless windowshades that never seem lifted to the light. As if a shade has been drawn down over some portion of the mind likewise. Telling herself: Yet maybe I could convey it someway now after all, could even try it from above maybe, the bed itself and the man asleep *faceless* and the woman beside him simply . . . simply what? Inert and dead and gazing. *L'Absinthe*, by Fern Degas. On one more of those melancholy, sepulchral awakenings that mark her days. "Yet like that Munch I threw out last winter," she tells herself. "But in reverse. So that looking at mine you would ask: Why isn't that girl screaming?" Fern Munch. Fern Winters. Fern Holmes. Dressing, she finds a typewritten sheet of paper on the chair beneath her raincoat. For a time, puzzled, she standing reading:

Department of Sociology: Field Survey Abstract, Communications Research. Interviews: Upper Nile Delta. Women Moslem, isolated. Rapport between interviewers and respondents generally bad.

Frowning, half within the coat, and reading:

"I desire to see films but my husband forbids. It is not by him considered decent. I get up in morning and

milk cow and draw water, then take cow to field. My day is this."

Reading:

"*Women who go to movies open minds to bad things such as songs. Children will imitate and grow up without character. How could I let a daughter hear songs and see shameful things? However I would permit a son to go. He would benefit by seeing scenes of woods.*"

Beginning to smile now, reading:

"*—Benefit by seeing scenes of woods.*"

"*I like police reports on radio. They teach much and show morals. Once I heard of lady traveling on a train. Give a bag to someone to hold and bag contained things stolen. Since then I am afraid of seeing a bag beside me which does not belong to me.*"

The man, Goslin, is still asleep. Smiling, she carries the sheet with her, continuing to read as she descends the stairs:

"*All I can do is be kind to my husband and grow up children. Movie is nothing but exhibition dancing. What is the meaning of dancing and songs?*"

"*Women who go are not good women because they sit with men. Gain nothing but nonsense. Nothing is better than bread.*"

"*Nothing is better than . . .*"

In the street, laughing, she folds the sheet into her pocket. The streets are empty, there is no traffic yet. Unreal city. It is six, no later than six. Laughing, she is still not thinking. Nothing is better than. "Because it is still not I," she says, "not Fern. It is only that broken gimcrack puppet I watch, in this fugitive small drama of my night without stay." I get up in morning and milk cow and take cow to field. My day is this. In her own apartment again she showers, then goes back to bed. When she awakens this time it is two, perhaps two-fifteen. It is hot again. Taking another shower she does not dress immediately. She makes coffee, standing in the narrow kitchen and waiting as it drips, hearing the dripping. Dancing and songs, what is the meaning of dancing and songs? Glancing into the living room she remembers that she has forgotten the turpentine and the paints. There is adequate turpentine in the can if she wants to work. She does not work. Beyond the windowless huge warehouses across the street the sun is blocked, though the heat will not lessen. For a time, still not dressing, she tries to read, the chapter called "For Madmen Only." Less than pages into it she stops to think: Or would it be better not to show myself at all, not Fern nor the man either, but the windows themselves? Not to see me, but the very things I myself see? Some drab, remorseless, half-drawn shade, as an objective correlative for it all, for the lifetime of awakening and gazing? For the twice four hundred days?

Sea change. Of his bones are coral made . . .

She has closed the book. She thinks: But the lighting would be hard. As in that other I have so often thought of but know I cannot do, Adam, through all of those distant years when he would take me to church, alone, afternoons, to sit not speaking in that immense, groined silence with my hand in his . . . or isn't it the lighting at all? Because I do not know, cannot even remember now. But even after the first two, three, six, when you awaken to understand that no insignia marks your forehead in the morning simply because you have gone to bed with a man the night before, still, how, when does it really start? Because Adam sooner or later she has got to learn to play with the other children. *See* change. My day is.

Why isn't that girl screaming?

The book is abandoned, now she is staring at the telephone. No Marion, nothing. Nothing is wrong. Nothing is any different today than it was yesterday or last week or. "Except that the deformity mother is not even any longer of the flesh, I fear, but of the soul."

Then she begins to laugh, alone in the apartment, rising, begins to laugh aloud. It is not mirthless either. "Oh, Jesus," she says, "I am. I literally am. I am going out of my imbecile mind." Van Goghing out of it. She dresses, laughing. It is four o'clock. And probably am half-ready to slice off an ear by now too, she thinks, if only there were someone around to appreciate the gesture. Gauguin, where you gone? She seeks out a film, the first she can find. When she leaves the theater again, after the air-conditioning, it seems even hotter. She is wearing the raincoat, though open now, with tennis shorts and a blouse beneath it, her wrist bearing the weight of her left arm in that pocket. She eats a salad at an air-conditioned lunch counter. It is turning dark when she returns to the apartment, still well before nine. I desire to see films but my husband forbids. Undressing again she snaps the switch for the neon above the easel, then takes out the new canvas once more. Sitting in her underpants and with nothing else on she stares at the grays, at the darkness already intimated, thinking: Because Marion the deformity is not of the flesh now but of the soul. Laughing anew, aloud she says, "Jesus, you are a pompous fart." She stares at the canvas. After a time she says: "And like those windows. I am beginning to look at the damned things just the way I look at those windows." She thinks: I would be happier in a world without windows. Still laughing, she says, "Would that be anal or oral, now?" Gazing at the grays, thinking: Or isn't it a window? It it some mirror of my spirit, then? She continues to laugh. "And you're going to do it again, aren't you, shitface? Shitface canvas? You and that dopey stinking inevitable dark hole into which all of my puny imaginings must plunge?" She has lifted a palette knife from the stand. Now she traces it lightly across the cloth, point to. "But I haven't got the guts for that either, have I?" she says. Then she is holding a tube of black, the most opaque, thinking: But Jesus, I could just smear the whole thing, why not? So no matter what I did afterwards there would be no place to go but up the chromatic scale. Would that solve it? Wouldn't it? Abandoning the canvas again, its back outward against the stack, for some moments she stands near it, before the bulletin board. She is not looking at the reproductions, at her sketches. Her face has turned grave now, now there is no mirth in the laugh. "Marion, I am sick," she says. "Oh, damn it, I am sick, and that is no joke, no longer a joke." It is ten o'clock. Then it is midnight. Because a son would benefit from seeing scenes of woods. She tells herself, "So today was eight hundred and one, only I forgot to count." She turns on a radio, long enough to hear that news is being broadcast, not listening to the news. She says, "But that means it is past midnight, even. So now it is tomorrow and eight hundred and two. If yesterday was the Wednesday I thought it was."

Standing. Gazing about the shadowed room, at the naked easel, the bleak windows. At the raincoat where it has been flung upon the bed with one arm draped limply, trailing along the dusty floor. In the heat, the room, the night.

My day is this.

Then for some days she did not leave the apartment. More often than not she did not dress either. She rarely made the bed, could not recall when she had last changed the sweated, abused sheets. Sitting in that dishevelment amid the debris of half-eaten meals and strewn cigarette butts, in the fetid air, she thought: But maybe the one I ought to like is Goya, then. As at the end, when he conceived all those horrors on his own living-room walls. She was not painting. She did nothing at all.

Then one night she realized something. She was seated upon the stool before the easel. She was completely naked. Her legs were drawn up, her heels resting upon the upper crossbrace beneath the seat, and her arms were on her knees. Beside her the same eight or ten squeezings of pigment lay caked and brittle on the glass now, and there was a faint odor of linseed in the room. She did not know how long she had been sitting there, and the thought did not seem new, but she had never put it into words before. She said, "But it is because it does not hurt enough. It should hurt more than this."

She stood then, quite still, quite abstracted. She thought: So how long is it that I have been sucked dry of even that, of the dubious comfort of pain? Thinking: Yet it is true, almost as if I am mechanically measuring out some penance maybe, but without even contrition. Let alone remorse. Like one of those cartoons where they show the soul leaving the body and the body just lies there. Lays there? She did not smile, taking a cigarette, thinking: I am the one who dies. Turning to confront the telephone, holding the cigarette, she said, "Jesus, yes, I ought to suffer more than this. At least I ought to suffer."

At the telephone, staring at it, stubbing out the cigarette she thought: But dear God, how could I, how even begin? Thinking: No Marion no Mother I do not mean three or four do not mean six or eight but fifty, more like fifty. Thinking: Mother, Marion, I have slept with fifty boys, at least fifty, and while I feel nothing, nothing, nothing, it is that very emptiness, perhaps, that is the realest grief of all. Her eyes were closed, her breasts rose and fell, her lips were compressed. Trembling, she said, "But I have to talk. Must."

Then she was at one of the windows, something was

in her hand. It was paint, one of the blacks. When had she picked up the paint, what was she doing at the window? Shaken, her free hand at the glass as if to assay its grimy, smeared texture with her fingertips, trembling still she thought: Oh, I am mad againe, I am indeed. She said, "But something is going to happen to me if I do not talk."

Sea chains. And a drift of sandy bones . . .

It was two o'clock in the morning, possibly two-fifteen. Clothing lay scattered, about the floor, on the disarrayed studio couch. Still the day's heat clung like film, and she could taste sweat upon her upper lip, could feel it under her arms. "I ought to shower," she said. Instead, swiftly, she went to the closet and removed her raincoat. She drew it on with nothing beneath it at all. Buttoning it, she thought: Or will I eventually leave this behind one day too? Taking only her keys and a dollar bill, stepping into her older, tongueless tennis shoes, she locked the door and went down.

She did not go to the tavern, however. In the street, hesitating, breathing deeply, at last she turned in the opposite direction. Then it was aimless, without thought, though she turned again after perhaps six blocks, toward the docks, the Hudson. There was nothing here, no traffic, and she passed almost no one. Then there were no sidewalks either, where warehouse truck platforms extended into the streets. She was vaguely aware of loading pens, depots, an overhead railroad ramp. Her hands were in her pockets, and she could hear the slapping of her loose shoes. Then, finally, she believed she could smell the river.

Some blocks ahead of her there would be an open pier, she knew, one of the few accessible from the streets themselves. Once or twice she had been there, at this same hour though not alone, watching the dark running currents, the distant lights, sensing the sea beyond. Once too, even as she had been thrust, standing, against an upright piling to accept the impatient, dreary, inevitable violation, even as she perceived across the man's shoulder the contamination of oil and slime upon the tide, she had almost been tempted to swim. Remembering it now, she thought: And someway it would have been clean, too, cleaner than what I am, what I know. Thinking: And no grave to draw me ever, but lost beneath it all, my imagined, drifting father, Sandy Bones.

Thinking: No, not strangers, Mother, but down there in the Village where it is so easy to meet people, where all I have to do is go out, appear somewhere. Deliberately, she did not walk on toward the wharf. When she changed direction at the next corner, she thought: Herman Melville? Is it somewhere near here, a street named Gansevoort connected somehow with Melville? But there appeared to be no sign. The street she followed now extended for only one block also, and was inordinately narrow, though here too there were warehouses. At the corner where she would have to turn again the streetlamp had been smashed. For a moment she paused in the darkness, in the acute silence. She thought: Yes, you can smell it here.

Then she realized that there was an isolated apartment building on the corner after all, diagonally opposite her. It was five or six stories tall, but run down, with a look of abandonment. Several of its upper windows were even boarded over. Yet beyond a columned portico dim light burned in a vestibule, and within a first-floor window to its left another light was visible also. She thought: Jesus, but it would be like living with death, with all that emptiness above. Then she thought she heard music.

Curious merely, her hands still in her pockets, she went across. It was tuned quite low, something baroque, and liturgical, perhaps a Mass. Bach, would it be? Vivaldi?

Just without the fall of light from the window, below the outer column of the portico, she stood listening.

Crossing, she had discerned the light that of a naked bulb at the end of a cord. Otherwise the room had appeared virtually barren. But now, scowling, she confronted the painting.

It was large, at least thirty-six inches deep, though unframed, its edges ragged at the stretchers. Nor did it seem to be hung, rather it would have been resting upon some piece of furniture, tilted at the wall. It seemed a portrait.

Then it took her oddly, of a man, perhaps forty, with a flaccid, gaunt face. The eyes were remarkably deep, remarkably dark. She knew it to be the angle of her vision, some chance reflection of the unshaded bulb on the dull glaze of varnish, yet the figure might have been staring directly at her. And there was something febrific in the look, something driven, or wild, beneath the uncombed hair, above the open collar. Yet, fleetingly, for some reason she felt she knew the face. Then she thought: Or have I seen the work itself, reproduced somewhere? Was it good enough for that? Glancing about herself, toward the cheerless vestibule, at the scarred walls, she thought: But here? Who would be able to own it here?

Abruptly then she drew back. In the room, near her though still out of sight, someone had moved. Yet she could not have sworn she heard anything either, not with the music. Then she did, a sound that might have been a bottle touching a glass.

He emerged into her line of vision finally, though his back was turned, a man with thick uncut utterly black hair, seeming frail, standing as if preoccupied. Or was he too contemplating the painting? She saw not, since the face came into profile then, a face fiercely haggard, drawn, yet seeming to gaze at nothing. She thought: Or if no one here could afford it, maybe he is the painter, then? Then she thought: And my God, yes, because he has the features for it too, thinking: And it is El Greco I mean. That he looks like someone called El Greco should look if you had heard only the name and had never seen the self-portraits.

And I only am escaped alone to tell thee . . . what was she thinking of now?

The man crossed the room then, considering the painting after all, even lifting it as if to examine some detail more closely. She thought: Oh, come on, don't tell us you think you can make it even better yet? But it was not that. Even as she thought it, thinking also *Jesus I would like to take a look myself, would like to solve that technique*, he had turned its face to the wall. Then he might have been staring at her where she watched.

She did not move, however, sensing that he was not seeing her. It was not because of the darkness, the angle, rather again he seemed not to be looking at anything, simply abstracted, constrained. Yet for the moment she was confused, even startled, thinking: But he is ten years younger than the one in the painting, maybe more than that. Or was it some kind of vision, had he projected himself as he was going to look at that age? Could you? The eyes, the gravity, the subtly fevered gauntness, all were identical, though she saw now too that the man was not slight, that it was his slackness of posture only. As if wearily, he lifted his hands, palms upward, studying them. When he turned again, moving out of sight, the light died also, though the music continued.

Then she stood in the portico, hearing it still, for a time not moving as she listened. *Domine Deus*, was it? Anyway an oboe behind the soprano now, with string basses. Thinking: Or am I just romanticizing the whole thing, did I just notice him in a bar somewhere, sometime?

Neither the vestibule door nor the one beyond was locked, both stood ajar. There were mailboxes, several of them smashed, perhaps vandalized, their covers wrenched awry. There were few names.

The inner door was at her left, anonymous and paint-worn in the weak glow of the solitary bulb which illuminated the corridor. At its center a peeling gilded *A* was barely discernible. There was a bell in the doorframe.

Again she stood quite still, again listening, hearing the chorus, the Mass. But it was more distant here, muted, behind the door. Her face was thoughtful, her tongue was between her lips. Her hand lifted toward the bell, hovered there. It did not ring.

For a moment then her breathing was unnatural, the inhalations somehow languid and implosive at once. Then, quietly, not quite laughing, she said, "Jesus, what can happen to me anyway?"

She rang then, hearing it faintly from just within, over the music. Instantly her eyes darted to the vestibule behind her, to the street beyond. She drew backward a single step. Then she stopped again.

The music had ceased, had choired momentarily and was gone. But the door did not open. Waiting, she thought: And the choir would be boys, though once they would have used castrati. Thinking: *Gloria in excelsis Deo*, isn't that it? Because I am so intelligent too, so very admirably intelligent, have engraved like a lapidary all manner of wisdom upon the bright jewel of my mind. Almost aloud, her hand at the outer door again now, she said, "Oh, I am, Mother I am. Because you do not do this in New York, not even with someone you have very likely seen once in some familiar Village bar—"

So she is finally retreating when the door opens, when she glances back to find him there, yet having heard no sound and with the light behind him in the room still off also, only the dim bulb of the corridor accentuating the strained, grave face. Absurdly, she laughs, tossing her head, her golden hair, saying, "Look, that painting. I was outside. Excuse me, it was just impulse. Anyway, I'm not really here at all. It was only—"

She stops, not believing she will wait, waiting. Her left hand is raised, it hovers where she stands watching him, where he watches her in turn. He is not looking at the hand. Perhaps he has already seen. His expression remains as she has viewed it through the window, constrained, inviolable, Gothic. Then his own hand lifts, to reach within, though he does not look in that direction. She assumes it will be a light. It is a radio, the music. He is still watching her as she hears it return, though softly now, the boy's choir, the old invocation.

"That coat. I suppose the pocket would be just the right height to disguise it, wouldn't it?" he says at last.

FIVE

She talked to him. It was improbable, it was not even real. Days were to pass before she understood that he himself said almost nothing. Yet it would save her. Thinking *I do not believe this*, nonetheless she had found sanctuary, surcease. After all the embattled nights, the disquietude, the agony, began to ebb.

Yet in the beginning, astonished even at the profoundly unfamiliar timbre of her own voice, she could not have said whether it was the man at all. Thinking *This cannot be, such things do not happen*, she felt it as if she had someway manufactured him out of her own desperation and need, that assuredly she was imputing to him a sympathy that did not exist. Because it was not conversation, was not even wholly acceptance. Even after weeks she would know it always she who went to him, without protest on his part perhaps though without prearrangement or invitation either, simply appearing at the apartment, ringing the bell. Sometimes he would not answer, though only rarely, but then a few hours later would open to her again, remote, withdrawn, more often than not with the very atmosphere about him stagnant with that same despoilment that had informed her own existence for so long. Then, still not knowing him at all, she would nonetheless speculate that he had not been out but had simply failed to answer her ring. Yet she did not think this with any distress. She said to herself, "Or maybe I am just afraid to question it. Maybe I don't want to remind myself that I do not believe in even this much."

So she talked, in the hot nights, conscious sometimes of hardly more than his quiet breath in the bed near her, of his eyes not even always open to the monologue. She did not know what he did with his life at all, with his time when she was not with him. He lived poorly, less in frugality than in a kind of ruthless indifference to comfort or indulgence. The apartment was of one room and a bath only, the room itself much smaller than her own, almost anchoritic. There was a single armchair near the one front window, one straight chair at the unpainted table upon which the painting stood. Shelves in a closet served him as bureau space. His clothes themselves were undistinguished and few, tweed jackets possibly costly but far from new, khaki pants, white shirts. There were no suits, and she never saw him wear a necktie. He seemed never to eat. There was no evidence of any work, any occupation, in the room, and save for a single cluttered bookcase none of leisure or avocation either. Except for the bookcase and his portable radio the room might have been that of a transient rented for a week or a month. He told her he had lived there a year. The building itself was in fact being abandoned, though gradually, as tenants departed, and he was one of three or four remaining. Coming and going she would never see or hear the others, would never see other lights either. He seemed conditioned to exist in such emptiness, such silence, disseminating an aura of solitude fierce and unmitigated even when they were together. She sensed that her presence had not yet even begun to penetrate it.

He had no job. When she asked about this he told her he received an income, not large, but adequate to such independence as he possessed. He appeared to have no friends either, or at least none he saw currently. When it occurred to her to inquire in the bohemian bars, among those habitués who might have known him if anyone did, none recognized the name. Then she thought: So maybe he is listening to me because his life is even emptier than mine.

Yet the serenity, the calm, persisted. She did not know its source, what gave her license to talk, yet she was secure in it on even that first night. She should have been circumspect, even frightened, yet she was able to say to herself, "I can stay here, I am safe here." It was dawn before he crossed the room toward her, came to her where she sat huddled upon the bed she had not even yet seen, toward which he had dismissed her when she entered. Until then she had discerned him again too only in darkness where he leaned at the table save for those moments in which a match would flare, when the intense, sharp features would emerge hotly out of shadow with his eyes fixed upon her own so that she would endure the sensation of having been held, impaled by the same gaze even when she was not able to situate him at all. She did not move when he took her hand. Nor did she look up, not immediately, though he was visible now in the pale light that broke beyond the undrawn shade. Then she did, incredulous, as he lifted it, her lamed wrist, thinking: *Because no one else, not ever, not even in bed after a second or third time.* His eyes seemed to glitter, not pained, not even concerned, just thoughtful. "You don't have to do that," she said. "What?" "Be kind. Not react." He was looking at her, not at the hand. "Jesus," he said, "what do they do, just ignore it?" "Mostly. But you watch the eyes, see the—" "Desire?" he said. "That too, yes." The expression changed then, he laughed without sound. So then she knew something else, though he had not even spoken his name yet. Thinking *How can this be?* she sat quite still until he released her, failing to believe it even as she gave it voice, as she said to herself, "But I am not going to watch. For the first time in my life, I myself, Fern, and not the puppet, not the effigy."

It was scarcely love. Perhaps it was there only for her, perhaps he shared none of it. One night, possibly the second or third, her body flung across his own in sweated fulfillment, in their sweated collapse, she said, "Jesus. So I can still at least fuck like I mean it, anyway." She did not intend it as it sounded. She was thinking: But I have not murdered everything after all. She asked herself: Fifty? Could there have been fifty? Thinking: And yet I did not have any idea before, never knew. She said to herself, "Who, then? Who is he?"

She found that she had even stopped counting the nights. Even when she would walk the seven or eight blocks from her own apartment to ring and receive no answer, would stand in the dingy vestibule or in the corridor just without his door itself thinking *He is in there, can he be, just sitting?*—even then she was undisturbed. Soon she was painting again too, tentatively, not quite extirpating the darkness but anticipating that, quietly pre-meditative. Then one afternoon she went to a museum. When she arrived she realized she had not been there in more than a year, to that or any other. She could not even recall when she had been uptown last, properly dressed as she now was, walking the streets in common daylight. So it was peace. Even if it is spurious, she thought. She told herself it had to be. But still she refused to question it, or to let herself dwell upon the self-containment, the reserve. She did not want to, not even after some weeks had passed. Tranquil, astonished at the reprieve, she said, "Because for now I will settle for this." She said, "Dear God, won't I though?"

But he had begun to speak by then anyway, as she herself finally began to cease. Perhaps he had simply been waiting for her own urgency to be appeased, she did not know. Yet still it was strange, unnatural, sometimes he could allow hours to pass in which nothing was said at all. Or else everything seemed fragmentary, disjunctive, an effort of will, as if he were struggling to hold inviolable something that the very act of speech might impair. He would pause. In the harsh gaps between sentences, even phrases, she would believe him thinking. Then he would say nothing else.

On one of their first nights together she took down the painting, studying it under the naked bulb, not the figure this time but the artistry itself, the craftsmanship. She found it archaic, almost Netherlandish in its detail, yet brilliant, as good as anything contemporary she had ever seen. She told him so. Then she was not certain she had heard him at all. "A priest painted it?" she said.

"No. Christ." He indicated a scarcely legible signature that she had not yet discovered. "That's the name. Ferrin Priest."

"Fern—?"

He spelled it. As he did she perceived that it was dated also, from thirteen years before. Scowling, she looked back. "But seeming so much like you," she said. "Yet the model would have had to be at least twenty years older than you were when it was done—"

"Yes," he said. "The eyes, at least, they—"

"But who, then? It can't be just something you picked up because of the resemblance—?"

"It's . . . no one."

He turned it back to the wall. She watched him, though she asked nothing more. Later he told her that he had met the painter, Priest, long before, saying that he had been taken to Mexico at the age of fourteen by a widowed father, that the man had lived nearby. When she asked what other work he had done, thinking she might search it out, he said there was very little, that Priest had accomplished nothing in years. This time she did not have to ask, the next question could not have been more self-evident. A moment passed, however. They were in bed, smoking, sharing a cigarette. On one elbow she leaned above him, waiting. "He's a drunkard," he said finally. The cigarette rested between his lips, jerking as he spoke. She took it from him. After another moment he said, "You are right that he is good. There is probably even . . . genius, but the standards were too high, he never did much. This one alone cost him almost a year. And he was getting worse even then. I don't think he finished anything at all in the years I lived with him. He—"

"Lived with?" she said. "You mean near—?"

"With," he said. "My father died. Ferrin took me in. Became a kind of—"

Again she waited. Then he said only, "It was two years. It's long ago—"

That was during the first week. Sometime later he mentioned that Priest now lived in Vermont, on a farm. She had taken down the canvas once again, would often do so, repeatedly impressed. Yet a sense of its familiarity persisted also, for all that she saw him, Chance, in it himself. "Why do you leave it against the wall?" she said.

"Why do I—?"

"Or would it just overwhelm the joint?" She laughed. "But what a shame. That he doesn't do more work, I mean."

"I ought to return it to him," he said. "Except that it would probably—"

"Hurt him? Remind him of what he used to be able to manage—?"

"Yes. That, and—"

He did not go on. "Is he married?" she asked finally.

"A second wife. I haven't met her."

Tilting the canvas against her left hip, steadying it with that hand, she was tracing its textures lightly with the fingers of the other. "How often do you see him?" she asked.

She had not been looking at him. When she did, it was to find him gazing at her oddly, as if confused. Then he approached to take the painting from her. She saw it the signature, the single word, *Priest*, at which he seemed almost to glower. He returned the canvas to its place. "Jesus, it's . . . ten years. More. Sometimes I—"

"But—?"

"Since I left Mexico." He glanced about himself, as if searching for something misplaced in the room, in time, one hand at the back of his neck. "Damn it," he said. "And I haven't written either, in—" He went to the window, his head lowered. Watching, she said nothing, though the question formulated itself in her mind, had already done so more times than she might count. Never mind Priest: who are you?

That night she did not sleep, not for some hours. Lying next to him, she realized she had never before been awake when he himself was not. Ordinarily, she would be conscious of a kind of controlled, self-possessed stillness about him, in which he seemed scarcely to breathe though in which she sensed him always alert, staring into the dark.

Now his breath was turbulent, an ordeal. She thought: And as with speech, as if there is something he has contained secretly within himself for so long that the very cords must conspire in silence. Thinking *But what is it? What?* she sat up finally, smoking. He had said that his father had done little but drink also, that they had chosen Mexico at his mother's death because the income would afford more dimension there. One night she had asked him about the town in which they had lived. He had described it well, with far more ease than usual, conveying the sense of a timelessness she herself had long envisioned, the weathered, immemorial countenance of things that do not change. That night she had thought: So he is capable of response to two things at least, to the man Ferrin Priest and to Mexico. This was before he had told her how long it had been since he had seen the painter. Now, sitting, watching him sleep, she thought: And then his father died. When he himself was sixteen. And he lived with Ferrin Priest for two years and was in the army for perhaps two more, making twenty. Had he said the army? Thinking: And what, where, in the years since?

On another occasion she had asked him if he wrote. She had been glancing through his books. For a time he had looked at her queerly, as if the question contained no meaning. Then he said, "I suppose I thought I might. Once. As a boy. But—" "Did you do any at school?" she said. "School?" Then he laughed. "Jesus, I never went, after I was thirteen or so. There wasn't . . . not even a grammar school for the Indian kids in town, let alone anything for—" "But—?" She turned back to the books. Her own were predictable, the standard classroom currency of the moment. Save for scattered volumes of poetry he had none of these. Most of the others she could not even identify, they were by authors whose names eluded her, arcane, obscure, many of the editions themselves quite old. Some were in Latin also, others in Spanish. Frowning at him she lifted one out at random, then read: *Proslogon: Anselm*. She glanced at others: *Ars Magna*, *The Kuzari*, Dante, something called *Adversus Praxean*. "Ferrin got me into things," he said finally. "Some of those . . . his signature is probably in a few. And my father, he—" Again he laughed. "I'm not . . . illiterate, if that was what you had in mind—"

If that was what I had in mind, she thought. Smoking, facing the books now too, she could still hear him where he slept, thinking: Am I supposed to accept this? Any of it? Really? Then she remembered something. Once, some months before, she had been at a party. She had been drinking, and then there was marijuana. After the alcohol it had made her ill. Eventually she had awakened in a bed, no longer sick but with no sense of time or place at all. There had been music, jazz, from another room. Then she had become aware that she was undressed, that she was not alone. She could not see the man with her, could not recall who he was. Then she turned sick again, in that accusatory darkness, searching helplessly for her undergarments, for her raincoat, finally weeping. For some reason she did not turn on a light, rather she stood shaking, repeating over and over: "Who is with me?" When she fled the party she did not leave her apartment again for weeks, not at night. Remembering it now, she thought: And I believed it a kind of perverted apotheosis of sorts, like an epigraph for the discalced narrative of my life, weeping there and asking who it was with me in that darkness. Seated next to him now, discarding the cigarette finally, she thought: Chance? Steven Chance? She said: "So who is it with me in this?"

So the sense of tranquillity could not wholly persist. Sometimes, remembering how it began, approaching his street at evening perhaps, or later, in the summer's prolonged dusk, she would say, "One night I am going to turn that corner and the streetlamp will have been repaired. And then the building will not even be there." Or else she would think: Nor would he care. Less than not care, would not even remember were I to cease coming that I had ever appeared at all. He had not once been to her own rooms, called for her, asked to see her work. Yet it was none of this either. She thought: Because why has it taken me almost a month to learn that I should have been just a little afraid in the beginning after all?

It had happened twice that she knew, although perhaps on other nights also, because only awakening unexpectedly did she see. The first time she had not realized immediately that he was not with her in the bed. It was still dark, not yet morning. When she did realize, she could not have said why she held herself still, why she did not speak. But then for a moment she did not even breathe. He was seated upon the straight chair near the table, utterly motionless, fixed there almost rigidly. He was staring directly ahead of himself, his hands gripping the frame of the chair beneath him. Even in the darkness she believed she perceived a quiver, as from intolerable strain, in the muscles of his jaw. Unmoving herself, she had no idea how much time occurred before it ceased, before he appeared to collapse inwardly as if in exhaustion. Nor did he return to the bed until sometime after she herself slept anew.

When she awoke to it again several nights later she found it almost diabolical, the rigor unyielding for so long that even disconcerted she believed she had actually dozed again before he stirred, before he arose to throw back his head as might a swimmer emerging from insupportable depths. But still she did not speak, did not ask.

Then one night she did. Coming awake to find him not at the table but in the armchair, slumped there wearily in the shadows of a demitting moon from beyond the win-dow, so that she told herself, "It is finished now, whatever it is, it is over for tonight," still not quite moving and almost guardedly, she said, "When do you get any sleep, Steve?"

He did not turn toward her. His head was back, resting against the back of the chair. Finally he lowered it. She noticed the book in his lap only when the match flared.

"You can't read," she said, "not in that light." She sat up at last, drawing the sheet about her thighs. "Or do you just sit there reciting to yourself, maybe, like—what do they call them?—like a hafiz, or something—?"

He laughed finally, the sound abbreviated and severe, puzzling. "I could," he said. "This one anyway, it's—" Then, abruptly, startling her, he flung it aside, his arm seeming hardly to move although the book struck the table across from him before slapping to the floor. Shocked, she stared at it where it lay.

He said nothing more, however, not looking toward her nor at the book either, his face set. At last she arose, still considering him as she crossed to retrieve it, watching him even as she knelt. Then she had to seek out the title page, its enlarged typeface, the imprint on the colophon not legible where she had squinted at that first. Reading: *Eric Chazen: Collected Poems.* It was something she had noticed before, on his shelves, sensing the writer's name vaguely familiar at best, and with an impression of the work as being so unimportant that she had even wondered at its presence. Rising again now, she said, "But why would you—?"

Then she stopped, stood facing him. For a minute she could not quite reach it, thinking: Books, all the unneces-sary books I have read. Thinking: Some obscure, minor poet, what do they call them?—experimental—who died young, telling herself: "But I know something else too."

She thought: Hart Crane? Why am I thinking of that Siqueiros portrait of Hart Crane? Thinking: Or because Siqueiros is Mexico, is that why? And because somewhere not even paying attention I must have read that Eric Chazen was . . . that Eric Chazen died in. *Died in.*

The silence was absolute, though it was her own now, a peculiar stillness engulfing her. But she knew where she had seen the other painting before also then, his, had been right about seeing it, not needing to glance down at the book again but already feeling the glossy coated sheet next to the page at which it was opened, telling herself: "So it would have been in some library once, I must have opened this same edition to the extent of noticing the frontispiece at least." Then she went over, still carrying it. Squatting at the chair, below him in the silvered light and peering upward at the somber, alien face, for a minute she said nothing. Then she said, "So that would be why. One of the reasons, anyway. I guess I wouldn't think about painting either, wouldn't try, if my father had been—"

Again he laughed, perhaps scornfully, though still not turning to her. Then he stood. "Except that isn't . . . why anything. Writing or not, do you think if I . . . wanted to, it would make any difference who, what my—"

Thinking: And I can hear my heart, suddenly I can hear my own heartbeat. Then she thought: Or why not? Granting he is no Dylan Thomas, but still, a book, any book. But it was not that, she knew. With his back turned he had lifted the shade, was facing the gray street. Her voice was quiet, not quite natural as she arose. "All right, Steve," she said. "It was my intrusion, and I'm sorry. You don't have to tell me anything. Anyway, I've been— am—pretty damned content as it is—"

"What is there to tell, Fern? Just because the man

happened to paste together a volume of halfway readable poems—"

Turning, he had raised a hand, it hung as if presaging continuance. She was close to him. When the hand fell it brushed against her breast, was drawn back. Then he seemed to scowl at it, or her, as if momentarily bewildered by her nakedness, perhaps by her very presence. She thought: It is. More than intrusion, it is violation. Yet in the same instant she sensed something else entirely, was almost astounded to decide: And yet he would. He would answer anything at all, if I only knew what to ask.

"Steve? Listen. If you want to . . . end this, sometime, you won't just . . . disappear or something—?"

"Won't—?" He continued to scowl, his eyes lifting. "Fern, you're not . . . haven't let yourself—?"

"No," she said. "Not that. But—"

"All right. I won't just . . . Jesus, anyway, what do you mean, disappear? What do you think I—?"

"Steve, Steve. What do I think you . . . when there is so much that is missing, all the mystery—"

"Mystery—?"

She smiled then, the beginning of amusement quite real. "You really mean it, don't you? You really think that because I know this much now I even begin to understand the rest—" Then she paused, let it cease. Probably he had not been listening anyway. Yet it was his hand again, the touch of his knuckles lightly at her groin, at which she drew in her breath, at the tentative, barely perceptible impress of flesh against flesh. Because he would not do this in bed, or not often. Poised, seeming to contemplate her womanhood as if it were he then who confronted an unreality, often for a long time he would not touch her at all. Yet it could have been no different if he did, since inevitably, surely, she would respond, flooding toward him always as if the night's first conjunction were a renewal or a continuation rather than any beginning. Yet there was never haste either. Finally spent and without breath, amid their sweated, flowing odors, each time she would exult less in her consummation than in its degree, its totality. Remembering such moments now, she thought: Or is it still only me, only I with all that dissoluble, hollow ravagement in my life, who have finally found it? He was gazing beyond her, the hand fell. Telling herself, "Yes. Because, dear God, I am all right now. Except now I have to wonder if it was I who needed saving to begin with."

Some days later he told her more of it, another morning then and still close even in the hours before sunrise, in the heat that had continued untempered into late September. A light burned in the bathroom only, spilling across the bed, and they had not yet slept. Earlier, she had been reading in the book itself, the poems, surprised at a hard, transcendent lucidity in certain lines that she sensed were already implanting themselves into memory, yet more often baffled, finding their meanings incomprehensible. She had been to a library one afternoon also, but there had been next to nothing, he seemed known to some few other poets merely. "Shouldn't there be more interest, Steve?" she said now. "Compared to some of the stuff you read—?"

"Someone keeps asking Ferrin," he said. "Writing to him about a critical biography, something, and . . . wants my address too. But I've told Ferrin no, it's—"

"But—"

"The work. It's . . . better than you know, Fern. Even if no one reads it these days—or ever did. A poor man's Traherne, maybe. But that's all that is . . . anybody's business. All that Eric gave a damn about himself, when he was in a condition to give a damn about anything. He—"

Seated in the armchair he lifted his chin to indicate the book where it lay on the table now, before the reversed portrait. "Those few lines you like. Jesus, I've said Ferrin is an alcoholic today, but Eric was . . . immeasurably worse. The best of all that dates from his early twenties, maybe a little later. Even when I was a kid, it had already stopped, there was only the bottle—"

His voice was quite dull, toneless. He was not looking at her, gazing into the column of light, or perhaps beyond, perhaps at nothing. He was drinking. "Even Ferrin doesn't know," he went on. "Not really. And I've never told him, I suppose because he is too innocent about people, or too generous a person himself. And he . . . liked Eric too, it would hurt him. But even down there in Mexico, he never saw. He and Lydia, his first wife. They were the first Americans we ran into, in a store that sold liquor, as would happen, but long after we were exchanging visits he never had any idea. He wasn't in . . . remarkable shape himself anyway. But we only met them once a month or so—they were in another town—and when we did, Eric would talk. He was . . . Christ, articulate enough, more than convincing, and he believed himself too, the . . . illusion, going on about work he had conceived and was ostensibly drafting. Usually a notion based on some book he had managed to read ten pages of in a sane moment the week before. So even when Ferrin did see him drink, it was infrequently enough that he thought it meant nothing, that Eric had gotten into that condition for the very reason that we were taking time out to visit. And then when Eric . . . he fell, one afternoon, drunk, down a . . . when that happened Ferrin took me in. And stayed sober himself for months, because I whom he had seen perhaps twenty times in two years happened to be just sixteen and alone down there, without legitimate papers even, since it turned out that Eric had typically forgotten to renew them, and became more of a—"

He stopped, considering his glass. Then he shook his head. "I'm not putting it well. But you've seen the painting, it's . . . Eric was a little mad. Frustrated by lack of recognition too, maybe, but still . . . so that I could walk into the house and find him . . . discussing something, original sin, the *Gita* . . . with Avicenna. Maimonides. Alone at the kitchen table. And he was not . . . a good person, finally. My mother . . . had deserved better. While Ferrin is incredibly the opposite. Equally drunk now, I can tell from the letters, from all the things he doesn't say, but there is a . . . kindness there, a sense of . . . charity, that makes him perhaps the only person I have ever known who truly lives like a . . . Christian. And the . . . warmth, símpatia, is infectious, so that even down there, with the poorest Indian . . . well, you would have to live there to know, how no gringo ever manages to communicate at all, ever gets through to a—" Abruptly he dismissed it, rising. Then he chuckled. "Or, Jesus—singing, even. Teaching something like . . . 'The Rose of Tralee,' to a bunch of ragged peasant kids who did not understand one word of—"

At the table, the bottle, he stopped. Then it was the book he lifted instead, to discard it again with a grimace. Filling his glass, he said, "Well, anyway, it's scarcely . . . important."

Watching him drink, saying nothing, she thought with a futile irony: Scarcely. Yet it eluded her still, not quite pain, not abnegation either. Or was this not it at all then, did a lesser poet named Eric Chazen mean nothing to him perhaps, perhaps not even normally cross his mind until she herself brought him up? She told herself, "And yet I was right about one part of it, that he is capable of affection for one human being in this world at least." Still not speaking she went into the bathroom.

Seated, with the door not fully closed, behind it in a corner on the stained tile she noticed something that appeared at first glance a toy, a child's glass marble. When she lifted it she found it a stone, though unusual, with a faded yet luminous quality that suggested translucence. It was virtually colorless, though darkening into an almost perfect circle of gray at one point, and with yet a darker spot within that. Emerging, she asked, "Is this anything, Steve? It looks just like somebody's old ancestor's petrified left eye—"

Glancing up from where he was seated again, he seemed startled. "You found it. I thought it was . . . yes, the Indians would think it that. A bird's, maybe, miraculously preserved. They would use it as a talisman, probably someone did. I carried it, just loose, in a pocket, it's . . . absurd—"

It weighed nothing on her palm. "Talisman for what?" Turning to the table she set it upon the book of poems.

"I never knew. I suppose anything a given shaman happened to tell them."

A moment passed. Still it lurked, troubling her in a manner that left her hesitant. Intrusion. On the wall above the bed there hung a reproduced photograph that she had tacked into place herself, tearing it from one of her books as a kind of grim joke, of Toulouse-Lautrec, stunted and improbable. That other cripple. Frowning toward it now, wordlessly, she said, "But you too then, poor clown." Nonetheless, leaning at the table finally, taking a cigarette, she spoke it aloud. "And you still insist it has nothing to do with why you don't write yourself, Steve—?"

"What?" He seemed to stir, almost violently, yet she suspected that only his eyes had moved. She realized he had been staring at the charm, the stone. "Write? Listen, why do you keep . . . and Ferrin too, in all the letters, just because he once read a few things that I—"

"Read—?"

"Childish. Stuff I tried when I lived with him. I couldn't think of anyone else, so I sent them to a friend of Eric's. They were . . . in print somewhere. I hadn't asked him to do that, only to tell me whether—"

He drank. Incredulous now, thinking *If I only ask*, she said, "But isn't that all the more reason you should still—?"

"Oh, cojones, Fern, don't start sounding like some sort of . . . homely, ministerial . . . as if it has any meaning, or—"

"Yet—"

"Oh, all right. Yes, maybe it has. For some people who . . . have to, but you're wrong that it's out of . . . listen, that was more than ten years ago. And that long ago I had . . . maybe enthusiasm is the word. I could get . . . involved. But for Christ's sake, I don't even . . . read, any longer. I take out a book that I've . . . something I've cherished, and it's only—"

For a time she did not reply, appraising the magic eye again, remembering her own savage futility of so long, the unassayable blackness in those canvases, some of which, still now, stood against the wall in her apartment. Then she said, "I am not bright enough, Steve. But all the negative books, gosh, since who?—Nietzsche, would it be?— when the vision is so despairing that reading them is like . . . I don't know. Yet they get them written—"

He dug his fingers into his thick hair, his head lowered in consternation. "There has to be a lie in it, Fern. Real despair, a real sense of the . . . Jesus, just the boredom . . . and there wouldn't be any point in . . . words—"

"But then couldn't the very act of writing itself be a kind of—?"

"Salvation? Creation as an act of faith, which either Kafka said somewhere or Ferrin did once, about painting? I don't remember. Maybe, maybe. Except before faith comes—"

"Belief?"

"That's a way to put it, I suppose. Yes. I—"

"And you don't believe?"

"Good Christ, what—?"

"Excuse me." She laughed, deliberately. "You may rest assured that is the first time the subject has ever come up in my so-called adult life. Even entered my mind. But—" She crushed out her unfinished cigarette. "Yet I still do not understand. I mean I understand, perhaps, but do not accept. Good heavens, I've told you about all of my own . . . relinquishment. Yet, still, I painted. Or tried to, at least—"

"Do you sincerely think it adds up to . . . your precious little game of art, every damned fool and his sister playing at it, when it is probably the more real distinction to have the sense not—"

"Well, damn it, now, you haven't even once come to look—"

"I'm sorry. Not you, anyway. I was just thinking about . . . life, I suppose. Or maybe about . . . Rimbaud." His fist opened and closed. "But Jesus, I might as well write at that. All this talk, it must be—"

"—Five o'clock."

"And that, too. You and your mystical . . . cosmic chronometer. Horological Fern—"

"Make sure you spell it properly—"

He stood, smiling, then nodded toward her lamed wrist. "But it's because you can't fit a watch there, isn't it? The other gift, by way of compensation?" He retrieved his glass. "What were we talking about? Listen, all I mean is that I simply do not give a damn about . . . books, art, all the recondite, agonized reasons why anybody . . . writes or not. Or your own Nietzsche then, wasn't he the one who said it? That only the sick, the weak . . . it was they, naturally, inventing heaven, the redemptive drops of blood. And that simple-minded Van Gogh you like so much, all that . . . weeping in front of churches, living with that whore. Why? For humility's sake? Man's? When all he got out of it was a gaudy dose of—" He laughed. "But that's why you're attracted to him too, wouldn't it be? That story you told me, from childhood, about sticking your own hand into a . . . Christ. Listen, can we just go to bed now, maybe? Something as unilluminating and banal as—"

"Sleep and be cursed. Anyway, I scarcely meant to impute anything like—"

But it died then, suddenly halted even as his hand touched idly at the book again, as her glance followed. Or was it she alone? Because only now did it spring into her mind, for the first time and yet realized somehow wholly, complete, as she thought: Chazen? Eric Chazen? Already thinking too: Or isn't that why he changed it at all, not because of the who but the what? Not even self-consciously, she said, "Good heavens, it should have occurred to me a month ago, shouldn't it? You're a Jew, then—"

Their eyes met, though his own were no more than interested. "I suppose I am."

"You suppose?"

"I never . . . think about it." He shook his head. "But Jesus, maybe you're right. Maybe you're . . . good for me, even. Sometimes I don't know what I *am* thinking about, what I seem to be doing with—" He glanced about them, at the shadowed, empty quarters, as if only then becoming sensible of the isolation, the shabbiness. "And yet this queer light, too. Standing that way. You look almost vestal, or—"

"Ready for immolation. Even if indisputably deficient in one of the primary requisites. For heaven's sake, Steve, how does someone not 'think' about being a Jew?"

"It's just . . . never been a factor in my life. Does it have to be?" He was grinning at her. "Or like the beasts before Adam names them, I have no consciousness of it, until someone—"

"Intrudes—" The word had come instinctively, though his response was only speculative, perhaps still amused. Then he turned, was refilling his glass. She waited, watching him a moment longer, saying nothing else. Beyond the window dawn was intimated, it would be hot again. And suddenly she was tired. Reaching within, she extinguished the bathroom light.

Then again she paused, locating him in silhouette now where he leaned at the window frame, peering out, his brow against his wrist. She thought: Or doesn't that begin to solve it either? Because anyway, as if you actually need a reason to begin with. To be squeezed dry of any evocable remembrance of pain, suffering nothing at all, suffering only because you do not suffer. I had not thought death had undone so many. To herself she said, "But there is more than that, still. With him it is more than that."

And then she did something that in their singular, un-stipulated relationship she had never done before. Waiting, as he came across finally in the lifting gentian light, suddenly she ceased to wait, suddenly she drew him down with unappeasable urgency. And yet it was not need, somehow she was even laughing also, trembling, thinking: Oh Jesus, and I have chosen so well too, so impossibly well, even as her lips searched out his face, his mouth.

† 101 †

And then she was athwart him, inverted there with her face at his loins instead, laughing inwardly still and yet driven, quite mad, as she brought him to readiness with her lips, her tongue. Nor did it diminish even as she felt her own weight being raised then, her hips shifted and spread upon him, at his own tongue's reciprocation. Not even when his warm seed at last burst within her throat would it quite stop, nor when her own thighs quivered and stiffened and locked. And yet it was he too then, laughing beneath her himself when she had finally flung herself back to spew it insanely between them where they kissed, viscous along his cheek, until he wiped it away with a forearm, his wrist. "What?" she said. "What are you—?"

"Nothing. That damned dwarf up there, your . . . Lautrec. In those whorehouses, the old joke. Did he . . . go up on all those women, could you say?"

Then one evening he did not answer her ring. She came at eight and again at eleven. Somehow she knew it different from those nights at the beginning when she had believed him sitting only, not answering then either but there nonetheless, within, unassailable in that private darkness. Now it was intuitive, a certainty of absence. When she returned at two in the morning she waited in the portico for more than an hour, idly, not quite thinking anything, not yet.

Then it became days. She was still not troubled, though it surprised her. After the first few trips she did not need to ring, since there was something in his mailbox, an advertising circular most likely, that she could see had not been removed. She continued to return a second and a third time each night. Curious, she thought only: Because I would not have believed there was anywhere for him to go. Once, on the third night, the inner vestibule door was unlatched when she arrived, and she paused for a time next to his apartment entrance itself. Her hand touched that bell. She had not meant it to. Hearing it buzz within, in the emptiness, she rang it again.

Then, about to leave, already entering the vestibule, she thought: Why have I never seen anyone else in this building? Thinking: Someone comes and goes, someone left this door ajar tonight. Behind her the ill-lighted corridor was uninviting, dark stairs mounting into a well of shadow at its rear. "Ghosts, then?" she said. "Eric Chazen's, at least? Art there, ghost? Truepenny?"

Walking home, still only pensive, questioning, now and then touching her money and keys in the pocket of her raincoat, she thought: Father Chazen. While in a way I have two as he does, have Adam and Raymond Holmes as he has Eric Chazen and Ferrin Priest. Thinking: Or why not Ferrin Priest for me too then, since I seem to have pretty much given myself a choice? Adam, Ferrin, or poor old decomposing Sandy Bones? Or does it take a heap o' living, to make a house a Holmes?

Then she paused, thinking: But Veracruz, to have him sail from? Or am I whacky altogether, because didn't Hart Crane jump off some ship that left from there too? Absently, thinking *Oh, well, I will ask Steve tomorrow*, she went on. She said, "Ferrin? Ferrin Priest, will you be my daddy?"

By the next afternoon she realized that she was doing nothing, had occupied herself not at all when she was not going and returning from his apartment, was not painting, had not opened a book. "Now, damn it," she said. "Damn me, I can wait better than this." Thinking: Because there will be an explanation for this too, as much as there ever is for anything. She said, "And who wants an explanation anyway? I just want—"

And lay hands upon the man, the blinded, dreaming man

. . . and what was that, now? She remembered, some line of his father's she had not been able to decipher at all. *I just want . . .*

"Steve?" she said.

After five or six days it began to rain, a steady, unceasing downpour. In her raincoat as ever, but without hat or umbrella, she went again and again, walked in the rain. Then, once, with the door again unlocked, she explored the building. Her hair was matted, her shoes sopping. The stairs were accessible for only one flight, after that they were obstructed by a lashed-to plank at the railings. There was one dim bulb only, and there were four doors. Up here the atmosphere was musty, yet pervaded with an odor that had nothing to do with the rain. Nor could she hear it, that or any other sound, in the corridor or at any of the doors. Standing quite still in the silence, drenched, conscious of the dampness beneath her coat where she wore nothing again now, no undergarments at all, in the eerie light, she said, "Why do I never see anybody in this place?" Then, quite loudly, poised at the head of the stairs, she said, "Herman Melville, are you here? Captain Ahab? Or how about Vivaldi, then?" There was no sound, no response. Or hadn't she spoken out loud after all? Deliberately now, she called, "Listen, who is here? Is everybody dead? If everybody is dead, who opened that vestibule door, then?"

And I only am escaped alone to tell thee . . .

Downstairs, again at his own door, once more the rain existed, it hummed and spattered. "No one lives here," she said. "No one ever did." Thinking: He is gone. Dear God, but didn't he promise? Didn't he? Ringing the inner bell, hearing its muffled, distant buzz, hearing the rain. "Steve?" she said.

A clock at which she had not needed to look read three-seventeen when she entered the all-night pharmacy.

The store sells oddments also, miscellaneous household wares, assorted gifts. It is at a focal intersection and even at this hour is crowded with people eating, browsing, avoiding the rain. Ignoring the rack to which she herself has pointed, a clerk informs her, "We also got this, lady, only two dollars more. You could look, it says 'Momma' when you spank her." Shaking her head, tasting the rain upon her lips, she unfolds the soaked bill from her pocket. "Thank you," she says. "That Raggedy Ann will be quite adequate for the child I have in mind."

SIX

And began to speak my joke again, my weary, sad, despairing joke. And browsed through an old monograph on Utrillo, who was mad likewise. Those are pearls that were his eyes . . .

And then I had a dream, that night a dream, and it was odd because in the dream I was having an abortion. And kept telling the doctor, trying to explain about Raggedy Ann. The nurse had gone out of the room, a white room, and the doctor was waiting for something to sterilize. Looking like a moribund owl, and he seemed younger than he should have been. But then how old must a murderer be?

All scattered at the bottom of the sea . . .

How odd, the dream. Waiting. With sterile eyes. And trying to explain, saying, "Because in all of my life, through all of the years, whenever I have had something to flee from." Raggedy Jesus, Raggedy Ann. And when I called for the appointment the nurse said, "And what name should I put down?" That seemed subtle. Being subtle in turn, I said, "Kindly make the appointment for Miss Multitudes."

Because no Marion not three not six but fifty, more like fifty. And my daddy sterile lies.

Multitudes. I, Fern Van Gogh, dreaming, contained multitudes.

"Yes," the doctor said, "it is merely tension, quite natural. One moment, the nurse will be adjusting that saddle."

And having no idea what night it was, the night I bought the doll and dreamed. Walking in that rain and finding the circular still in the slot, in the rain that had not ceased for days. For how many days?

In the rain, when it was eight hundred and forty-some days.

So I was counting again then too, making my dismal joke and counting the days, knew even that we were already into October. When for all these weeks now, not. Because of him, was counting again. Because of not him.

Steve?

And had money in my pocket, keys in my pocket, again too was touching my money and keys.

And was painting my blacks again also, in my head painting them. One day I sketched. Lying on the bed I used charcoal on the backs of some old watercolors, and all I kept shaping were skulls. Skulls that gaped. Like my daddy, who had sand in his sockets. I lay on my back holding the stiff sheets overhead in my bad hand and making believe the bed was a scaffolding. Sand in his sockets, watery pockets, my daddy has fish in his eyes. My daddy is a. And then I signed the sketches Edgar Allan Winters. On the scaffolding in my cistern chapel I signed them.

A priest painted it?

Off Cádiz, all drowned. And when I had told him about

that, saying: Which maybe solves the problem of my own leaky soul.

Dreaming. After standing on a street corner in the rain, holding my doll and maybe sensing even then that it was beginning, hearing the faint far-off gushing whisper of the blood. But forgetting again when I went home to sleep. Forgot that my period was beginning, and dreamed instead of my insides drawn out.

And then finding it a Sunday because at noon he was still not there and walking again still in the rain I met someone *Eddie, was that his name?* and he was carrying the *Times*. Standing in the doorway of a store that was closed while he said: Why not, what else on a miserable day like this? And then he said: And listen, I've got a pocket full of.

Give me some, I said.

Well sure. But come on to my place and we'll.

No I said it's the wrong time of the month anyway. But give me some.

Taking three of them and putting them into my coat and walking again. And then back home and smoked, all three but slowly, through the long gray wet Sunday afternoon, and at least did not count anymore. And was psychic too, because leaving him I found the sociology interviews I had stolen from his room but had not seen since. Reading them again, smoking and reading. Women who go to movies open minds to bad things such as songs. Children will imitate and grow up without character. Reading and smoking and thinking: I would not have believed there was anywhere for him to go. I get up in morning and milk cow and take cow to field. My day is.

But had too much. Because when I went out again the rain was all smoky, my head was full of smoke. And why was I carrying the doll? I said: But if he is still not there I will leave it in the vestibule. And then if it is gone when

I come back I will know that someone lives there after all, who would steal a child's favorite doll.

"—Listen, Steve, how old must an abortionist be?"

"—Fern? Are you all right? You look . . . Jesus, and you are soaked. You better get—"

Thinking: Oh God, thank God. Saying: "I brought you a doll. You were away just long enough, I had to have somebody to play with."

Taking my coat, flinging aside the covering sheet on the bed. Telling me that I did not look well. With my eyes pale probably from the marijuana and my heart pounding because he was back, no breath to breathe because he was back. And yet with my voice so different from the one within, in my eternal pose, saying only, "Pardon the vagueness but someone gave me a gift. A whole potful."

"Good Christ, get some sleep for a while, Fern—"

Saying: "And also I contain multitudes. Of gauze. It being that time of month when thou mayest in my groin behold—"

"—Sleep—"

And kept disappearing. It was dark now, and with the marijuana the hours were awry, it could have been nine or it could have been midnight. But it was a Sunday, I knew, and he was back. Oh God, back. And with my head all smoky still, wanting to tell him about my dream, but I would hear him and then not. In his mask of shadow, was just sitting, here in this house of phantoms where no one lived. His suitcase was still near the door *since then I am afraid of seeing a bag next to me* and then I was trembling, standing and shaking at the bed. Because no word, none. And I wanted. Wanted—

"Did you go somewhere, Steve?" I asked him.

"Yes."

And knew something then, knew I did not like him at

all. Even as I knew I could have died for every moment he had been away.

In light from the bathroom only, a crack of light from beyond the almost closed door. And sick, still, from the marijuana, sick from the wash of relief that had churned my very bowels even as I had come upon the circular crumpled on the vestibule floor. But God, then, what? How? That fatality that drew me so inexorably? Thinking, eternally: Who is this with me in this darkness, who are we together, both, in this inguinal dark? Fern Winters Utrillo Nijinski Multitudes Goya Holmes Priest. Saying, "Ain't nobody asking but me, Steve. Only Miss Bones—"

"Fern, I—"

"What, Steve—?"

"Nothing. Go to sleep. It's—"

And then would hear him move, so silently move, or drink, or sigh, over the sounds of the smoking rain. And I in his bed again.

Anon.

And then remembered the dream anew, that dopey dream. But could not remember what the D stood for, in D and C. Dissolute? Disreputable? Disembabied? Though if real I would have been truly wadded now, with more than gauze. Equally needing to pause. Because of gauze we pause. And that damned pot, damned Jan Van Eyck and his pot. Gosling? Remembering that I was going to make a list once, of everybody I had ever. And then reading *Ulysses* and Molly Bloom's and Joyce was wrong because you cannot, not that quickly. Not to mention the anons. Because the deformity Marion is not of the flesh but of the.

And not sleeping, knowing I would not sleep. As the ceiling lifted and fell, and the light from the bathroom wavered and wandered. Marijuandered? At last I reached over to his shelves and lifted out a book, any book, tilting it into the column of light. Heaven help us, reading: *En-chiridion Fontium Historiae Ecclesisticae*. But before I put it back a slip of paper fell out of it, yellowed and creased and very old, and I read: *The knowledge of God is very far from the love of him*. And underneath that it said: *Pascal*.

"Did your father copy this, Steve?" I said.

In the darkness he came across. "It's his handwriting," he said.

And Utrillo's father could have been?

"Steve? What's: 'And lay hands upon the man, the blinded, dreaming man'?"

"Saul of Tarsus. On the road to—" Folding away the sheet, replacing it in the book. To lie forgotten for ten years more. Damascus? And disappearing again, gone, into shadow. The love of Chance is very far from the. And under that I would write: Winters.

Then I thought I would write to Ferrin. Dear Ferrin, I would write. Dear Priest. Who is Steve Chance? You whom alone he seems to love, can you know or say?

And dilatation was the D. Dilatation and curettage. Unless the C was for Cádiz. The sea, for Cádiz. Dear Ferrin, I would put. In the genuine handwriting of Saul of Tarsus.

Renoir or Degas, Utrillo's father could have been?

Dear Priest. Help me, Priest?

The laws of gauze say pause. Was it yesterday that I lay in my bed sketching, or was it Friday? Holding the sheets overhead, moving the charcoal very carefully. Because my daddy went down in the C. Sometimes I would hold the charcoal still and move my other hand instead, drawing with the sheets themselves, almost, against the stationary coal. Passing a plane across a point in space, recording its passage. *Fern Adam Winters is not your.*

And Baby Jesus, alone in the.

And that same afternoon, while I sketched, the telephone. Hearing: Nothing Fern, just to chat, your father and I were simply.

Hieronymo.

Fern Valadon?

Yet it was diminishing now, the marijuana fading. The pot passing. And with my hair falling about my face, shrouding my face, where I sat upon his bed for the first time in one week *eternity* and clasped my arms about my uplifted legs. Was he watching me? Across the room did he even know that I was sitting, was not asleep? The piss potting? Holding my bad wrist in my other hand, at my ankles, gazing at my interlocked hand and wrist. And even humming to myself too, what was I humming? I remembered. That aria from *The Pearl Fishers*, Leïla's, that nobody ever seemed to have heard. What is the meaning of dancing and songs?

Why was I here? Why did he let me come here at all? Priest?

And still that dream, hounding me, the doctor with his face like a dying owl's, and with an instrument like a rake, a tiny silver rake. As if your womb were something mowed. And then awakening to find that I had started to stain in the night and knowing it my period but for the moment confused, for a long moment almost believing it the dream yet again. But did not say: I am going out of my mind, Marion, out of my aborted mind. And flowing freshly now still, streaming. So that I should have brought an extra. Or if real then after all, the dream, what then, this seepage in my thighs? In the temple of my thighs, whose seed in peril lies? Perilize. In the sepulcher of my thighs, what slain El Greco sighs?

Or yet if real, and his? Dear God, if real and his? In the seeding of my thighs, what spawn of Steven might arise?

† 112 †

Filippino Lippi's mother was a?
None.

Dear Priest, I would write. Dear Ferrin. Because through all of my life, every time I have had something to.

And if not a dream? If—?

Murder. My day is.

But back. At *thank* last *God* back.

And then slept, for some while evidently slept. Awakening to the rain again, and with something beneath me in the bed. The talisman, the petrified eye.

Or was I sleeping still, dreaming yet again? Because when I awakened I could hear him talking.

Talking?

Here, in this room? Hearing his voice and then another, a woman's? A woman's? Some woman's other than my own? Hearing:

"No, leave the light off. There is someone in the—"

"What? Now, Steve? This quickly, you—?"

"Sleeping. In the—"

Hearing them *this is not a dream!* I lay almost rigidly, clutching the stone, the eye. How long had I slept? Had he gone outside, into the rain? It was chilly, damp, the door was open still. Who had come in with him, who? Here to this unreal refuge where I sometimes believed no one truly existed at all, where no one other than I had ventured in all this time?

The love of Chance is very far from the knowledge of him. I was not dreaming now. In his bed, my face toward the wall, I knew the week was over, that unbearable week, he was back. But there was more, now. Thinking: I am here in this room and he is here, but who else? What? I did not move, facing the crack of light where it lay upon my arm and climbed the wall I did not. Watching as it was broken by the shadow of a hand, his, hers, from somewhere behind me where they whispered. Dear Ferrin, I would write. Dear Ferrin: Who is this other? Who?

Hearing her again, hearing the woman:

"Steve, good Lord, we can talk in the car, then. Not here—"

"No. Damn it. Lurking out there in . . . that rain. Watching the window, were you? How long were—?"

"I'm all right. I'm—"

"Jesus, first her and now . . . Lee, anyhow, take off those wet—"

"No. I'll be—"

"—Shower—"

Dear Ferrin, dear Priest. Hearing the rain, that seeping. Sensing the other, in my thighs. Pearl eyes. Lee? Did he call her Lee? And who, this woman from out of the seeping rain? Here, with him. Lee, he said. He said:

"Lee, there's a . . . any damned towel. There must be a robe someplace too. You—"

"I . . . yes. All right. It's been hours. I was walking, mostly. Steve, believe me, I did not want to come. But the minute you left, I—"

"Damn the—"

It stopped, the light folded away. Not moving still, after a minute I heard the shower drumming behind the bathroom door, louder yet than the rain. I could not hear Steve, though I could hear everything else, a rustling at the shade, the spatter of a passing car. And the minute he left, she said. Dear Ferrin, that means he was with. This week was with. Lee, he called her, Lee. Under me I could feel the stone, the eye against my heart. *Dear Ferrin that means she has been, has existed in his life through all this time from long before I.* Feeling the stone, waiting for the shower to cease. Hearing that at last and then awaiting the door too, the light where it would fall again upon my hand at the wall. And not the marijuana any longer. Nothing, any longer.

I am the one who dies when he is not.

And then not wanting to listen, not understanding when I did, hearing:

"Why? Damn it, Lee. Wasn't the . . . once enough? What more do you—?"

"Steve, my arm. You are hurting me—"

"Coming here? Following? What meaning do you think it—?"

"Steve, I had to. Could not keep myself from—"

"Had to—?"

"You're . . . tearing it, Steve. Are you drunk? Do you want to wake her—?"

"Yes! Why not? Jesus, you . . . both of you, thinking it's—"

"Steve!"

"—Something sacred, maybe, when it . . . or must I show you how meaningless, profane—"

"Let me go—"

Losing the light again where she stumbled against the door. Yet I could see them now, where I had turned, shadow intaglioed upon shadow against the night's vaster dark, hers that I did not know, his. For a moment they were locked, they seemed to struggle. Who? What? Then I could hear his breath, rushing and torn, heard it even above the sudden wild whispering in my head: *Dear Ferrin dear Priest all of this week he has been with—*

"Steve! She's awake! Look! Stop—"

Was I still sick? Was it still the marijuana after all? I had lifted myself, was facing them with my weight upon my arms, though still I clutched the stone. "All right, then," the woman said. Realizing it was she who was breathless, not he. Hearing her sob. "Tell her to leave, then," she said. "Whoever she is. Steve? Because we have to talk. I cannot simply go back—"

"In Maurice Utrillo's mother's ass," I said.

Whirling toward me, twin shadows, suspended. Was it really me? Aloud? Yet no one else, in all the days, not here at least. "Damn it, Steve," I said. "I've got something like squatter's rights, anyway. Or tell me, then. From how long? Because if you just wandered off someplace and happened to shack up for the week I could not care less. But I won't be—"

"Steve, you must. I need—"

"Need—?"

Seeing then that he held her still, at her wrist. As he said: "Damn . . . all of this. Both of you, now . . . all this talk about . . . willingness, need, as if I were—"

But in darkness then she jerked away. Following, he held fast, so that for an instant, insanely, they loomed directly above me, she with her robed arms outflung to hover like some great pinioned bird. Uncomprehending still, I heard a sound that might have been a moan: Dancing and songs, what is the meaning of dancing and songs? And then he flung her down.

The robe had been torn away, had fallen to the floor. Feeling the sudden crush of her weight upon my legs I sprang back, though instantly she too recoiled, hung poised. "Steve!" she cried. "God! What are you—?"

Uncomprehending, dismayed. Was it the pot? Did I wake or sleep? For the moment *dear Ferrin* able to do no more than wait, than watch, even as she.

"All this talk . . . love . . . do you think it—?"

Again she sobbed. "No," she said. "Damn it, Steve. Not what I think, what I know. Because even this, whatever you believe you are—"

"Love—?"

"Whoever she—"

And then he was gone, had strode away. And only breath then, hers, mine. Hearing that, and hearing the blood as well, the secret ebb and drain of blood. She moved again, drew aside, and I felt again the faintly sweated touch of her calf against my own.

But was turning myself, then, upon my hands and knees, to reach the switch beyond the bed. Having lost the stone, the charm. Feeling her withdraw behind me yet farther at the light.

Then lifting my head alone, poised there still, crouching, to look back.

As she, at the bed's opposite end, identical. Naked, to gaze upon the other, each.

And then stunned, so that for the minute even the unreality could not intervene: at the dark chopped hair still wet from the shower or from rain, gleaming there, or that stark, impossibly beautiful plane of cheek hewn into a purity of line so rare that not one in ten thousand would know to cherish it. Her eyes were wild, feral, mad, and from that perspective in the lamp's indirect accentuation she might have been some ravaged saint or virgin out of an agonized Caravaggio heartbreakingly long conceived but never dared, never fulfilled. Looking at me—thinking what, in her own turn?—until her tongue touched her lips and I could discern the terrible pulsing of a cord at her neck, its flutter in the inconceivably pure column of her neck.

And then how strange, as she ceased to look at me at all, but gazed instead at the small, worn stone where it had rolled to lie between us. Frowning, reaching to take it, she did not. Instead she rose up then, upon her haunches, her head lifting and her hands too, as if to blind her eyes, her rising breasts far fuller than my own and whiter also in contrast to flesh that had taken the sun. And beneath one of them I saw a scar, like a tiny, distorted etching of a cross. Then her hands, her body, fell, she hung limply with her head lowered, to sob once without sound.

Then she fled, that lithe, tall, unimaginably beautiful girl. With that face. Dear Ferrin, you who paint, how you would weep to see that face! Light flooded from the bathroom and then was devoured as the door jerked after her.

Near the window he could have been watching or not, I had no idea. For the moment I sat merely, the sheet somehow across my thighs. Then I began to laugh. Did I say it out loud? "Now, shit, what do I have to wait for the bathroom for?" Standing, I went across and took down my raincoat from where it hung on a nail on the outside of the closet door. It was still soaked, practically dripping. Like my psyche, had I said? Schizo-Fernic. My shoes were still drenched also.

But she came out then, in a wet, clinging blouse. She wore pants. I knew she would. "You are in a drawing," I said, stupidly. "Of a young boy. An Andrea del Sarto."

"*What—?*"

"Nothing. It wasn't anything. Just one ultimate insanity."

Staring at me, the light taking that same melting delicate plane beside the gleaming black hair, the slender beauty of her neck. Not looking at him at all, nor the eyes tormented now, only sick, only lost. "Yes," she may have said.

When she went out I waited, but it was for her only, to give her time to go. Confronting him in the emptiness, hearing the rain anew, thinking of nothing now, not really, or only sick again myself, or just tired. At the door, not expecting to, maybe still only waiting, I said, "All right, Steve. It was violation after all, then. But you always let me in, I had no way to know there was someone from before, or . . . whatever. If I shouldn't have been here tonight, I'm sorry. I mean that much, sincerely. The rest was fun. I'll remember it when I go back to being the town pump—"

"With a broken handle," he said. Watching me now he seemed to laugh, and yet with incalculable strain, soundlessly, pained. Finally he said, "Not from before. Jesus, you and your . . . what did you say, squatter's privileges? Do I owe you an explanation, really? Violation, yes. To the extent that it is your fault, in part, since—"

"My—?"

"Words. All that . . . talk, making me think about . . . I went to Vermont. That was Ferrin's wife. I—"

"Ferrin's—?"

"Priest—"

"Oh, Steve. Oh, Steve—"

Mad.

SEVEN

It was because of the horse that Harry Talltrees saw them arrive in Mictlán. The horse was the reason he had come to Mexico originally, or so he proclaimed. He mentioned Rousseau, and "man's natural estate." People like the young painter, Quigley, spoke rather less tenuously about the dubious configuration of the animal's spine, or its age. "It just hasn't eaten well," Talltrees insisted, "having belonged to an Indian."

He stabled the creature in his garage, which was large. No one rode it except himself, and this perhaps twice a week. His home was some five blocks from the zócalo, and as a practice he would lead the horse almost that far before mounting. Then he would circumnavigate the block-long square at least once, with what he conceived an aristocratic indolence, before appearing to depart for destinations unknown. Removed from the zócalo he would dismount again and direct the animal to the nearest hillside that appeared pasturable, where he would loaf for some hours. Probably people knew. Certainly his wife did, though she offered no comment. Then again she rarely offered one about anything.

She was virtually as docile as the horse (which Talltrees called Oedipus, for no reason that he would remember; his wife's name was Marcia). She had been the nightshift file clerk in the photographic morgue of the San Francisco newspaper on which Talltrees had been a reporter, a largeboned but not heavy girl, and quite pretty. Talltrees had been twenty-six when they met. Journalism was not the place for him, though he had no notion what was. When he told Marcia one night that he believed he could devise a better mystery novel than the one from her bed table he had just read, it was only talk. Nor would he have cared if he failed. What did startle him was the figure on the check, his advance against royalties from the publisher. "Fractured Jesus. All those hours in somebody else's office," he said.

They had been living together for a year, and they were married just before they drove to Mexico. When Talltrees had completed a second book within four months of their arrival, Marcia said only, "That's grand, Harry. It means you can do three a year. So we won't have to stay here too long, will we?"

But he did not write three books in the year. He did not begin another for ten months, and when she questioned him he said only that he had no ideas. He had had none when he began the first two either, but he did not tell her this. Both times he had simply commenced by setting down some reconstructed opening scene he recalled from other of such things he had read, and the remainder had somehow worked itself out. He knew he could have started a third book on the day he posted the second. He knew also that the third would be blood sibling in kind and quality to the earlier two, as would a tenth to the third. When he finally did begin the third it was because their bank statement indicated that they would be penniless in precisely five months.

They did not fight. In fact they rarely discussed it, any more than they discussed the horse. When he led it into the garden for the first time Marcia simply stared, not even closing her magazine. After two years, when the pattern had pretty much been established, she said only, "Are we about to camp here forever, Harry? With all this excitement?"

Then it was because of Oedipus (he still possessed both then, horse and wife) that it was he who saw them arrive. This was in October, a year ago, and he had contrived a new approach to promulgating the image of his equestrian rejuvenation by then. There had lived in the town for some period an elderly, incommunicative Englishman named Roderick, with a wife younger than himself but more often than not bedridden. Several months before, the wife had died and Roderick had departed. The man owned an isolated house on a thrust of land overlooking the lake, remote from any of those others owned or rented by foreigners, and he left the keys with Talltrees. The house was small, but its garden was some forty or fifty feet deep. Under the strain of his wife's infirmity Roderick had not tended it. Now, two afternoons each week, Oedipus cropped it while Talltrees idled in the comfort of a straw chair on the patio.

"It was just accident that I was there," he would tell Joe Quigley later. "I had decided to try Oedipus on an uphill sprint, and then I thought I'd air out the place. I fell asleep out front."

"I don't follow," Quigley said. He had long since ceased to comment about the horse. "You mean nobody had told them the house was empty, and they were just look-ing—?"

"Yes," Talltrees said. "Standing outside the gate." They had not knocked or called out, and Talltrees did not know what had awakened him, unless their car. It was only the man who troubled him, actually, not the girl. She herself might have been no more than a misdirected tourist in fact, no more than curious. But even after Talltrees had sat up and stretched, unbending himself from the chair, the other neither averted his eyes nor apologized. Nor did he speak, a man roughly Talltrees' own age and with a dark, two-day stubble of beard, wearing a tweed jacket too hot for the afternoon, the season. "But I still don't get it," Quigley said. "If they didn't know the house was for rent—?"

"Yes," Talltrees repeated. "On top of which they had not even stopped in town. The girl mentioned it, later, after we settled things. I said something about the unpacking she was probably anxious to get to, but she told me no, that she wanted to go down the hill first and look around. And then she mentioned that she had not seen Mexico City either. So in other words they had driven all the way from New York and it wasn't Mexico and it wasn't Mictlán either, it was that house. And only to stare at, evidently, because she also said that when they saw me taking my siesta and Oedipus cropping the lawn they assumed it occupied. And so would have gone away again if I hadn't awakened. But meanwhile he has to have lived there once, whenever he was here before—"

"Did he say so—?"

"He didn't say anything. Or almost nothing, anyway. It was she. That he had spent time down here before, no more or less. Outside of asking me the rent and telling me he would take the place, I don't believe he spoke nine words. But it was obvious enough, even though he did not come inside when I invited them either. At first I thought it was just the view, the lake, because he had wandered out to the edge of that bluff. Too close for comfort, actually, though I decided he was old enough to know better. The earth seems solid, but it's a sheer drop for the first thirty feet or more. Well, you can imagine . . . if no one ever put in a fence you can be sure the property is inaccessible from below. But then the girl and I were in the kitchen for a while, talking about getting the water turned on, that sort of thing, and when I glanced out again he wasn't there. He'd gone down. I—"

"Down? Is there a way—?"

"Out the gate and along the crest, where the decline becomes more gradual. Though it's still a lot easier if you're a goat. I suppose I was even anxious for a minute, but I was about to show the girl the lake anyway. He was directly below us, down among those first rocks where all that split-eared philodendron grows wild. Just kneeling, picking up dirt, letting it run through his fist. There's nothing to see, nothing down there at all. Yet the girl didn't call to him either, as if she didn't want him to know we were watching. I guess it might have been ten minutes before we strolled back out a second time. And that was when I saw him with that Indian—"

"That Indian, yes," Quigley said. "Just how in God's name would—?"

"You tell me. But even if it hadn't been evident earlier, I would have had to see then that he was no stranger—"

"But that one? Isn't he the one Betty Tinkle thinks stole something out of her car last year? She didn't report it, naturally—a woman, living alone—"

"I'm not sure I would either," Talltrees said. "Manolo Ortega, yes. But be that as it may. His shack is on the leeward side of that hill up there. So if he were coming up from town he would use that callejón and then cut through the alley behind Roderick's place itself. Anyhow, they were down that way when I spotted them. Probably

I still would have thought it inconsequential, Chance knowing Spanish and merely stopping a passerby to ask about something, except that he had his hand on the man's shoulder. And they must have been together for most of the ten minutes too, since what they were doing by then was saying good-bye. I don't understand this at all, really. At least if he were some sort of local official, or a mestizo shopkeeper, even. But an illiterate Indian—?"

But the bewilderment was only to increment itself even that same afternoon. Because it was as he led Oedipus through the gate, finally, that he thought to invite them. "For dinner," he said. "But I mean in an hour or so, since we all generally eat on a Mexican schedule. Why not three o'clock?" The girl, Fern, seemed tempted to accept. "Especially once I explained that Roderick hadn't left any gas tanks," he told Quigley. "So they cannot cook today even if she wants to. Even if they do get the pumps working. But it was Chance. Maybe he was just tired, all that driving. And if they didn't make the natural stopover in Mexico City, who knows how far they came this morning alone? But still—"

That was in October. A pattern had already been intimated, although Talltrees could not know it yet. Some days passed before he again saw the girl. (It was Quigley who would verify that they were not married, which Talltrees had inferred without interest. "I heard her in the post office, renting a box," Quigley said. "For la Señorita Winters.") When he repeated the invitation she put him off, vaguely. Within another week Talltrees had stopped asking.

But it was Chance only, not the girl. As time passed he began to see her quite often, about the town, and often painting too, work that would have had to impress him if only because it was so much superior to Quigley's. Frequently she did sketches only, with a quick, decisive line that seemed to force comment from the whiteness of the sheets themselves, through the very absence of shading. Sometimes there seemed a kind of wonderment in her attitude, almost the incredulity of a prisoner at unforeseen reprieve, though he assumed this no more than an artist's response to the place, its tones. In no time at all she knew the devious hillside byways of the town better than he himself, and within months her Spanish was remarkably fluent also. Now and then, too, he would notice her with an attractive Indian girl he recognized finally as Ortega's wife, shopping together amid the makeshift sidestreet stalls on the town's market day, and with the other animated in a manner that impressed him also, since he knew it only Fern's ingenuousness that had broken down what to other Americans would remain an enduring barrier of mistrust. Insofar as he knew her, though he knew he did not, he decided he liked her.

Yet there was a kind of reserve about her also, different from Chance's, far less deliberate, no less real. Something precluded personal revelation, always subtly cut off such conversations almost before they began. He accepted it as an innocent privacy, since she could not have been more friendly otherwise. Once, leading Oedipus through a marshy field below the town, he met her at the lakeshore. She was alone, though not sketching. It was twilight, and the lake itself was molten, but she was intent upon something else altogether. It was a volcano, the Nevado de Toluca, its jagged rim barely visible beyond the nearer hills usually, yet seeming to soar now, and with the snow at its peak an unearthly, bleeding crimson in the sunset. Talltrees had been in Mictlán for the two years without knowing it visible from anywhere except higher ground. Then he realized he was seeing even more of it than he had from elsewhere. "Jesus," he said, "it is even changing hue while you watch."

"It's different every night," she said. "I suppose because the mists up there act like a prism." They had begun to walk. "You can drive up, do you know? There's a trail, through a fault. And then you're inside an enormous bowl of snow. Like a half-eaten ice-cream cone. Dear heaven, when I think of cities—"

She did not complete the line, smiling self-consciously. "Let me tell the old-time residents a thing or two," she said. Taking the horse's bridle she laughed. "Poor old doomed Theban beast. You don't really ride him, Harry, do you?"

"Don't tell Marcia," Talltrees said. "It's basically a spiritual thing."

That was still in the beginning, in the fall. He knew about the road into the volcano, had driven it himself several times. But he could not imagine Chance doing so, or not simply to show it to someone. Actually, he had seen very little of the man, and it was Quigley who mentioned the cantina. "The one with that ridiculous name, just off the zócalo," he said. " 'Think on the Dead.' Late, practically at closing time." Talltrees had never entered the place save for once in daylight, and then only on an occasion when the outdoor kiosks were shut, purchasing a bottle of beer which he carried immediately to the square again. He had not intended to carry it out. He could not be certain that the silence had fallen at his entry either, that anyone had been talking before that. The room was sunless, and fleetingly perceived objects like candy skulls or photographs of bullfighters in death had cluttered the shelves behind the zinc bar. There was a stench from the open urinal. Perhaps it was not fear, not atavistic. "Hell, go look yourself, then," Quigley said. He would not, not deliberately. But one night, returning alone from the town's once-weekly film, passing, he saw an Indian struggling to hoist a sack of meal onto a burro, too drunk to manipulate it. In the cantina doorway three or four others stood laughing, not assisting as the sack slipped and thudded to the cobblestones. Chance was among them. The laughter subsided as Talltrees approached. Still grinning, Chance nodded, though their eyes scarcely met, he was watching the drunken man again. Only when he moved on did Talltrees realize that he had not seen Ortega, that Chance had been by himself.

Then he dismissed it. Or perhaps he just accepted. "Anyway, I wasn't remarkably distressed over the absence of someone named Steve Chance from my life before they got here," he told Quigley. Perhaps he already sensed that at the end of a year the few words that had passed between them on that first morning would remain more than would occur in any conversation thereafter. He did not let it annoy him, or thought not.

So he was not particularly interested when he saw the other girl arrive either, long months later, the one called Lee Suffridge. It was summer by then, and he happened to be alone in the zócalo, brooding over an unresolved scheme for the new novel he should have started weeks before. It was well after midnight. Seated with his back to the street on which anyone arriving from the main highway would enter the town it was not the car he saw but the play of its headlights first, on the shuttered storefronts at the corner of the square before him. With his eyes closed he would not have been conscious of the vehicle at all, it came that slowly. Even when it had turned into that side of the zócalo its engine remained almost soundless, although the car itself was by no means new. He would not have to notice the Vermont license plates to know that it was new to the town, however. He watched it for no reason other than that it existed.

It had come to a stop along the square's raised inner curb, below the mall, seeming almost to cease moving of its own inertia rather than to be braked. The driver was leaning forward, hands high on the wheel, and it was some time before she materialized as female. Lounging upon a bench some distance from the curb, out of the headlights, Talltrees knew he himself had not been seen.

Then he thought it funny. "Because she was scared," he would tell Quigley. "Even if you would have to be pretty naïve about Mexico to make a drive like that to start with. A woman, girl, alone, in those mountains. But even accomplishing that, with no way of knowing if the town was the one she wanted, let alone how to find the house she wanted in the town itself." Watching her, grinning, he thought: And she cannot speak four words of the language either, probably. So now is wondering if she is going to have to sit in that heap until the sun comes up.

Still he did not approach her. The square was utterly still. Diagonally across from him in the farthest reach of the headlights a burro was tethered between that corner and a building evidently about to undergo renovation, a butcher's, and behind it, squatting at the wall, a lone peasant had glanced up into the lights once, then buried his face again into his raised knees. A streetlamp burned dimly over there also, although he became aware of it only when, finally, the car's lights were extinguished. He discerned something of her appearance then, the sharp plane of cheek, the dark chopped hair.

"Englitch?" he said quietly. "Spik Englitch?"

"What—?" The girl started, her head jerked toward him where he sprawled. "Oh, Lord, yes, do you speak—?"

"Englitch, sí. Spik Englitch mucho fine."

"Oh, please—" The girl might have sobbed. "I'm quite lost. Is this town called Mictlán? I'm looking for someone named Chance. An American. Señor Chance—?"

Talltrees arose finally, shuffling toward her. "Ah, sí.

Spik Englitch muy swell, you bet." Then he desisted, since, drawing back, the girl had actually started to roll up her window. "Wait," he said, "I speak it better than that. Here. Yond Cassius has a lean and hungry look, he thinks too much. Such men are—"

"But—" She was peering at him. "But you're an American—?"

"Forgive me," Talltrees said. "I just like to practice my Spanish."

She did not smile. Probably she understood that he had been drinking, however, since the window at last descended again. A little contrite, he gave the directions at once. Then he said, "I can show you more easily, if you'll let me get in—?"

"No." It was almost vehement. She said, "I'm sorry. What I mean is, I'm not . . . he doesn't—"

Talltrees studied her. Finally he shrugged his shoulders. "It looks impassable after the lane ends," he said, "but you can drive right to the gate. Take it in lowest gear." He was gesturing, indicating the way. Thanking him, she said nothing else, did not introduce herself. He watched as she backed off, past the corner, then shifted forward to disappear into the right avenue. Then, alone again, he said, " 'He?' Not 'they' don't expect her, but 'he' doesn't?" He took a cigarette, still gazing toward the corner.

But he was still not interested, not really, even when the talk started. It started quickly. "That's a pretty cramped house to have guests in," Quigley said. "There's a cot," Talltrees told him—"the one that serves as a couch in the living room." "Right next to that open archway, isn't it?" Quigley insisted.

But he had another reason for not pursuing it too, since he got busy then. In those rare periods when he did work, he worked unconscionably, day and night, immersing himself in it to the exclusion of all else. Partly it was guilt, almost Calvinistic, after the eight or ten months of unremitted idleness that had gone before. Even so, it would take him three months to complete the task.

But it was only two months later that he found himself interrupted after all, for a day or two at least, though it had nothing to do with that house, with the gossip. Instead he would go into mourning. It would be for the horse, for Oedipus, although at the time he would have to wonder whether he was not about to lose Marcia too.

This would be early in another October. She had not been complaining. In fact he had assumed her resigned, especially since she had said nothing even when he bought the saddle. It was not secondhand, like most of their Mexican purchases. Of impressively tooled leather, from Taxco, it was actually inlaid with silver. Nor did he keep it in the garage. Still smelling after months of its own newness rather than of horse, it hung from a spike driven into the living-room wall. In passing, now and then, Marcia merely drew in her breath.

And then one afternoon Oedipus was gone. He did not realize it immediately. Probably he could not have said why he looked into the garage at all. He had been at the typewriter for hours. Wandering briefly into the garden, he decided that what he really had in mind was a rum and tonic. Then he had already started back to the house before he glanced across. The rear garage door was open. "Oedie?" Talltrees said. He entered to peer behind the car, not really thinking yet, not quite asking himself: "Now since when do you have to step around a Volkswagen to be able to see a horse on the other side?" The bamboo front doors were closed but not locked. They rarely were during the day. He turned back to the garden. It was expansive, treesheltered within its walls at the rear, and it was empty. "Oedie, baby?" he said.

In the house, crossing through the antiquated kitchen

and calling loudly when he did not find the maid, in English he said, "Hey, now. Hey." Neither was the maid in the living room. Nor was Marcia. Perhaps he sensed the extent of the stillness. "Marcia?" he said. "Marsh? Have you seen Mother Fucker? Now what could have happened to everybody—?"

Then he saw the saddle. Or rather he saw the peg. For a moment, idiotically, all he could think of was a line he had read once, not remembering where: "There was my rifle, standing in the corner, gone."

"Marcia?" he said. "Concha?"

Again neither wife nor maid answered. But he was running by then, in and out of the two bedrooms, the nondescript corner room opening onto the garden where his work table stood and which he called his study, into the garage once more. Only when he was in the street, the cobblestoned road, moving less rapidly then but not walking either, with only Indians in sight, Indians and an apparently untended herd of goats, did he remember that he was without a shirt. He thought: Now, Jesus, can you go to a Mexican police station without a shirt? But he did not stop, turn back.

Then he found the maid, Concha. She was an ageless Toltec, enormously fat, with a tendency after even three years to giggle hysterically in his presence. She giggled now, even before he had accosted her, although at first sight he would have assumed her in some state of exhaustion or fatigue. He had almost passed her by, where she sat heavily upon a stone step at a storefront, her face in her hands. Springing back he realized it had been laughter, however. Alone here in the street she giggled and giggled. "What?" he said. "What is it?" Snatching at her shoulder, he cried, "Listen now, listen! The house is unlocked. Go back. Where is my horse? Where is my wife—?"

But he would not be wholly startled then, not quite

surprised. It was the crowd he saw first, running on, and then Joe Quigley, Quigley running himself and yet essentially in place, this at the nearest corner of the zócalo as Talltrees approached, springing forward and then back and with his arms raised and shouting something too, though in fact it was the horse that Talltrees was hearing now instead. Darting toward the elevated mall, almost at once Quigley had bounded again into the street which was the extension of Talltrees' own, that became the square's lefthand side as he himself at last entered it. "Go!" Quigley shouted. "Come on! Come on!"

Then he continued to hear the horse without seeing it, a steady, rhythmic, ringing canter which, had he not known it must somehow be Oedipus, would have bespoken nothing unusual at all, neither exertion nor effort, certainly nothing deserving Quigley's enthusiasm. But he had never ridden Oedipus himself at anything like this gait, even for the block or two which remained the extent to which he had ridden him ever. Then she, Marcia, came into sight finally from around the far corner of the mall. The elevation was greater at that end, and there was cactus along that walk, so he had not seen her traverse it, had not even been certain where she was. It was she he stared at initially, astonished, or more than that, gaping at her where she sat poised in the saddle, casually accommodated there, with a straw sombrero that may well have been one of his own lifting and falling in her right hand as she switched it repeatedly against the horse's flanks. Perhaps he was aware that her face as it bore down upon him was completely expressionless, not intent and not even in concentration, but displaying nothing at all. He could hear his own breath from the effort of his run, that and the steady, intensifying *clop clop clop* of the horse, and then Quigley also again. The horse was sweated, lathered, he did perceive this now as it approached, its mouth struggling against the bit as it swerved into profile and commenced to turn less than a dozen strides from where he stood, yet achieving this too somehow with grace. "Go!" Quigley cried. "Nine more! Nine!"

Then he understood that the horse was not moving so fast as it seemed. It took an exceptional amount of time to negotiate the corner, or time itself became disjunctive somehow, so that the beast seemed to hang in suspension almost, hammering, its forelegs rising and falling, the CLOP CLOP CLOP ringing terrifically now and yet the sound illusory too, somehow without origin, so that as Marcia gazed down upon him finally, still sitting easily, her right hand still rising and falling in concord with the horse's own rhythm and the hat swishing through air before it swatted sharply against Oedipus' rump, her face still devoid of everything except calm, a look that he saw was somehow preoccupied and vacant at once, he found that he could keep pace without even running hard. "Now listen, Marcia, what do you think—you stop now, do you hear? You—"

But he was reaching out then too, lunging, as to snatch at bridle, reins, perhaps even Oedipus himself, only to have the creature whirl, to find it drawn away more smartly than he would have believed possible even as he realized he did not believe it at all, clattering upon the stones and then increasing stride in a manner equally dumbfounding, to plunge onward until safely out of grasp and then settle into that same unhurried earlier canter again. And still Marcia seemed not to have glanced at him, not to have seen him at all.

Then Quigley had grabbed his arm. "Why not?" he cried. "Why not? Let's see if she can. It's only nine more, eight and a half—"

"What? Nine what? Around the—how many has she—?"

"We bet," Quigley screamed. "Twenty-five times, and

she's made it sixteen already. As long as she doesn't walk, that's the only stipulation. For crying out loud, it's only Oedipus—"

So he was running again then, as fast as he could this time, diagonally up onto and across the raised mall and past the central bandstand to head her off, conscious too as he went that there were more spectators than he had known, Indians, merchants, and here and there ragged barefoot children racing along the borders of the square themselves, shouting after her, gleeful and disbelieving at once. "Listen now, Marcia, listen, you will murder him, what do you think you're—?"

But once again they, horse and rider both, were to astound him, leave him literally flatfooted. (It was Oedipus he was thinking about primarily, this with the dim vestige of his mind capable at the moment of thought, the sheer exertion, that plodding, determined, more than twenty-year-old reserve of whatever it was that propelled him, perhaps memory alone, so that it had not struck him at all yet to recall that he had never seen Marcia on a horse before, had not known that she could ride, let alone with such effortlessness, such ease.) Because when he cut her off, leaping from the high far corner of the concrete mall to the cobblestones again without seeking the steps and then dashed out in front of them with both hands lifted they reined up in an instant, less than that, impossibly, the horse actually mounting onto his hind legs as she yanked him in, up and up, towering over him finally in excruciating unreal hiatus against the bright sky and then turning, seeming to turn on two legs only, and were moving again in the opposite direction even before reality itself allowed incredulity to be denied, had reversed themselves and thundered back toward the corner around which they had just come. He sprang back onto the mall, decidedly not thinking now, a little deranged, but this time he was far too slow, either that or they, it, had called upon even more of that inconceivable reserve, the horse belying every truth of its existence now, antiquity and gauntness and near-blindedness at once, and long before he crossed diagonally back to where Quigley danced screaming they had departed the square entirely, were pounding into a street perpendicular to his own, the improbable unrelenting CLOPCLOPCLOP seeming still faster yet and yet diminishing even as Quigley rushed toward him once more, shouting inanities he did not comprehend at all now—into a street where perhaps a hundred yards ahead the cobblestones ended and the road became little more than a trail amid pines and laurel and Indian shanties, toward the water, the lake.

He fell. Not hard, not hurting himself. But when he got to his feet again they were out of sight. Nor did Quigley wait either, do more than glance back. There were youngsters ahead of him now too, racing wildly on. Then he sensed someone, just behind him. It was the girl, Lee Suffridge. He had not noticed her among the onlookers. In fact he had not seen her more than four or five times since her arrival, after a morning when both had laughingly apologized for what had not been a meeting at all. Yet even working without interruption he had been aware that he was attracted to her. Perhaps it was her style only, the unaffected manner, though he knew too it was the notion that she was alone down here, that itself arousing him. So he understood also that he had been more attentive to Quigley's gossip than he might admit. Now, grinning at him, a little distant, amused, she said only, "I had the impression the horse was yours?"

Talltrees grimaced, brushing himself off. "So did I, until about eleven minutes ago."

They walked together. Down below, Quigley and the others had long since disappeared, where the path swung to the right. There would be a dock, some twenty feet of planking low against the water, built by an anonymous departed American in fact, an extension of the path which otherwise turned yet again to follow the shore. Quigley and several more kept rowboats there. He refused to hurry now. Even self-conscious about his missing shirt, his bony shoulders, he would not. Nor did he when they commenced to hear Quigley again, an inexplicable, lunatic outcry. "Row!" Quigley was yelling. "Row! Row!"

He made the turning and halted, the girl still with him. They had come to the last rise above the lake, and there were no trees below them. He could see Quigley and the children at the end of the pier, the boards taking too much weight so that the group might have been ballasted upon the surface itself. Then, glancing toward Lee where she had looked toward him in the same instant, as if both simultaneously in the other's face sought corroboration for what their first view of the water had told them they could not be seeing there, Talltrees said, quite calmly, even reasonably, "I didn't hear the hooves on the planks. But she must have ridden right out across the dock first, do you suppose?"

Quigley would indicate later that she had, though he was never to get the details perfectly ordered. Now, still not startled, almost impressed rather, he stood quite still, scowling just a little as he watched the three objects, wife, horse, and flat-bottomed rowboat, these also seeming immobile but not quite, drifting outward even yet from where the initial momentum of the horse's leap must have snapped the light hawser they trailed and set them afloat, one astride the other like some classic equestrian monument misplaced in time and space both, and with the boat beginning to swing about then on an invisible mild current too, so that the tableau was slowly turning into profile. Then there were duplicates as the lake began to

still, as a second horse, second rider, second boat, materialized in inverted reflection beneath them. They were
twenty yards offshore. Oedipus' head was high, held as if
in some ultimate assertion of pride, or grandeur, though
his flanks were heaving. Then, once, a nervous snort was
wafted to the bank as he stomped one foreleg into the
water with which, inexorably, the scow was filling. After
this the creature might have been bolted into place, however, not moving again except to turn its head, its eyes,
toward the land, sinking straight down and steadily now,
forelocks, joints, withers, the eyes fixed directly toward
Talltrees where he stood, or so it seemed, Talltrees himself still possessed of a kind of quiet, imperturbable tranquillity while Oedipus confronted him with one final look
of question or reproof, or in admonition perhaps for the
usage that had led him here. He went under the same way,
attempting neither to struggle nor swim, unprotesting, and
with Marcia still mounted upon the inlaid silver saddle
and still clasping the reins and making no move either,
placid, premeditative, in her case without a backward
glance at all, her visage set upon some distant and, to
Talltrees, undiscernible point on the horizon. For a full
minute, even as the bubbles of Oedipus' final profound
exhalation at last ceased to rise and burst about her, still
she had not looked back. Nor did she even appear, if
disengaged, to be treading water. Then, cleanly, effort-
lessly, she turned and breasted the seven or eight strokes
necessary to bring her to shore, emerging without expression, her blouse and slacks clinging to her but her
face, her hair, hardly damp. Talltrees did not even remember that he had not known she could swim before,
either.

Nothing changed. He was the last to leave the dock
(though it would not occur to him until morning to

recruit a boy to dive for the saddle, by which time it would already be gone). When he returned home Marcia was packing, a single overnight bag. "May I take the car?" she said. "I'm going to Mexico City for a few days. For a concert or something, to do some shopping. I guess I was just edgy, Harry, is all." "Oh, yes, sure," he said.

He finished the book sooner than he expected, in some three weeks. Then, immediately idle again, as if the three-month habit of persistent toil had nothing to do with the posture of life as he construed it, he found that he was gossiping himself, with the new doctor who had arrived within days after he had posted the manuscript. He determined the man shallow, and was amused at his instantaneous, unintentionally overt interest in Fern. He told himself it was this alone that prompted him, that he was baiting the doctor because of his very credulousness, since even now with time to think about it he could not decide whether he credited Quigley's suspicions or not.

Quigley was twenty-three, yet already three years married, already the father of twin boys. He had money. His painting was little more than an embarrassment, nor was he excessively imaginative. But what Talltrees meant, what he thought, was: And he has never cheated either, was wed to the first girl whose pants he ever took off and all the rest is juicy fantasy. So then he realized he did not believe what he was repeating to the doctor after all.

Then he was to think himself certain of it, at least initially, on a night when he ran into Lee again. It would be the first time since the death of Oedipus, though he would recognize at once the extent to which she had been in his mind in recent days. It was not late, only ten o'clock. This was a Wednesday, shortly after the doctor's arrival, and for some reason he found himself approaching the dock. He carried a flash. In its beam she turned abruptly, where she was seated upon a grassy slope just above the shoreline. "Oh, Lee," he said, averting the light, then extinguishing it. "Hello. It's Harry Talltrees."

He sensed that she had been momentarily blinded. "Oh —hello yourself." Then she laughed. "Of all places. Forgive me if I'm intruding. Do you come here to mourn?"

Laughing, he approached along the trail to halt below her, their heads at a level. Then he moved up. "Do you mind?"

"No. Do. I was just sitting—"

"Anyway, he's probably already resurrected. Or transmigrated. Into another sex too, I read somewhere. So that will make him Jocasta now. Or maybe the sphinx—"

He was pained by what he presumed an undisguised awkwardness, conscious too of her own apparent ease. Yet he thought also: But I was right that I was wrong. Because maybe this is what she does with her time, all of it. Encouraged, though hesitant still, at last he managed to say, "You're a pretty good-looking girl. I mean, to be down here alone for so long, just visiting."

Below them the lake was still, all but invisible. She may have been considering him. "Well, thank you," she said finally.

Then he surprised even himself, even as he despised himself for it too, knowing it oafish and characteristic at once, his only ploy. The slope was unnavigable, and it was clumsy, but he achieved her shoulders with his hands, her face with his own. At once he was rejected, firmly, her head jerking aside, her palms pressing at his chest. Yet there was something else in it too, something fierce, too desperate, so that he thought even as they struggled: Oh Christ, yes. Because there has been nobody then, not since she got here. Thinking *Oh Jesus, yes, you poor frustrated lovely bitch* even as he forced her down now he at last encompassed her mouth again, brutally impressed his own upon it as his hand foraged beneath her sweater also, clutched at her breast.

Then it stopped, ended, though he would not realize it instantly, was fighting her still and with even pain at his lips before he understood that she was no longer moving at all, had neither surrendered nor acceded but was simply inert, supine beneath him. He had displaced her brassiere, that hand was within it. Pinning her there, one knee thrust into her groin now too, he lifted his head, sucked in air. She herself seemed to sigh, to collapse even more slackly. "All right," she said. "If it's just a stray piece of ass from the first cheap slut you happen to run into . . . just let me get my—"

"Shit, now. No. I want—"

But he allowed her to slip from beneath him then, his hand tracing along her stomach, lifting after her as she arose below him on the incline. "Wait, then," she said. Then it was unreal, too swift, as her arms crossed and then lifted to withdraw the sweater over her head, the remainder following even more swiftly than that, scarcely silhouetted in the darkness and yet with the gestures more than recognizable, indubitable, elbows akimbo as the brassiere was unhooked, one knee, the other, rising, repeated, as her pants, her underthings followed. Already he should have known it too irrational also, too unlikely. Instead, again, he thought only: Oh damn, yes. Yes. She was below him still, facing him, her arms apparently spread, because when he lunged forward to draw her near again it was her buttocks his hands clasped then, the unseen matting of her groin into which his face plunged as he caused her to stumble. When she shuddered and stiffened as he rolled with her, seeking her with his tongue, he believed it only frustration still, only urgency.

"Wait," he said. "Just wait, and I'll—"

Then he lost her, in that darkness where still caressing her he had heard her gasp even as he had arisen himself, as he commenced to jerk his own sweater from off his shoulders. He halted, the sweater trailing in one hand, sensing it even before he saw, realizing that he saw nothing. There were trees above him, pines, the path and the water below. The darkness was almost absolute. Again he was without breath. "Lee?" he said softly.

Then he laughed. Continuing to undress, amused only, he said, "Hey. Come on, there—"

But it might have been even more impenetrable now, and more silent, except for the distant, windborne call of a dog. Nor did he even seem to hear the quiet lapping at the shore. He became aware that he held an ultimate garment before himself, his shorts, in spite of the blackness. "Hey, now? Lee?" he repeated.

Then he thought he saw her after all. She was behind him, on the dock, at its farther end. She could not have been poised there more motionlessly. Nor could he tell whether she faced him, whether she was looking toward the water instead. For some seconds he did not stir either, though he could not have said why. Nor could he have defined what it was about the instant that made him ill at ease, suddenly uncomfortable. And suddenly it was cold too, suddenly he felt a breeze.

Then he understood that she was facing him in fact, but only as her arms lifted where she appeared to rise upward upon her toes, her body arched and reaching so that even knowing he could not do so he believed he saw the rising of her full breasts also, the thrust of her pelvis, and then for longer than he believed possible not moving again, the gesture pagan and extravagant and almost unbearably lascivious, and yet as if supplicatory too, an adjuration, an unuttered cry. Talltrees was transfixed.

Or was he demented, was the whole thing illusion?

He would have sworn his gaze had not faltered, he was positive of it. Yet now the dock was empty, a blur against the deeper dark beyond. Or did he hear her swimming then, a faint, cloaked ripple? "Well, God damn this," Talltrees said. Yet again he did not move, was listening intently. Then he was sure of that much at least, already she was well away, distant and rapid. "Why, you stupid, dismal cunt," he said.

Yet he lingered, finally sighing with a kind of bitter humor as he commenced to dress again, deciding it a total vindication. "Because she is so frustrated she doesn't know which end is up," he told himself. Thinking: But damn it, I will show her that, all right. At last about to leave, conscious of her out there still although beyond any possibility of sight now, not even quite able to visualize her any longer either, secret, elusive, wild, he cupped his hands at his mouth. "All right," he shouted. "All right, I'm going. Get back before you catch pneumonia." Perhaps he understood that what he felt in several ways was more of relief than annoyance. Nonetheless, he thought: But anyway, the next time it will be so bloody easy it will be a joke. Thinking: Damn, yes. Because I will give her a week or so to stew over it, and then all I will have to do is whistle.

So he was halfway home before he stopped, before he halted for a long moment with his jaws locked, to stare senselessly at his watch. He had not the slightest idea how long it was. "Well, fractured piss," he said aloud. Then he went striding back. Eventually he sprinted.

She was gone, however, her clothing had been retrieved. Pausing for breath, gazing about disgustedly, he explored the hillside with his flash. Then he noticed that there were no imprints on the dock, seemed no evidence of her emergence at all. He knew it improbable, the time far too brief, yet he thought: But that means any grubby peon who came along could have made off with them. "Lee?" he shouted. "Hey? Lee?"

In the morning, quite late, awakening dully, he had to sense Marcia asleep beside him first, before it came flooding back. First it was guilt, not wholly unfamiliar in his life, and an unformulated, dreary embarrassment. Then, abruptly, it was panic. Dressing hastily, quite credulously he thought: Oh, Jesus, and Quigley and the rest will be down there talking about it already, where some dumb fisherman threw in a net and dredged her out. Marcia continued asleep, oblivious, though Concha giggled and giggled as if out of an ancient mockery while he gulped coffee, until he fled the house.

But he was lucky. His watch read eleven, and before noon, slumped abysmally upon an inconspicuously shaded bench in a remote corner of the zócalo after a brief, unseasonal rain, he saw her emerging casually from the clinic, the new doctor's. That was a Thursday. So then there was nothing for him to do but remain at home, sheepishly, though for Marcia's sake feigning concern over the forthcoming report on his manuscript, while he struggled to convince himself that it would pass, that when they met again they would both pretend it had not happened. Then, drinking, as it came into new focus repeatedly, he thought: Or Christ, did it anyway?

Then he received a telegram, the next morning, Friday. It was delivered early, the knock awakening him, though when he commenced to study it, to read it disbelievingly for a third or fourth time, he saw that it was dated two days before. It left him stunned, to the extent that years thereafter he would be able to call it to mind at will: MANUSCRIPT AN UNACCEPTABLE BOTCH BUT CAN PERHAPS BE REVISED STOP LONG LETTER OF COMMENT WILL FOLLOW STOP REGARDS KNOX. He said nothing to Marcia, perhaps because he could not yet find credence for it himself. The book had been finished so recently that without the perspective of time, that objectivity, he had to believe it surely as good as the others, thought it even faster-paced, more fluent. Sick, he shuffled to the post office twice, checking his box, although the day's mail had already been distributed, there could be nothing until Monday at best.

Then he sat in the zócalo for some hours, drinking beer sullenly. It was market day, drab Indians came and went bearing pottery, fowl, vegetables, meal. He could not have been less concerned about running into Lee Suffridge now, or about much else. No matter how many alternate computations he contrived, he established irrefutably that he possessed exactly enough money to support them for eight weeks, give or take some incidental unforeseen expenditure. So he was not really himself when he saw Chance either, when he hailed him.

"Steve? Can you spare a minute?"

The other glanced back where he had been passing some distance away, from near the absurdly Victorian bandstand, in shirtsleeves, the eternal tweed jacket slung across his shoulder. Arising, Talltrees met him more than halfway. "Hey, listen. Those degenerate crime things I write. Hell, one a year and I can live the way I want. But evidently I've screwed up the new one. Do you think you could read it, maybe, just so I could get an outside opinion? I get too close myself, probably—"

Chance shrugged. Only later would Talltrees pause to realize how ingenuously, or yet how without surprise. "Drop it off this afternoon, if you want?" Chance said.

"Hey, swell. Sure. Or . . . no, tomorrow would be better, actually. I just heard. I ought to reread it myself, really—"

Now Chance seemed amused, though still it was not ironic, not patronizing. Yet he was already departing too. "Tomorrow is fine," he said.

Watching him walk away Talltrees did not even indulge in the luxury of amazement, at the occurrence or at himself. He thought only: Well, chingado, who else in this God-forsaken place? Some moments later, pausing only to purchase an eighty-cent fifth of native rum, he returned home.

Then it was late, long after midnight, when he awoke in a chair. He was in his study, with the drastically depleted bottle at his side. It was a minute before he recognized the scattered sheets of his carbon copy on the desk before him, that failure he had not been able to disentangle at all, and when he sickened over it anew he did not recall that he had suffered an almost identical anxiety over something entirely different only a day before. Nor did he remember that it was Chance to whom he had turned for help. Wretchedly, at the banging, the knocking, he thought only: Damn it, now, they are going to wake poor Oedipus.

Arising, he knocked aside a prized stone statuette, pre-Columbian ostensibly, of a Nahuatl rain spirit that he had purchased once in Veracruz, in an illegally executed dockside exchange. Only later would he discover it shattered irreparably, a simulation of laminate plaster.

Meanwhile he stands dumbly at the indrawn bamboo doors of the garage, still clutching their heavy padlock though the chain has slipped through it to the impacted earth at his feet, the flash he has instinctively picked up on his way through the kitchen averted now too although at last the face, Quigley's, pale and wide-eyed, is impressed upon his agonizingly awakening brain, the words have begun to assume meaning. "Dead?" he repeats. "Lee? Lee Suffridge?" But he does not believe either, it is the last sort of intelligence with which he seems able to cope. "But . . . who? How? Why would—?"

"Jesus, do I know?" He is remotely aware that Quigley is practically shouting. "I can't even swear it actually happened, can I? Not with Fern as incoherent as she was when that ass brought her to the house. And now he's got her under a sedative. But I saw the machete, and there was blood on it, all right. Brother, was there. He said he would wake the jefe himself, Chief Huerta, since it involves Americans. I'm supposed to meet him in the zócalo later, as soon as he gets away—"

"He—?"

"Santiago. Aguilar, the doctor—"

"But . . . where is Chance? The house, wasn't he there—?"

"Fern says no. She says she and Lee were alone. And then someone came in. Evidently Fern scared him off, waking up herself, but not in time—"

"And Lee is dead? *Lee?* She—?"

"Hang it, now," Quigley says. "Hang it now, yes. I mean it damned well sounds that way. But what else can I say until we see Santiago again? Will you for crying out loud grab a sweater and come on? I'll wait here—"

Then he stops, as both simultaneously become aware of Marcia where she has appeared behind them in the oblique light from the inner door, where she has halted listening as dumbstruck as he. She is completely undressed, in that sensuous nakedness in which he has almost forgotten she sleeps, a robe clasped inattentively at her bosom merely, tousled from the bed, astonishingly pretty, so that the shameful wash of relief he has felt amid all the rest is somehow human enough to be permissible. In fact he loves her—his book is shitty and that strange, untamed girl whose own cool flesh he had handled is dead, and he wants to reach out to her where she stands. Instead he says only, "Did you hear? With none of us having gotten to know her at all, even. Lee Suffridge—"

"Lee Priest," Marcia says, or so he thinks he hears. Her voice is thin, hurt, and she is gazing at the dirt floor between them.

"Priest? What priest? Who is a—?"

"She was married—"

"What? Who are you—?"

"Somewhere in New England. He was Chance's father's friend, in fact. That poet. The one whose book you went to Polanco to find after we first got here, Harry, who died up in that same house. It's—"

Talltrees is staring at her, yet sick again, impotent, worn, confused. So it is not angered, not even demanding. "What?" he says. "That . . . Eric Chazen, do you mean? And her husband is . . . was, someone who—?"

Marcia has turned, sighing, perhaps not conscious of Quigley as she at last unfurls the robe, as she draws it about herself. Perhaps it is any of a hundred responses, perhaps only sadness. "I have to shower," she says.

"Marcia, God damn it—" He has finally taken her arm. "Damn it, now. You knew all this, and you never—?"

"Harry, did you ever ask?" she says, quite wearily, immemorially familiar, quite forlorn.

Still it did not seem real, though they had been in the zócalo for almost an hour now, where the doctor had not yet appeared. It was cold, and at the corners the streetlamps burned fitfully in the night's unreliable current. Only Quigley continued to talk, persistent, repetitious, savoring it to the full. "But to have been married?" he said now, said again. "And to someone who knew Chance even before she herself did—?"

Marcia was wan, huddled between them in a great woolen sweater, coatlike, purchased in the town itself.

"Joe, I don't know any more, really. Only that she was still married legally. It might have been why she was here, even, where it's so easy to get a divorce. Or while she was debating it, anyway."

"But that house, then? The three of them, all these months—?"

"Would she have talked about that? Would I have asked her? Even that little of it probably wouldn't have come up if we hadn't been on the lake road when we met, near the old cemetery. Actually, it seemed the most innocuous sort of conversation to make, mentioning a poet we've heard about because he happens to be buried there. So then she told me about Chance, who he is. In fact, that was innocent too, she was even surprised I hadn't known. After all, a town so small. And then the other thing just followed naturally, that her husband had lived around the lake in Chignahuapán at that same time—"

"But still, but still . . . that means it was Chance she came down here to. A man already living with another woman—"

"Joe, the girl is dead, must you—?"

But it stopped then anyway, Quigley noticing him first and leaping up at once, though Talltrees lifted his head merely, Marcia also, watching as he crossed toward them under the nearest light after emerging from the calle entering the square at that corner, from the direction of the municipal building a block beyond. Then Talltrees arose too, though for a time the doctor said nothing at all even as he halted to confront them grimly, in need of a shave, looking fatigued. Talltrees was vaguely aware that he and Marcia had not met, but he waited only. So then it was Quigley. "Well? For Christ's sake, Santiago—?"

"Chance is in jail," the doctor said finally.

For a moment, thinking about the girl, Lee, anticipating at least some verification of that first, Talltrees heard without really comprehending. But again there was Quigley. "Chance? *Chance?* But I thought . . . listen, I heard Fern myself, before my wife put her to bed, before you left—"

"Yes," the doctor said. "I told the jefe all that. That Fern is certain it was not he. But—"

Inhaling deeply, the doctor lifted a hand, then fumbled for cigarettes. Standing herself then, it was Marcia who offered matches. "Oh—thank you," the doctor said. He glanced toward Talltrees, back. "I'm sorry. You must be—?"

"Yes—"

"Oh, now damn it to hell," Quigley said.

"All right." Again the doctor sighed, however. "Yes. I woke up Huerta at home. Well, as I told you before, with Americans involved . . . but anyway, an ordinary officer would have stolen everything in the house before getting around to business. The gate was open, the door also. There were lights on. She—" The doctor gazed at his cigarette. "Whoever it was, for whatever reason, it was . . . shocking. As if perpetrated in utter madness. He had hacked at her so savagely—"

"Please—" Marcia turned aside.

"Yes. Forgive me—"

"But *Chance* then, you said?" Quigley insisted.

"No. I mean I don't know. He is in jail, yes. But only as a kind of material witness, for now. But it was strange. Because he walked in on us. Up there, while we—"

"He what? At the house—?"

"Came in the door," the doctor said. Again he paused. "I don't think we had been there five minutes. Almost as if he had been waiting, or . . . well, no, I'm sure it was just coincidence. But . . . and with the living room full of smoke, too, from . . a child's rag doll, of all things, that someone had thrown into the fire. Huerta and I were at the body. And then he was standing there, across from us. In that bloody shirt—"

"*Blood? You mean he actually—?*"

"No. No. Not from . . . it was from before, earlier. I did an operation, a few hours ago. My God, it seems a week. Chance helped me, and I was too busy to give him a gown. But—" Again, bleakly, the doctor contemplated his cigarette. "At least I assumed it was the same. When I told Huerta. Except who in Christ's name walks around for three or four hours wearing a shirt that's—?"

They waited; at last the cigarette was abandoned, unfinished. "But even forgetting that, still, it was . . . incredible. Because he just stood there. All right, yes, perhaps the shock had come before I myself looked up, before Huerta did, but nonetheless, he . . . as if he had known exactly what he would find when he came in. But I don't mean as if he had seen it before either, but as if it were somehow . . . inevitable? Does that make sense? Foreknown? Or maybe I am losing my sanity altogether, because listen, yes, and then he . . . there is a lamp, with some sort of queer shade, so that it lights only one chair. In a kind of cone. And there was a book. He went over there. Then. With that girl lying there like . . . and where you could not even see him, almost, in that smoke, those shadows, holding an open page to the light. For a minute, at least. Dear God, could he have been *reading* that book? Until he finally asked us about Fern. Just, 'Where is Fern?' And then did not even seem to be looking at me when I told him. He—"

The doctor's voice fell, enclitic. For the moment, staring at him, Talltrees felt a curious sense of displacement himself, as if time were someway abeyant. Almost absently, he thought: And just because we are all standing, talking, does that prove that any of us are even here? Finally it was he who spoke, however. "Nonetheless," he said. "If Fern insists it wasn't Chance—?"

"Oh—well, yes—" The doctor seemed relieved at the question's relevance. "Of course. I told Huerta he won't be able to talk to her for hours." He indicated Quigley. "Well, Joe saw. She was really close to the edge when I found her. Yet it's touchy, too. Whatever actually happened, Huerta is scarcely anxious to discover that it was some indigent local burglar he can toss into jail for a spell. In fact he's probably already back in bed mentally counting out the eight or ten thousand pesos he'll collect when some fellow gringo pays the bribe to get Chance out—"

"*What?*" Now it was Marcia who interrupted. "Dear heaven, all right, with a traffic ticket, with anything you need done officially. Even if it's part of the culture, so to speak. But with . . . and only six or eight hundred dollars? Then what would Huerta do—?"

The doctor shrugged. "Insist that Chance leave the country, I suppose. Fern too. And then register the killing as having been committed by person or persons unknown—"

"But Christ, Christ, now," Quigley demanded, "the girl is dead, don't they even care—?"

Now the doctor almost smiled. "An Indian died in my clinic tonight. Do you know where he is now? Slung over the back of a burro. And with the peons who brought him in probably asleep under a cactus somewhere, since they were drinking when they left. So that God knows where the burro has wandered to, either. They'll find it mañana, of course. Listen, American or not, this is still Mexico. Here, where people live with death like . . . or with a mortality rate that . . . well, surely, you've all been here long enough to know? But meanwhile, yes, since she did happen to be a foreigner there are complications of a legal sort. Huerta took her tourist card, whatever other papers he found—I didn't see. He'll notify the embassy in the Federal District on Monday. He also said he'll fill out a certificate of death and release the body for burial tomorrow. The house is locked, naturally—" He withdrew a set of keys, which he handed to Quigley. "I found these on a dresser, Fern will need them eventually. There will be a policeman outside until morning, at least. But all this makes it obvious too, the way he is deliberately expediting matters, getting everything cleaned up before la mordida. Does Chance have money, do any of you know? Does Fern—say a Toluca bank account? Anyway, we will have to arrange a funeral ourselves. And she wasn't Catholic, I don't imagine—? So we have that problem also, since I doubt a local padre will be sophisticated enough to . . . well, later. My God, I have to get some sleep. It seems like . . . and those people, that house, they—"

It diminished, ceased. But Talltrees had stopped listening anyway. He held a cigarette, not lighting it. It was Marcia to whom he looked. "Something else," he said finally. "Somebody ought to call Vermont. The man could be here in a dozen or fifteen hours, if he wanted to—"

The doctor was frowning. "She has a husband," Quigley said. "Had—"

"Husband—?"

Talltrees stared at his watch. It was some moments before three.

"Harry—?" Marcia was looking at him questioningly.

"Do you think I'm overjoyed at the idea?" He was aware that he would have to inquire at the police station to learn the address, that he would have to seek out the town's lone telephone operator at her home also. Yet he knew he would, knew he must. "Damn it," he said. "And it will take hours to make a connection too, if we even do—"

"Harry? Will you mention . . . do you think he knows who she was down here with?"

"What will it mean if I do tell him? Do we know that either? Do we know anything at all? It's—" Talltrees threw aside his unlighted Negrito. "Marsh, go home, why not? Get some sleep—"

But he saw it emerge even as the others looked up also, the headlights dimming though not being extinguished, where it entered the square and approached along that most immediate side to stop opposite them. Glancing at them, the doctor started immediately across. The jefe may have nodded, or even spoken, a muffled, "Señores, Señora," a man neither heavy nor old yet somehow conveying the impression of both within the car's shadowed confinement, with whom Talltrees had conversed at length only once in three years. Nor would it occur to him to walk over now, to accompany the doctor.

It took a minute or two only, however, the car moving again before the doctor had quite stepped aside, silently, the renewed headlights flinging shadows across them of the lean trees, picking out storefronts where it would circle the square before it departed. With hooded eyes Huerta may have nodded again also. Then the streetlamps flickered and almost disappeared while the doctor continued to wait, as they went to him.

And yet it was somehow almost unnecessary then, almost redundant. "There were only a couple of lines," the doctor said. "In Spanish. No motive, simply the facts—"

So again it was only Joe Quigley, while Talltrees himself was already looking ahead now, thinking: So now I will have to tell the man that, too. "Motive?" Quigley cried. "Motive—?"

"In the office," the doctor said. "At the jail. Chance, I mean. He wrote out a confession."

EIGHT

Telling myself not to think, to stop thinking. Saying: Do not think now. Or think something else, anything, think art. Think paintings I have loved and will hold in my poor privileged head forever, like the laughing faces of boys in Murillo, or those peasants who reek of the abiding soil in Le Nain. Think the unearthly, filtered, sourceless light in Piero della Francesca, think . . .

Oh Lee, Lee.

Think Leonardo, who bought birds that were caged, and set them free.

But confessed, Quigley said, confessed?

But no. But not.

Yet had to be standing there. Had to be standing between me and the fire.

But . . .

Or sleep, then. Sleep.

But could not. And lying in the guest room could

hear them anyway, remotely, talking about it still, although the doctor was gone again now. Joe's voice was tremulous, pitched high like a whine, and June's was thin and sad and tired, and now and then, too, would come a cry from one of the twins, a heartbreaking whimper in the night. And that poor strange girl, June would say, dear heaven the horror.

But confessed, Joe said, confessed. And this other man, this Priest. Because Harry went to wake up the operator and.

A priest, June said, she was married to—?

Yet the doctor says not, June, says the shirt was from. *In the name of Xipe, who is flayed* . . .

And she is dead? Like . . . Van Gogh? Like Andrea del Sarto? And Steve is in? In?

Oh Lee, Lee.

And Talltrees is? Went to?

As once in my head, so long ago, when I would write to him saying: Dear Ferrin, dear Priest. And now he?

Sleep. Oh God, sleep . . .

But I had not taken the second capsule. Leaving it on the dresser when he came and went that second time and with my keys too, saying the house is locked Fern you must sleep now you have had a bad. But I did not take it.

Facing the wall I lay on my left side, my arm outstretched, and I could see my hand in the treebroken glow of moonlight from the window, beyond where my hair was spilled, the narrowness of wrist and the curl of my fingers back to my palm. It was not yet dawn, was an hour or more to dawn, was perhaps four. The window was open and I could smell jasmine, though it would fade and return. In the moonlight that she would never more see, and gazing upon my hand.

And yet remembering her in moonlight too, one night when she had been here a week and we had not yet talked, perhaps not a week and it was hot, the air dry and sterile with thunder from a storm beyond the mountains that would not break, and I awoke sweating beneath the sarape and the bed empty but could see her in that shaft of silvered light that fell across her breasts *O Lee* where she stood at the wall beyond me. And asking me then, saying what does he do, Fern? Standing out there by that cliff, it is the third night that I have seen, have heard him get up and have watched. And going to the door together then, she and I, though he was not there any longer, was gone. Where his father fell then, she said. Yes, I said. In the heat, standing at the open door, and when I closed it turning my falling hand accidently touched her own. Go back to bed Lee, I said.

And dawn before Steve returned and we had not slept, had talked finally into the slow commencement of dawn. And had thought I was about to lose it until then, had been sick when she came. And yet did not, in ways I would never be able to tell anyone to make them understand, even after Lee *three* it was not to be spoiled.

You are in a drawing, a boy.

Saying Ferrin has done me. In a ratty old sweater. I think I like the sweater better than my face.

But does he paint then, Lee?

Three or four in the five years since I married him, she said.

And walking down together once, to show her the grave, the stone, in that jungle of fern and laurel so long abandoned to the ghosts of dead Aztecs now, to the spirits of the corn and the wild. But pulling away some of the growth too *all sunken there* to read: ERIC CHAZEN, 1907–1946. Fern at the ferns, Lee said, but it was Ferrin who had it put there, do you know?

There. And then tonight . . . dear God, tonight. And why to there, did I flee?

And before me in the anguished night, that candle, what poor deluded soul?

But had asked him too, long months before. Do you ever go, Steve?

I have looked at it, he said.

And gazing about the living room then, only at that moment, with a sense of something lost, forgotten, until I finally knew, and said: The painting, Steve? Because all this time and even driving down I never thought, didn't you bring? Looking up from his chair, scowling at me. And then to say only: Here?

And Manolo as well, still soon, when we had been here only weeks but with Petra working three days a week also by then and their Spanish far too fast, saying it was here that his father died, here at this house.

Steve, will you tell them, at least? I do not give a damn what the others think, the Americans, married or. But to deceive someone like.

And she is so lovely, Lee said, that chiseled, ancient, innocent face. And even so many months pregnant too, I had never known a pregnant woman could be so lovely.

There will be women there, Fern, a midwife and.

And perhaps already now *because I was listening for it earlier too, it is hours*, already tonight in that shack with no floor and its sentinels of stones upon the roof, its stones against the wind. And like a Bellini, his Magdalen her face might be, and so the child.

Or *dear God above* maybe even at the same time as, same moment, when.

Sleep. Oh, please, may I sleep?

These streets, Steve, did Herman Melville walk these streets?

Imposibilidad.

But still, about her eyes, something eternally sad, so grave. Is it just their poverty, Steve? Does Manolo's drinking have anything to do with it?

Fern, they are Indians. Can't you see what that means, truly means? And not even that she cannot read, or never in her life has dared to lift her hand to a simple telephone?

And carrying their water all the way up that hillside from the fountain near the zócalo too, until I told her, Petra, please, here at the house. And still then only at the outside faucet where she does the wash. Saying couldn't I, Steve, once perhaps, to go inside, to see the way they?

Fern, they have pride, it would be an.

But you, Steve, how many evenings do?

It is different with me, he said.

And all the years, Manolo said, I have remembered him all the years. Who purchased for me in Toluca with his own pesos a book, and instructed me to put down my name.

But stealing, Steve? Because Joe Quigley says he has been in jail for.

Fern he has starved. Petra is one of ten or a dozen children of whom three lived to see the age of twelve. Jesus read Malthus or Ricardo or somebody, at least try to think about it in some context other than your own self-indulgent spurious civilized neurotic way of.

And when you, then? All those hours when he and you?

It is like—

What, Steve?

As if nothing has altered. As if I have gone back to.

Fern that was Ferrin's wife, I am going back to.

To . . .

And because I had heard of him through all of that time, Lee said. Because Ferrin had explained who he was, of course, and now and then there would be a letter too, though always from such an unlikely place and with such irregularity that even Ferrin who was probably the one person in the world to whom he did write could not follow, would lose track of the rootlessness as he had long since of the motive behind it. And the letters so constricted, so full of an unvoiced despair. And hurting Ferrin also, for having lost him so, so that when they finally started to arrive from New York he would ask Steve to visit, would say that there was always a home for him up there if he wanted one, at our place in Vermont. And I myself finally, just postscripts really, seconding the invitation. Being absurd, I suppose, even patronizing. But I thought of him as a boy, do you see? Because I was twenty-four when Ferrin and I were married and Steve was just about the same age at the same time, but the Steve that Ferrin talked about was the one of fifteen or seventeen or so, from here in Mictlán and later from Chignahuapán. And there was even an old photo, so youthful, with a kind of mischievous, shy smile on his face. But that made the affection all the more genuine, actually. After all, any woman, hearing for five years about someone her husband had once almost looked upon as a son. And then when he appeared, was suddenly real ...

Lee, talking. Lee. Dear heaven, so that for the first time in my adult life there was actually a girl with whom I.

And now she. She.

And yet I knew too, knew even before. Because it was only the second night, the third, and they were in the front room beyond the archway and almost no word between us before that, none *from when I climbed the hill two nights earlier after the movie had run late and found the car at the gate and knew that too, nine months after New York without having to look was able to tell myself: That car is going to have Vermont license plates,* and then heard him saying no, Lee, sleep inside tonight, and there was a minute and then she came in to stand above the bed and myself asleep *pretending sleep* until at last it took her weight and a while later his and then it was I, me, to whom he turned. And again hearing no, you are here now, Lee, so stay here then, and I could feel him constraining her with one arm, feel her struggling there, and I myself fighting also until he said you too, Fern, but struggling still and yet finally not *pretending that too* and then upon me *entering* and not even with force *dear God so I have opened to him so instinctively even now.* But it was not I either then, for the first time with him as with so many others long before not Fern but watching myself, as from a distance, as from afar. And yet not true *lying to myself* even as I remained aware that he was still holding her *because God not, not watching but here, now, I, me, Fern, can this be happening? cannot* and yet without change, without difference *agony, sweet* until I heard a moan *hers? mine?* and then *within, within* was lost to it wholly *she is not here, there is no one else here* lost dying *hating* flooding loving *O!* Until *no, wait, wait!* he was gone and I lay seeping, flooding into that sunken collapse as if within me still *I have not put in my diaphragm, not since she arrived*—lay spent and drained and hearing a glass tinkle at last beyond the archway, a bottle *that could not have happened* until she began to shudder, to weep softly next to me in the darkness. And then knew, or sensed, knew even before I could have said that I was about to reach out to her finally, to clasp my hand about her own before I got up to go to the bathroom, to douche. And then before dawn awoke and heard him again *when did he come back to bed?* and it was she now, feeling her struggles as she would have felt mine and not moving at her cry *penetrating, he must be, did, the same inside her as in* nor through the rest either, endless, in that dishevelment, the rank sweat of that enseamed bed. Waiting, to fulfillment, and yet another cry, a sob, and then his breath, thinking: *And so I do hear him sometimes after all, this is when, but before this moment it has always been with.* As it sank finally, diminished and slowed. As Lee's hand fell from his back, struck my hip, slipped down. And still a moment *where are they, both, in this instant?* until at last he arose, had lifted himself *out, when?* and was sitting on the bed's side, until a match was ignited and flared and died. Only then did I move, saying: May I have one also, please? This is the last, he said. And shaking then, for a moment I could not stop shaking. But it was laughter too, part of it had to be, because I said: Well share it then, for grief's sake, do you think we might get germs? And she too at last, at last rising upon her elbows with her head flung back in that darkness, her breath still torn, saying: Oh God, give me a puff also, please. And who? Ferrin Priest's wife, yes, but who? And yet sensing it all the more surely then, and was right too because it could not have been more than days later *dear heaven is there actually a girl with whom I?* that morning when I was making the coffee and she called from the bathroom saying Fern I think the water tank is almost empty again, if you want a shower you'd better. And running then so that she was just stepping out *her hair gleaming, if he could love anyone, those bones* but had no more than flung aside my robe when it died completely. Well, now shit, I said. And Lee, laughing, saying: Here, I just rinsed this washcloth, at least you can wet your. Handing it to me. And drying her head then with both hands raised, with her breasts uplifted and I could see that tiny scar. But then not using the cloth either, waiting rather, holding it and looking at Lee. Until she looked back herself, paused and looked back. Quizzically for an instant but then not, then nodding, and with a smile beautiful and forlorn. As I said: Dear Lord, could we tell anyone this? Is there anyone to whom we could tell this, who would understand?

And because talking by then. Because alone so often in the house, the nights, hearing: *And I could connect those letters with him then, do you see? Because all of a sudden those five years of the strange, intermittent, evasive letters became real. The exotic postmarks, stationery from cheap freighters churning from one gloomy corner of nowhere to the other, the letterheads from second-rate hotels in cities that do not seem even truly to exist except in archaic books, or myth. Damascus, the first had been from. Him, there. And then Benares, Allahabad. Like some fugitive or wanderer upon earth. And then to have him appear, with no word beforehand either, of course, to glance out the front window toward the Vermont roadside that morning last autumn and see him standing there, gazing at the house. With that face, that look . . .*

To Mexico then I came.

Steve? You are going back to?

Fern that was Ferrin's as soon as I can pick up a cheap car or.

And back in my apartment the next morning heaping everything into cartons to ship to Marion and Adam's except for what I would bring, two suitcases and the best of my pigments and brushes and a roll of expensive linen, wearing my raincoat still *wandering around in that thing naked as some saint of the Jains, he had said, dreaming of Mahavira,* and after two days there were odds and ends I had forgotten, a pair of tennis shoes with the tongues cut away and an unopened can of turpentine that I had only recently bought and a pail of white lead too, almost full, too messy and too heavy to pack or send. And then standing for a long moment looking at nothing *this room was once an annex to the malebolge* while I realized that I had lived there for more than two years *how many days?* until I found a book I had also left out, my *Steppenwolf,* too lazy to open a suitcase again and so depositing it on the toilet seat for the next tenant. For emergency only.

Fern you should not come, if I have not convinced you already that I am not capable of.

Standing there. Between me and the.

But not, was not.

Steve?

Yet now is in? In?

And I? In this bed in Quigley's house and?

Yet not hearing anyone now after all, not Joe and not June, but I knew they were not asleep. Thinking: I am not the only person awake in this house. And dawn still far off, the moon darkening now also *telling me because Ferrin says he was strange even then, Fern, says something happened to him when his father died that transcended common grief. Closed up upon himself, Ferrin recalls, so that his first wife Lydia would have to shout at him sometimes Steven will you please for heaven's sake make some sound once in a while so I can tell when you are in the house. And only those few miles across the lake for two years and with friends here in Mictlán also yet never once came back to.*

Chase Zen.

And wanting a cigarette now, remembering I had seen a pack of Quig's cheap Del Prados on the dresser when the doctor had left my keys. But could not find any matches. While I was feeling for them one of the twins began to cry again, beyond a door that was closed. Shem and Shaun Quigley. And now tonight already perhaps Petra too has.

Were we led all that way for birth or for?

And a year, can it be? Mexico? And having seen so little, not three weekends in Mexico City. But at least most of the murals, Rivera and Siqueiros and.

Tamayo and Tamayo and Tamayo, creeps in this.

And that night when I remembered that Siqueiros portrait of. Who jumped off a boat, all mixed up in my head with. But if Ferrin is his surrogate father that makes Lee his *fornicating with his own* and didn't Siqueiros try to assassinate somebody down here once, Trotsky or—?

Caravaggio once committed?

Sitting on the bed now, letting my hair fall across my face. Because seeing it again then *Lee, tell me Steve was here a minute ago will you, but why a match when the lights are?* And then standing, holding the robe June had left for me, thinking I might be sick. *Miracles, there is a city of, and it is called. Called?*

And when I ran *God, help*, but why there, that jungle rank and sweet? In the dead vast and middle of the night. As in a dark Rousseau.

Rue. So. But you must wear it with a.

Standing, holding the robe. *Le Douanier*. And then thinking I could hear music, faintly, from a radio, perhaps in Joe and June's bedroom. But dying again, as it would, lost to the mountains between here and the city far away. As when Lee one night finding something too remote and about to tune it out when he said no wait that is Monk *a monk playing the?* but could not call it back. Filippino Lippi's mother was?

What's that you are humming, Fern, isn't that Leïla, *Les Pêcheurs de Perles?*

But his own mother, perhaps. Because asking him once, do you remember her, Steve, how old were you when?

Bach, she liked, he said.

And yet the rest *lunacy, sometimes* from where? As when I bought the little straw Don Quixote for the mantelpiece, asking me, did I know about Cervantes? I know he wrote *Don Quixote*, I said. Saying: No, his hand. The left, in fact. It was maimed. At the battle of.

At least I knew about Admiral Horatio Nelson, I said. And Captain Ahab.

Laughing at me. But Rimbaud too, then, he said. If you are counting legs. And Santa Anna, compliments of old Mexico. Not to mention Talltrees' horse.

Smart ass. So who was Utrillo's father, then?

Laughing, saying: You first, Valadon. Who was Dela-croix's?

Steve? Oh, Steve?

And told the police that he?

Serve. Antes.

There were matches right where I had been looking a minute ago, next to the capsule *sleep* and the glass of water the doctor had left. Because Fern you have come very close to. And with a considerable history of, I almost said, but did not. *Because no Marion not three or four not ten but.* And standing at those windows too *this room was once Golgotha* with the black pigment already at hand, as if about to.

Paint the pain?

Except how would you get the *Bizet* singing in?

Scarlatti also, he said. And Palestrina.

But it had stopped. Or hadn't there been music? And June's baby was quiet again now too, which? After I lit the cigarette I opened the door more widely. There was a lamp burning just outside. But even when I had not been able to find the matches, I knew why I had not turned on a light in the room where I was.

Because the last time I turned on a light.

And now what have you done Lee put on that same bloody shirt that he?

O heat, dry up my.

And watching her swim one afternoon, diving from that dock in a suppleness so fluid I understood even before I tried that no line could capture it, the grace of Lee in. Lee in.

Like Osiris, we hacked it into.

And only two or three nights ago, alone *oh you Diony-sian idiot* coming in at ten-thirty *her hair soaked* and if not sick from it probably would not have been sleeping near the fire tonight either, and so still might be, might still be . . . Veracruz, the true?

And wouldn't Stephen Crane have sailed from?

But mad, she said. Fern, it was mad. Because it was not until the last night, until after he had been up there a week. With Ferrin asleep, downstairs, where he had passed out in a chair. And then he went down again, afterward. I had not heard him going, swear I did not, not even leaving the bed although I know that I had not slept. Because lying there, torn by that guilt, sweating over it, and desolate over what I believed must be his own as well. Steve's. And then to hear them talking, him and Ferrin, who with that much to drink might normally not awaken until noon. And yet not talking either, but reading together. Aloud. Will you believe this, can you? The two of them, from a book of poems, I don't know whose but something they thought ridiculous, that they were mocking, laughing over. Naked, dripping from his seed that I had not even yet found strength to rid myself of, I went part of the way down the stairs, had to, to preserve my sanity. To see Ferrin whom he had somehow awakened striding back and forth with the book in his hand, declaiming, and Steve in my own bathrobe that Ferrin would think only innocently borrowed sprawling across the very chair in which Ferrin had been asleep earlier, giggling, hammering his thigh and giggling. And after almost no real communication between them during the week before this, so that I had sensed Ferrin's pain finally, after so long to have Steve visit and then not to reach him in any way. But now, there, that unbelievable communion, as if Steve were sixteen again and the ten or a dozen years had not intervened at all, let alone myself, what had happened between us not thirty minutes before. Did I say mad? Dear heaven, it had no reality of any sort.

To have made love to another man's wife, that man's, and then to seek to deny it by reverting to . . . and my God, how I believed I hated him then, Fern. How certain I was that it had not been he after all, finally, had been the mistake of five years rather, Ferrin, the sixteen years of difference in our ages, kind and gentle and wise and good as I knew him to be or not, the drink, the isolation and withdrawal of Vermont, that farm. And yet within hours of his departure had followed him as you know, and even nine months later still, with the contempt all the more bitter after what happened that night in New York, was still so lost and desperate that . . .

Lee. Saying: *Or was it only because there had been nothing before? Fern, will it make sense to you if I say I had gone to bed with virtually every man I had ever met? For three years, four, after college, just alone, not knowing why, not knowing who or what I was, for no reason? And yet not even suffering over it either, somehow, feeling nothing at all. Like some effigy or abstraction of myself, a marionette, being manipulated through the unransomed passing of the days . . .*

Like . . . you what? Lee? What did you just—?

And yet it is not even worth going into, Fern, not really. Because I imagine there are so many kinds of apathy in this life that the last thing you need is a reason. I will show you fear in a handful of dust. And yet I was as good a wife for Ferrin as I might have been. All right, yes, no utter fool either, precious little art major that I was. Knowing him a father for me too. But nonetheless. Until, until . . .

Lee? Do you know Edvard Munch, the cry, that bridge—?

Imposibilidad. And Hart, I meant.

Lepanto?

And yet did not know I was coming, Fern, will you

*believe that? Accept it? Any more than I had no idea
that you were here? Any more than I believed you could
have been important in his life when I saw you in New
York that night, believed anyone could be, after what had
happened in Montpelier? Had left Ferrin only, and after a
renewed torment too, since he spoke of Steve more than
ever then, after that final incredible evening and what he
thought was some rapport between them after all, accentuating my guilt until . . . but was going to New York
only. Or so I believed. Though there had been a postcard,
are you aware? One. After six months. With the Mictlán
cancellation but with no word, only some quotation that
even Ferrin who knows everything could not place. "From
future transmigrations save my soul." And then his signature, "S." But when I got to the city with only the one
overnight bag was suddenly on the George Washington
Bridge and not believing it even then though not stopping
either, never once stopping until I was so exhausted that I
could scarcely hold the wheel. Because I knew if I had
stopped at all I would have turned back. Am I out of my
mind? Or what? That fatality that drew me so inexorably,
holds me. Us. When I do not even like him, Fern, can
that be? You, of all people, can you tell me what—?*

Lee? You slept with—?

Any. All. Meaningless, it—

From future transmigrations save my.

Until—

I had no clothes, the sarape only, in which I had run.
But there was a skirt of June's on a hanger in the closet,
someone's bulky Toluca sweater too, too large *but that
army jacket of Steve's then, Lee, with the fur.* So that I
would even think her he, sometimes, in those khaki pants
as well, silent in the front room beneath that lamp, or
reading there *many a quaint and curious volume of* in one
of those ludicrous books of his into which I could never

do more than scowl. *But that probably Ferrin too, she said, the influence after so long, still, when he reads anything at all, the esoteric names Irenaeus Simon Magus Sadi Eckhart Laotse the whole house full of and teases about two-thirds of the ephemeral trash that I.*

Tertullian? Who in God's name is?

Don't you, Fern? Ever?

No, I said. Not those. I am an Emily Brontë sort from way back.

I do not mean the theology itself, she said. I meant—

Only to curse Him sometimes, I said. When I was younger. Because of my.

And the infant Jesus, in the secretive afternoon light.

No, she said. I mean now. I mean here. Do you, Fern?

It would be one hell of a time to, I said.

And because on one of those nights *together* when we. And cold too then, with no wood left for the fire, so that when he came into the bed he said Christ, how intoxicating, like crawling between two cadavers, but with an arm across my breasts at once and the other over hers also, I could tell. And then it was she and I started to turn away but he was drawing me toward them even while he shifted himself upon her finally, pulling at me until my hip pressed close against her own as he penetrated *in, do my shoulders jerk that way too?* And then was clasping me even more tightly as it began though I lay motionless only, Lee too it seemed *thinking what?* but then no longer, then suddenly accepting him utterly where her arms shot upward to lock him to her, her legs intertwined about him then also and a heat that was not yet sweat commencing as well, mounting. Then I myself somehow a part of it too finally *impossible yet dear God I feel nothing like jealousy or is it only a cheap thrill maybe? But not, am somehow sharing this, this gathering warmth, not theirs alone* and next had even altered position myself *or is it simply because I know what is happening inside of her?* to force my hand beneath her neck, somehow compelled, cleaving to them both now *closer, the heat, ours, my breasts crushed there, my groin where her jutting hip thrust into it* and encircling his back too, my leg upon him *loving her someway hating also but not.* And with sweat streaming between us now after all *adhesion, suction do I mean?* until she stiffened beneath him *and again into my crotch, dear God what am I doing?* in a shudder that possessed her rigidly for a long moment before she sank back into exhaustion and then lay gasping *and again what thinking, does she even know that I?* where I embraced them still, both, in that wetness, until gradually it commenced to slow, until it settled and died. But then understanding that it had been she only, not he, because he was spreading my own legs with his knee even as he lifted himself *out of her* then, my arm beneath her still where I shifted my buttocks and opened for him *oh God, inserting!* and yet so easily *because jellied from it, that is Lee's gush upon him, from inside of.* And myself more than ready *because it aroused me even more than I knew* so that I sensed it would take me only a moment, less *oh, Steve, yes!* and only then understanding that Lee lay against us in turn, had been drawn as closely as I, her face at my throat as I thrashed to contain him completely *within me, Steve, do not stop, more!* And then came *coming!* clutching at both of them *bursting!* but losing them again as I cried once *did I?* and fell away *drifting now, all flooded, lost* until eventually it became real again and I was aware of his breath at my mouth, much slower than mine, in a new quiet *peace* but knew too that still he had not come. And let him withdraw then *out, loss!* with no strength to hold him anyhow though I felt Lee's leg beneath my own somehow and part of his weight upon me still, across my thighs, even as it was she once more *and my own juices all over it now too, my God he must have slipped into her as if falling* so that still we lay interlocked *upon me but not, in her, he* with one of his hands clutching my upper arm until he came at last *suspended, quivering* and in that same instant I had caught my breath, held it, until that too ceased and all was spent, fell heaving into that final slowing wash and drain of blood. The three of us, though streaming still, and rife, commingled, upon the soaking sheets.

Then he was gone, was beyond the archway somewhere where a match flared and faded, though Lee lay against me yet, one arm outflung, her cheek at my breast. Nor did she move, although she spoke, at last said: Dear name of Lesbos, so are we somehow that way now too? I was smoking, had reached across and found cigarettes. It is not very likely, I said. Sick perhaps, but not that. *Loving her however in some way I could never articulate, and knowing that she as well.* She turned upon her back finally, yet not off me completely now either, the weight of her neck at the hollow between my hip and ribs. Sighing there, as the outer door opened, as we felt the brief chill. May I? she said. I held the cigarette to her lips, watching as its glow intensified while she inhaled, seeing the dark, lovely contours of her body also, that shadow at her groin where it was she, not I, who would feel his discharge seeping. Until at last she too arose, was gone.

And then did not return. Steve had not dressed, would be on the lawn only. But from beyond the other door I had heard the hissing of the bidet, distantly, and then too long a silence. Knowing her already, sensing it.

Lee?

In the darkness of the bathroom, that chill, naked and trembling.

Fern, I cannot.

Lee?

† 172 †

Or is it even because it does not hurt enough? As if my very soul is dead.

Is this Mexico, that she? Is it New York, last year, I myself?

Fern, when he enters me with you in the bed I want to scream, why aren't I screaming? And instead I.

Am I she? Is she I?

Fern, lesser desperation than this has been the burden of people who became.

But laughing then, deliberately laughing as I took her arm, saying all right, Lee, we will renounce the world together then. Saint Lee and Saint Fern. Weeping before churches we will go hand in hand into the desert places.

But trembling still. Don't, Fern.

All right, I said.

You are not any happier about it than I.

No. Nor any more able to do anything about it. Nor perhaps even able to desire to do anything about it.

Fern, I am afraid. I am afraid of this.

Cold. And Lee afraid. And now . . . where soon, all sunken there, to read her name upon a stone?

That word, she said. On the Day of Judgment I am going to borrow one of your brushes and paint it on my.

Oh you damned imbecile, swimming at this time of.

Had to be swimming there. Had to be swimming between me and the.

Love? Lee?

But the fire. Because the very next night—was it?—and neither of us asleep though with fresh wood now, heaped high upon the grate *more, Steve, I don't know about you but Lee and I both froze our delicate fannies off yesterday* until the light seemed to dance through the archway upon the inner walls, the house sweltering, and when he came in *his shadow looming, folded back amid the beams* I said Steve tell me something why do you read all that mystical occult theological whatever horseshit if you do not have any shred of belief in?

Not answering me. Sitting at the bed's end *his shadow, but it is earlier tonight above Lee on the cot I am thinking of,* smoking a cigarette. Tell me, Steve. Why?

Order, maybe, he said.

Piss on order. Why?

Cur Deus homo?

Talk English, damn it.

Jesus, aren't you in a stercoraceous little mood?

Never mind my never mind mood. Do you believe in sin, Steve?

Drooling Christ, now.

Do you, Steve?

Though as a matter of fact in . . . evil, perhaps.

Evil?

If only as opposed to.

But chuckling then, abandoning his cigarette and moving between us, beneath the light that flickered and sang. Watching me, his eyes almost merry, or was that too only the fire?

Tell Lee there is no such thing as sin, Steve. Or retribution or any of the rest of that Saint Thomas Aquinas crap.

And chuckling yet again, his hands beneath his head, as he looked to Lee who lay with her weight upon one elbow and studied him in turn, looked back to me.

Tell her there is no such thing, I said.

Laughing. Saying so it is happening already, is it? The pair of you aligned together against me now.

You can always move in with the scorpions in that broken-down maid's room out back, I said.

Laughing still, saying so you are. Except not quite severely enough yet, perhaps.

It's pretty severe. In fact we both hate your stercoraceous guts.

Do you, Fern?

Laughing. Watching me as I turned for cigarettes. But then suddenly had snatched at my wrist, yanking me back so abruptly that I came to my knees above him. Hurting me, even. God damn it, Steve?

And the eyes different then too, seeming to glitter. Or was it my own shadow upon them?

Do you, Fern?

Damn it, what is—?

But had released me then, and yet not, my wrist only, with his other hand clasped to the back of my neck instead. And then was drawing me down.

Steve. Damn you. You—

And seeing his free hand dart toward Lee then also, where I could sense that she had been about to spring away, shackling her there. As he forced me downward still and with pain now too but then not, even as I ceased to struggle against the pressure becoming aware that the pressure was decreasing. But with my face pressed upon it anyway by then *limp, in that coarse darkness* and for the moment not moving, not knowing whether he would hurt me again.

Because neither of you, he said, not really. Not quite severely enough yet.

But then not holding me at all, his fingers easing gently into my hair rather, spreading lightly upon the base of my skull. And still upon him *hating him, yes, because can he actually think that even this?* But then *impossible* did, did, had lifted my face slightly *his fingers delicate upon my spine* and was seeking it with my tongue after all, my hair tumbling in firelight where my mouth encircled it *flopping away once* until it began to rise at last *it, his, he* and then swelling terrifically as I sought out the vein *and a word for this too.* But then was being eased away, his hand within my hair again, and could hear Lee saying no, Steve, don't, until she also then, pressed upon him herself on her hands and knees and his hand at her neck exactly as at my own *and yet he is not forcing her either because he knows that she likewise*. And then shutting my eyes but a moment later not, watching her from just above where I saw the plane of her cheek hollowed because of the pursing of her lips and with her own eyes open too as it slipped away, flashing to mine *insane* even as I felt the renewed pressure upon my shoulder *no, not after* and he forced me down yet again *spit, it was only, no more than a sloppy kiss*, and then yet again did, was swallowing it as completely as I could *will we get germs?* And then without thought any longer, devouring it *every gland in my throat is salivating* until I almost choked and jerked back my head and then it was Lee just as heedlessly, her mouth rising and falling upon it, seeing the constriction of her neck too before her own breathless gasp, and then alternating, I, she, I, she, until I sensed it finally even before his body stiffened and Lee's head snapped up although she contained it still, my thumb and forefinger ringed about it now beneath her lips also where it throbbed and pumped within her and with his hand grasping my thigh, digging into my flesh even as I swiftly replaced her yet one more time, slipping upon it *gulping* to accept the final spurting ejaculation. And then to wait, to hold, to succor its tremulant, expiring pulsations with my tongue.

And then we lay upon him, both, our faces each to the other's upon his shoulders where he had guided us up, one of his arms about each of us as well, in the persisting heat, the light that hovered still about us at the walls.

Because Adam, Adam, Adam, she has simply got to learn to play with the other children.

And yet no, yet not. Because it was somehow even tenderness now, his lips as they brushed lightly at my brow, turned toward Lee's. *Calm.* And you have still not told her, Steve, I said at last. This. Now. Will you tell Lee it cannot be wholly wrong?

My sister, my bride, he said.

Which is who?

Either. Both. Does it matter?

In the quiet, the glimmery light. *Am I Lee, are we one?* Or Demeter and Persephone, he said, my wives of darkness. Or Tinker and Evers, at least.

Who, Steve?

Nothing. A bum joke. Or anyway I hope it is a joke. *Hoc est enim corpus meum.*

Yet you relish it too, don't you?

Om mani padme hum. The jewel is in the lotus. Plural of lotus.

And all his supposititious little pseudointellectual puns, Lee said. To avoid real conversation. Do you think if we go through the whole routine again before breakfast he might tell us what that other word means?

He would still relish it, I said.

Would I, Fern?

All right. Cannot absolutely abide either, perhaps. Yet craving for something, and so plunge deeper. But still.

What?

In New York, that night, trying to drive us both off then too. And yet even if you did, it would somehow make very little difference.

But you won't leave anyway. As we just seem to have verified. With one of you as psychotic as the other, now.

So damn you for that too, I suppose. So what next? Do we just watch and see how much you can stand, is that it?

How much what?

Do I know? It is the one thing there is probably not a word for.

Depravity, Lee said.

Or does it perhaps reach some point after which it cannot be borne after all? Is that it?

Quién sabe?

And then, Steve?

What? When we can finally certify the reality?

Then, yes.

I suppose like Wotan. You are strung from the windy tree. And yet—

What?

For a moment, at least. Here, now. Truthfully. I almost—

Go ahead, Lee said.

Go ahead?

Finish one fucking sentence in your life. You almost what?

Laughing then, soundlessly, beneath us still.

He almost loves us, I said. Both. Together. Should we forget sucking him off and bake a cake, Lee, do you think?

Fuck him, Lee said. Him and his damned contumacious Jew's soul. Do you know about that, Fern? That Eric Chazen's name was really Isaac? About his grandfather too?

What? Lee? His grandfather was a—?

As the fire began to settle at last, the light to waver and fall.

Steve? Eric's father was a—?

Holding us, as the light withdrew. Nonetheless, he said. It is the . . . best I can do, perhaps. These moments. We almost reach.

Almost reach?

We?

But Israel too, he was in? When he left Ferrin's, at eighteen, to fight during?

Or why don't we write a novel about him, Fern? The first one about a Jew in which none of that has to matter, since he is besieged enough to begin with? And that absurd name he chose, out of some counterfeit adolescent notion of the existential—

Bach? And Arcangelo Corelli?

Or hadn't there been music? There was no sound now,

only a tremor of leaves beyond the window. I was smoking again, another of Joe's Del Prados. In June's sweater and skirt that I had taken from the closet, a pair of sandals also. *Fern you must sleep, you have had an extreme.* Sitting, watching the smoke drift into the shaft of light from the living room beyond.

Because the last time I turned on a.

I doubt he would have changed it for that kind of reason, Fern. Can you conceive of him ever giving a damn what anybody thinks? It was only Eric, the poetry, I'm sure.

Israel? The king my father's wreck?

The living room was high and beamed, much wider than ours, and I could see the glass doors to the garden at its other end. It would be five o'clock now, or not much before. Why was I up, why was I dressed? When I went across, the twins' spaniel came padding out from somewhere, sniffing at me.

"Is the gate unlocked, perro, do you think?" I said.

Following me outside, smaller than the dog I had seen earlier. Had I seen a dog? So gaunt, so hideous, or even as if tearing at some wound? Or like a terrible omen even *except too late, because already then.* In the garage the lock was set into the hasp but not snapped, and when I went out I placed a stone against the door to keep the dog in. He began to whimper when I did.

The street was empty and chill, and I could hear water trickling somewhere, in a drainage ditch most likely, yet sounding as if it were deep below me. Then I was hearing roosters too, though it was time for them now.

And the cry of gulls, the deep sea swell?

What was slinking around in my head that I could not quite put my finger on? At the corner a tiny shop was opening, its metal shutters clattering as a woman rolled them upward. A shapeless Daumier woman, using a stick.

"Buenos días," she said. "Buenos," I said. So early, but like the cantinas then, too. For the peasants, before they go into the fields, he said.

But the meat, Steve? To hang in the sun all day?

Can they afford refrigeration, Fern? One shop in town, as a matter of fact. But half the time uses the locked case to keep his money in.

Yet showing me where, in those first days. And asking one of them which he was selling, the veal or the horse-flies, but said it in such a way that the man grinned and told us another place.

For if the sun breed maggots in a dead.

Is it changed, Steve? From before?

Very little, actually. But no electricity at all, then. Even now, Manolo, if he ever gets a few pesos, still hoping to run in a line. Though Petra wants him to lay a concrete floor. Or buy a bed.

Fishing, he said. A flatbottomed scow I bought for about three dollars in American money. Sport for me, though it often fed Manolo and the cousins he lived with.

Can he really have had a childhood, Lee? Is there truly a photo?

More than that. Holding an injured bird, if you can imagine?

And you taught him to read, Steve?

Important to them. Maybe I did, yes. A cheap copy of Mark Twain, in translation. Yet learned more from him, finally. All that confluent Catholic and Aztec anthropomorphism, the superstitions they.

Still, Steve? In this day and?

What day and? Fern listen, Petra, with that child coming, already she is trying to placate the brujas, the witches who live on the four corners of the roof and might spirit it away. And that drawing of her, do you know what anxiety she kept hidden when you did it? Begging me later to make sure nothing happened to it, because the same thing might happen to.

Petra believes that, truly?

Fern they do not know what they believe sometimes, but it is what her mother would have. Christ, the first time she saw Eric strolling around quoting somebody like Marlowe to himself she told me surreptitiously that she could have someone brew something, if I wanted, a remedy to exorcize the.

Petra saw Eric, Steve? You never told me Petra was? Didn't I?

And ghosts, he said. Los aires. Manolo insists the shade of Eric, about the house still.

The king my father's.

Steve? The things you mentioned, the drink, all the rest. But do you remember him with anything like love, Steve?

Like?

I would give you some violets, but they withered all when my father died.

A sea change, into . . . ?

And then remembering, quite suddenly. And yet how peculiar, because not for months and months now, old Sandy Bones, my fantasy father Raymond Holmes. Veracruz! And yet knowing why I had forgotten also. Because Mexico, this town, and all those days of quietude before Lee. Or even since *because no Lee there is no retribution except perhaps that which we impose upon ourselves in our own pain. Or as we might hurt others. But you are not hurting me, Lee, even if I do not begin to comprehend how it is that you have not. And without that hurt there is no.*

Steve? But back? All right, Mexico, maybe. But here, this very house, as if?

As if what, Fern?

I don't know, Steve. That is what I am asking you.

Never mind Eric Chazen, he said.

But when it reaches a point beyond which no more can be borne we will have touched?

Fern, stop pushing it. The pair of you. Sensuality as a spiritual ordeal, for Jesus' sake? Or carnal indulgence as a way to?

What, Steve?

Do you think it gets worse, harder to take? Until what, some glorious, blinding revelation of contrition and remorse? Redemption? When we will all walk together upon the waters of Mictlán's burning lake? Can you really be thick enough not to see that with every passing day you endure less? Jesus, look at Lee, who she was when she came. What is it, two months? And if I suggested right now that she crawl down there and eat your snatch she probably wouldn't bat an eye.

Standing above the bed in moonlight, even angered. And all that soricine bullshit about your ostensible contempt for me to start with, your tearful solace at each other's bosom. So why not, in fact? Two wholesome, heterosexual cunts, authenticated, indisputable. See how amazingly little it lacerates your exquisite souls?

And Lee, next to me, staring at him. Trying to prove something, my ass, she said finally. He would simply like us to, is all. Is just perverted enough so that it would gratify one more of his warped senses.

Maybe, he said. Very possibly. Nonetheless, it would still make my point.

Watching him still. Would it? she said. Poised upon one elbow now, with something bitter and defiant in her face. Drawing in her breath. Jesus, you bastard, she said.

But with her head cocked suddenly toward mine then, fleetingly, the look tentative, inquisitive. And then before I might react had flung herself forward across me, her

† 182 †

grip almost savage where she jerked wide my thighs, where her face plunged between.

And watching him no longer as my own breath was sucked in then, the sensation shocking and yet not, that sudden wet probing, more startled at the swell of her white buttocks across my torso *Lee's, not his?* until it penetrated *she?* and I gasped yet again *because no different from when he, oh!* And then *damn him, yes* had embraced her own smooth lean legs and was lifting her nearer weight, spreading them even as I tightened mine about her head and was searching into her myself now *feeling it still, deeper* where our interjoined bodies rolled and settled. Licking at only her pubic hair for a moment *as sometimes when he with me* until almost unwittingly I had found it and then was pressing my tongue within *but how? there is a way I do not know* and tasting it now too while sensing my own beginning to open toward her absolutely *and oh beautiful, yes, what difference? Lee, do!* But then suddenly had no breath either, was unable to sustain it and had to jerk back my head even as she herself, both of us gulping for air as we released each other to fall apart panting. Thinking almost absently *I have done that with a woman, for the first time in my* as Lee lay heaving, glaring yet again, saying well, well? You sick fuck, is that what you?

Until he laughed. Oh, shit, your tan, Lee, he said. And your hair. Compared to Fern's. Rump over tea kettle, that way. You looked like the symbol for Yin and Yang, the Tao.

Oh, Jesus. Oh, dear stricken Jesus. Will you go play with yourself, Chance? Will you? But laughing herself now, with him, as I too even where I lay conscious of it still *yet the same as my own that I have tasted upon his* until in a kind of improbable affectionate capitulation she had grabbed at him, had pulled him down upon us. And then as if in denial or refutation of the other was crouched above him and encompassing it with her mouth, huddled and shaking there. Until after a moment it was I instead, but climbing to squat rather, to feel her saliva upon it where I inserted it into myself from below. Yet almost hurting too *because of the depth, as if I am spitted* while she moved to sit facing me athwart him. But then instantly grabbing at me, at my shoulders, to balance herself where I understood that he had pressed her upward slightly, was seeking her from beneath with his tongue. And then kissing also, upon him that way, our mouths fluid, insatiable, as we searched out our own vaginal reek within one another, until it was she who withdrew, though tentatively, her hands at my cheeks, to gaze for an instant into my eyes. And not mad, not even quite incredulous, but only in acquiescence. Then tilting her jaw to indicate that she would replace me, but encountering difficulty, unable to mount until with my own hands I reached to help her ensheathe it *I am putting his prick into*. While turning to perch above his head myself then, to feel his tongue immediately too *Steve!* and then bending forward *physics, like, some law, to spread more receptively* and braced with my arms about Lee's waist, my face between her loins *kissing their fuck, am I?* where she writhed even as I. Buried there, my lips. And then shifting, inverting, at times one's mouth to another's sex all three, Lee's tongue or his at my clitoris more than once again *sopping now, I must be* as mine upon hers, and ever cleaved to one another, grasping, in liquidity, in that ever more common sweat, the delirious yielding of compliant flesh, until I had one orgasm and then another and Lee also and there was nothing any longer *nada!* but that inconceivable joyous sobbing aftermath, that precious floating calm in which I knew he was right *loving, yes, he, she, all* and when I knew too that whatever happened over however many future years *nada mas!* I would remember this only with a wistful keen longing, would cherish it for so long as I lived.

And Lee, her abandon more fierce than mine, in which as if not having been able to accept at all before she could not accept more readily now. Sitting finally, in that sweat, that dispossession, between us, sighing still but with her smile defeasible and resigned, saying Fern if he opens his mouth to gloat that he told us so I swear I will cut out his liver.

With his knuckles at my breast where he lay, head raised, upon his stomach watching her. There is still Saint Mary the Egyptian, he said. For twenty years, screwing the Arabian ass off every man in Alexandria. But then for twice that many doing penance in the desert. Floating all over the joint when she prayed, too.

Except that you just proved not, Lee said. Must I write out some sort of deposition that it is only infectious now? That the only angst occurs when I wait for my darned viscera to fall into place again? Even if you remain an unmitigated shitface for all that?

Although there is a corollary to the devaluation of suffering too, I'm afraid, he said. But which I suspect you both know already anyhow.

Steve?

The Eliot kind of thing, I suppose. The ultimate disaffection. Or *Sisyphus.* When you become aware that the worst of it is that nothing hurts at all.

As if a shade had been drawn down over some portion of the?

But am I not only Lee then, but he too? The three of us, even more akin than I ever?

And yet, evil? If only as opposed to?

Back, Steve?

Fern? Have you by chance seen that old . . . my stone

eye, that talisman? Had it in my pocket for the first few months we were here, but for weeks now, I.

As if nothing has altered. As if I have returned to.

Homeopathy? In 1960, as if?

My father's spirit, in chains. All is not well.

And lay hands upon the man, the blinded, dreaming man?

Steve? If Ferrin is a kind of father doesn't that make Lee your? And so you are.

Should we couple her with gimpy old Oedipus, would you prefer?

But not hurting me, Lee. Could not believe that you wouldn't. Dear heaven, that first night when I came in from that film and found you and him on the. And within days, in Toluca, three or four stores before I could locate.

Fern?

Nothing. It was only.

But don't you, Steve? Ever?

I count religion but a childish toy, and hold that there is no sin but.

Damn it, can't you once stop quoting and talk like a?

Petra saw Eric, Steve? And so she remembers you also, from?

Fern, I did not have time to see even then, thought still that he was alone down here. Had sat in the car outside the gate for ten minutes, twenty, until I became aware that he was standing on the lawn, watching me. Without a word when I went to him finally either, except to lead me within. And then . . .

All right, Steve. Whenever you are finished. But this time you might have the simple courtesy to introduce us, at least.

Or like Giacometti, Fern. Those three or four years before Ferrin, until I finally understood Giacometti. Be-

cause my own life pared down and down until only that sliver remained . . .

And Goya, Lee? Or people like Grünewald, and Bosch? Fuseli? For so long, the only ones whose vision I could identify with, because of my.

And not only at school, but with all of Ferrin's books in the house too, she said. And yet all I remember half the time are things like Michelangelo wearing his boots to bed. Or Titian, not dead until ninety-nine, and even then it took a plague . . .

Do you know Cosimo, Lee? Living like some animal, not answering for even a pupil like Bronzino, and keeping dead bodies in a trough, to study the bloat?

Was that Cosimo or Pontormo? Though El Greco too, that name alone! Or with his studio forever in darkness, to create by the fires within? And in Toledo at the same time as Saint Theresa, maybe knowing Saint John of the Cross as well? And that impossibly gorgeous story about Van der Goes, Fern? Almost out of his mind with melancholy from painting so many broken Christs, until he could only work when friars comforted him by singing psalms?

Or Van Gogh, Lee, oh my God!—eating his paints? And what they did to beautiful Modigliani, taking a death mask and not knowing how?

Yes, yes. And that girl, so lovely, and with his child, who leaped from a window only days after he? And because I used to have a fantasy, Fern, did I say? Alone, before Ferrin, those endless, undifferentiated mornings when it seemed I might even have charged money for it, for all that I. That instead of awakening to some faceless man whose name I could hardly recall was mistress to some mad brave heedless artist in his youth, was Fernande Olivier, say, when Picasso was no one but twenty-two

and flaming, or Suzanne Valadon even, in all her pro-
fligacy, but bearing the seed that might well have be-
longed to—

Oh, Lee, Lee, and do you remember . . . but surely,
you were with Ferrin then. But I, alone, in the kitchen
at my parents' home in the summer before my last year
at school, with no one to tell it to who would even have
responded to the name, and weeping silently there, when
I read that Jackson Pollock had died . . .

Fern, dear heaven. And they were born in the same
year, so that Ferrin had envied and loved his every
achievement. And went into the fields and chopped wood,
endlessly, for hours as he fought the grief . . .

Oh, Lee. Lee . . .

But she too then, can it truly be? Like so many others,
but all so long ago? Like a girl named Jeanne, who
adored and died for Modigliani?

And does that mean I will leave here now, leave Mexico?
But might even meet Ferrin Priest first, might see Ferrin?
And will say? Will say?

Oh God, someone, Steve, please help me, I . . .

But I was only in the zócalo, was only alone, upon
the mall. And still it was not day, although there were
great bleeding strokes of magenta and gold upon the
clouds above the delectable distant hills, and there were
Indians, clustering, as if spawned by the awakening land
itself. Why had I walked down from Quigley's, where
was I going? In the cool, sweet, awful beginning of light,
alone on the Mictlán square?

And with a burro hobbled at my side, the furry demar-
cation of a crucifix upon his bony spine.

Because it is told that one of them carried our Lord
Jesus, Manolo said. Did you not know? The legend here,
that all thereafter, so humble, and yet with that glory
marked forever more—

Steve? Steve?

But it was a block or two away, in that part of town where the streets were flat. And the largest building in Mictlán too, since a barracks also, the municipal offices. But still not knowing why. As I started walking, on a diagonal across the square.

High, pot in use.

But only five thousand pesos or so, June, is apparently all it will take. More money than Curro Huerta earns in months, even if only a few hundred bucks American.

And our tourist cards then too, Steve? When we didn't go back to the border last spring? You simply paid somebody to arrange?

Fern it is a way of life, no petty official ever earning enough without. Is it so unusual, can you think? What difference from the priests, indulgences in the Middle Ages? Or even Greece, the very sibyl at Cumae, selling favorable oracles for.

La mordida. And the bite, it means, the bribe. Yet, softly voiced, what sadness in the word . . .

And then I was across the street, standing in front of a church. The building *prison!* was ugly and squat, built of greenish stone and with a broad stone stairway climbing from the street to the second floor, with under that an archway and an iron gate. Behind a window on the ground floor there was one light, and there was a soldier below the stairs in a wrinkled green uniform, half asleep upon his gun.

And somewhere inside was?

With the soldier aware of me now. Turning to lean his gun against the wall, stretching and looking across. And younger than I, a boy.

And Steve was in?

And in our bed, all three? That streaming sweat, our bodies cleaved and crushed? And in all of my unocca-

sioned days, what greater revelation? Because what more, what else, if not that heat, that juice, that joy? And now she? And now he?

And yet again, still, Steve and I perhaps, again alone together we?

Oh God! Oh God, forgive.

And then had started to cry. But not even for that. Before the church, with my back to the soldier now, my hands at my face, crying. Because walking with him once beside the lake when we first arrived and there was a dead goat, were giant vultures lifting off and fluttering, hideous, and he said but the dogs too, Fern, I have quite literally seen one dog eat another here. Hovering and poised, so dreadful, as we passed. Saying any family who can afford it would pour concrete into the grave to prevent the.

Anus inward they usually begin the most accessible part or the eyes tearing at the.

And in the house still, she.

Crying. But then fled, ran past the corner to a wall where the soldier would not see. *For if the sun breed maggots in.* Saying Fern for Jesus' sake it is only a goat, actually a service they perform, can you imagine the stink of the countryside without? And even a federal law *kissing carrion* against the destruction of.

And goatsong, Fern? Don't you remember the derivation?

And then was across from the zócalo again, at the steps to yet another church, its doors all worn and stained, and obscurely carved. With the light in the square seeming someway filtered now, sourceless and unearthly, the sky a limpid Tuscan cerulean above the tall palms. Goatsong! And sobbing still, in the cool, sweet, delicious commencement of the Mexican day.

And she is dead? Here? Where all of us should have come to benefit from seeing scenes of woods?

But then how strange, how inexplicably unreal, the very facade of the church seeming to waver and recede, the silvered crucifix at its spire melting distantly into the drifting morning's mists, and the square itself as it came alive both familiarly lovely and desolately alien at once, some gloriously insane Turner suddenly conceiving the sky now too, until I felt queerly tense, queerly expectant, and with something exultant in my head as well, Bach-like, the terrible beauty of some passion or requiem or credo never before heard, and with a sense of infinite peace also, as in that ceaseless ebb and drift of love, or the Tao, where something unimaginably miraculous was surely about to occur, or lay even upon me, myself, so that in that very moment I might have raised my lamed hand to deliver all, might have cried forth the dead, invoked radiance before the blind! Or was I only mad yet once again, and lost, as forever, lost?

Steve?

And if I, Fern, would remember Lee Suffridge Priest for so long as I lived, who when I too was dead would remember me?

Because Fern, Fern, when the despair is genuine, can there be room for words? Stavrogin's endless confession, do you know the book? Is it anything more than just another self-indulgence, like all the rest of his dissolution? But when it touches bottom truly, when the emptiness at last becomes real, his suicide note is not one sentence long—

"—Fern, Fern, sweet fractured Christ on a jackass, now what are you—?"

"What—?"

Taking my arm as he turned me toward him. And then shaking me, even, until I indicated that he could release me. But closing my eyes then too, to taste it one more time. Los aires. "Oh. Harry, hello. It's only—"

"Fern, for Jesus' sake. You are supposed to be in bed—"

"Yes. But I wasn't sleeping. Did not want to wake Joe or June either, so I just—"

"But the doctor said . . . listen, all right, fine. But let me take you back, though. Didn't he even give you pills—?"

"I'm all right, Harry. Thank you. But you yourself, at such an hour. What—?"

"Calling. All sorts of complications—"

"You—?"

"This man, Priest. In Vermont. It took me all this time—"

"Oh, God! God! Harry? You actually told him that she—?"

"Yes. I had to. He—"

"Harry, it wasn't Steve. Could not have been. I—"

"Fern, he confessed—"

"But . . . and called—?"

"—Priest—"

Father?

Save!

Oh!

NINE

"*But he is returned, truly? Can it be? The young Señor Steve, from so very long ago?*"

Because she remembers still, although it is almost half of her lifetime past. And what she remembers most vividly is a bright, hot, windless day of summer, when she was in her fifteenth year. Remembering even that on that very morning, at awakening, she had discovered a fearsome yellow scorpion upon the rim of the outdoor sink, but with a torch of newspaper had driven it off.

She had been employed at the house of the gringos no more than a month then, but long enough so that already in the nights, when the demon-haunted father would have stumbled into his bedroom and the boy would commence to read at the fire, she would slip across the dark lawn and out the gate and down the gradual slope beyond, to meet Manolo Ortega at the water's edge. Knowing already too that one day when he would request the permission they would be wed, for who else among her suitors possessed a friend like the young norteamericano so wealthy, or could solve words that were printed upon a page?

But this was a day on which the other, the father, had departed, and so Manolo and the young señor were together upon the patio, where they would not often remain with the father at home. Petra was at the sink still, on that side of the house near her own tiny room, but she could hear them as she worked.

"No, amigo," the young señor said. "Written down by a norteamericano first, in English. And then put into Spanish by someone who can speak both tongues."

"But I do not understand. You say it is not a true thing that really happened?"

"Only a tale, to give pleasure. Better than truth. Such as when we are in the flatbottom boat, but for a time forget that it is only a scow on Lago de Chignahuapán and convince ourselves that we are mariners upon the great sea."

"But if he desired to make it better or more pleasurable than truth, why then do Huck and Jeem have only a poor craft even as we? Why are they not truly adventurers upon the oceans—?"

When they were gone, she realized she had not really been conscious of cessation, of their departure. Nor could she have said when she became aware it was more than silence she heard now either. But even as she paused, some soaked garment of his own in her hands, she knew it instinctively the other now, in their place.

And yet she believed she had become accustomed to it finally, that sense of his lurking, dire presence. Perhaps she almost was, in those moments when her few necessary encounters with him were anticipated. But now, the shirt in her hands still, only with concentration could she force herself into the rhythm of the scrubbing again, at the corrugated stone rack. And she would not lift her face, not look toward the sunny expanse of lawn at her right, even as she wrung it out at last and turned to deposit it into the straw basket at her side.

Then she was convinced she had seen him anyway, at the garden's farther end, a shadow furtive and threatful, slipping past. She rinsed socks of the young señor's, white, but thick with the mud of his many explorings.

Then he was within the house. She heard a chair scrape, and after that, through the window near her, a metallic sound from the kitchen, the banging of a pot. Again it clattered. Petra wiped her hands on her apron.

The earth beneath her had been wet, and at the front of the house, before the patio, she scuffed her bare feet into the grass. The door was open. Drawing in her breath, her lips compressed, she entered.

Half-empty, a bottle stood upon the table, a full glass beside it. It would be rum, she could tell from the insignia of wolves upon the label. Just within the kitchen, his back toward her, he stood at the stove.

"Do you wish to eat, señor?"

"Eh? What? Qué quiere?" He had turned as if startled, but for no more than an instant could she endure the fervid, penetrating eyes. Lowering her own, waiting, she fingered the small, cool, familiar object that reposed in the pocket of her thin dress.

She had entrusted herself to it for some weeks now, almost since arriving at the house, her protective amulet against those spirits that possessed him. She had an aunt in Mictlán, a sister of her deceased mother's, and it was she who had brought it to her. This was after she had told the aunt about the voices, the mysterious intercourse. "You are certain it is not simply of the drinking?" the aunt had asked, but Petra had been insistent. "I believe it demons," she had said.

So she clasped it surreptitiously now, waiting. "Ah," he said finally. "Yes. Sí. Gracias." Then he muttered something more, gesturing, words she did not comprehend at all although she sensed them an attempt at Spanish. But already she had noticed the three American sausages lying at the stove's edge, the beans as well. She nodded. His shirt was unbuttoned, his hair uncombed. At last with some further incomprehensible signal he was gone.

He had struck flame to three of the four burners, although the pan he had filled with water stood over none of them. She located a second utensil, emptying the beans into it, to be refried. Then, stepping into the other room to set his place at the table, from the patio she heard it commence yet again, the ceremony, that forbidding and always terrifying ritual so alien to anything she had ever before experienced, the sounds indistinguishable and yet not, a demand one moment or an exhortation the next, the ensuing silences in which he attended those responses that he alone among mortals might hear. And then the shout, perhaps, sudden, vehement, reciprocative, of further argumentation or denial. "—Not!" he protested now. Again with her fingertips at the charm Petra held her breath.

But it stopped. Or perhaps he was drinking again, having carried out bottle and glass both. Returning to the kitchen at last, waiting as the sausages boiled, she muttered herself now, the word in English for these which the young señor had taught her: "Hah-dawks." Over the free burners she warmed tortillas. When the silence persisted, seemed secure again, she said, "Yes. Sank your. How awr your?"

More quietly, questioningly, she said, "Steef? Steef Cho-sen?"

On the patio he was standing, abstracted, scowling toward the hills, tall, flaccid, and yet perhaps weary too, who seemed to sigh so often, or to gaze at nothing at all.

Just without the door she waited until he became aware of her, then again averted her eyes. "It is ready, señor."

Watching only the pale, sandaled feet as they turned, as they paused perhaps a meter before her. Yet conscious too of the bottle clutched in his bony hand, that bulk towering there. As he voiced some solitary new phrase, remote, profound, meaningless. "Sí, señor. It is on the table." Until he entered, again was separate from her.

There was a rope at the cliff, a line the young señor had strung for her, and it was there that she hung the clothing. Retrieving the basket, she did not glance toward the house as she carried it out. And then for a time she did not see or hear him either, although she sensed that he remained at his meal, or was seated merely, looking out. But the window was ablaze with reflected sunlight anyway, she could not have located him if she wished.

And then she even forgot. In that loveliness, that placid noon. Below her on the blinding lake there were boats, and here and there like frail insects' wings the nets of the poor fishers rose and fell. In the hills beyond, tall columns of white smoke were drifting, and the nearer breeze bore laurel and goat and pine. As she hung shirts and trousers and underclothing of the sort worn by the rich, and then paused too, to gaze toward a low wooded hill upon the most distant curve of the shore beyond which, invisible from here, her own village lay that she had left for the first time only a month before, their cane and thatched hut near where if he were not distressed by the pains in his spine her father would be occupied at his potter's wheel by the stream now, her two younger brothers who still lived at play near him. And surely now, with all so calm, no spirits were abroad.

And so forgot, did not even think to remember her talisman. Glancing again at the water below, at the ripple of a small, secret wind across its surface, she searched out that place where she would meet Manolo in the nights, near the proud, planked dock that he and the young señor had constructed together before she herself had arrived. And then remembered too that afternoon only weeks ago when she had opened the gate to him for the first time and he had looked at her and asked her name and then the name of her village, surprised and puzzled still that the young señor should have a friend of her own people, her own kind. And yet it was not really Manolo she thought of now either, rather it was of those moments when she would climb in breathless satiety up the outer slope with the odors of damp grass and of his young urgency still clinging to her, but then would pause, arrested, most often upon the patio but always just beyond the glow of the kerosene lamp which burned still in the house, even as when she would have departed, to see the other, the boy, seated still at the fire and with some book in his hands or those pages upon which he so often wrote, held for a time by the somber, intense face, the white flesh even so long accustomed to sun so different from her own, or touching her own curiously perhaps in that darkness and not remembering her talisman then either with the haunted one, the father, long asleep beyond the archway within. Or perhaps would whisper it to herself then too, that name that eluded her still. "Steef?" she would say. "Steef-on?"

And to be alone so, to frown so often upon the pages of so many books? What could be the meaning of reading, or of so many books?

Until one night when, as she returned, he was not within the house but on the patio, seated there in darkness, and without sound. And yet did not startle her either. "Petra? Buenas noches. You were outside—"

It did not seem a question. Uncertainly, pausing, she said only, "Sí, señor." Days, about the house, they would talk on occasion, though it would be he essentially, indicating what was expected of her, she nodding merely, amazed at the slightness of demand, the manner in which that which should have been command was request instead, and voiced with kindness. But that had lessened too, with the passing of time. Yet he had arisen now, had crossed toward her.

"There is nothing needed in the evenings," he said. "It is all right to absent thyself as you wish."

"I do not go far," she said. "This is not my village."

"I know. You are unhappy here, Petra?"

"It is better now."

"Now? Because of Manolo, your novio?"

"Sí, because of that. But too—"

"Petra—?"

"With permission. I was afraid before. The señor—"

"Of my father? Has he—?"

"No," she said. "It is only—"

She was reluctant to speak of the demons. Yet she did not wish him to misunderstand either, to think it something other that would not have frightened her at all, since she had known what it was to be a woman from her eleventh year. Indeed, she had even believed herself with child once, but after two months, on an afternoon when she had carried huge cans of water to where her cousins were plowing upon a steep hillside, she had begun to bleed severely and then had not been troubled again.

Or was it not the father she thought of at all then, even as Manolo's seed drained still upon her thighs, there upon the cool lawn where in darkness she sensed his hand lift, to hover, lightly, at her shoulder? Thinking fleetingly too of her cousin Estela who had gone for a year to work in the home of some wealthies in Chignahuapán, and then when she was eight months large from the man of the house had been told by the wife that no second mouth would be fed for the same labor as had been done before, and so had returned home. Trembling even, as the hand hovered still, seemed about to caress her.

"Petra—"

"Señor—?"

"I am sorry. My father is . . . there is grief in him, do you see? For my mother, these two years dead. And for his own insufficiency too, perhaps, or his failing—"

And so then she did not understand at all, the words nor the gesture either, as the hand did clasp her once, strongly, and in that darkness he seemed to gaze into her face with what could only be sorrow. And then how strange, as he released her and turned aside, perhaps two years older than she and so infinitely more wise, to bear such pain? And yet the peculiarity in the house too, where as Manolo had told her the father was a writer of books himself and yet had touched no pen to the sheets in her own days there even one time? To be so rich without toil? And for the boy, to be so rich and yet so sad?

So she forgot. Disquieted by so much that evaded her, as she hung the last of the garments. And she had no premonition of him this time either, that sudden intuition that had somehow always preceded sight or even hearing. So there was only the voice, the single, sharp, meaningless word spoken almost at her ear itself, after which the hand might not have clutched her at all had she not spun about, startled, directly into it. Nor would she remember falling, darting back from the cliff's edge to stumble, or be quite conscious of her nakedness either, beneath the flimsy smock that had caught up someway at her waist, of the underclothing never worn because never possessed. Because still it was not the man, was only the demons, and not for hours would she suspect that it might even have been to assist her that he next leaned. She fumbled desperately for her amulet.

But then it stopped too, that suddenly, the hand jerked up from her wrist. Or rather the other began as she drew herself about in turn, the harsh, unintelligible exchange, words that without attending she knew beyond her grasp and so to which she did not even try to listen. And yet she did not flee either, not yet, but climbed only to her hands and knees. It was he whose voice remained dominant, prodigal, after the boy's first shout, above her again now and with the bottle in his fist that he had somehow retrieved, looming even majestically for the instant where he blotted the sun but with its burst from about him dazzling, a crown of light upon his shoulders. Until they came together at the edge, until they commenced to struggle. And then the demons swallowed him.

It was twilight, dusk, before she reached her village. Nor would she explain, saying only that she had departed the house.

Yet neither was the waiting to be long, since within a day Manolo would appear, would walk there even as she. "A friend arrived by chance to visit," he said. "Yet another gringo you have no doubt viewed, from Chignahuapán. Within an hour of its happening, and discovered the body. There was a bottle beside him where he fell, amid those white flowers with the twin leaves. It is widely allowed that he was an incomparable borracho."

"He did not fall from the drunkenness," Petra said.

"This I know also," Manolo said. "Because last night, when I had not yet heard of anything, I went to our place at the water. And instead of you it was Steve who appeared. Having contemplated in the darkest of the wood throughout the day, but expecting that when he returned he would be taken to the prison."

"Manolito, be more direct," Petra said. "And what has come to pass?"

"Nada. Is that not what I pronounce? It is only this

morning that I learned. That it is being spoken of as one might expect, that the father was drunk."

And that was all, and should have been the end. For when Manolo returned yet another day it was to declare that the young señor was gone, had traveled to Chignahuapán with the father's friend, and each time thereafter would say that he had not seen him again. And so indeed it did seem to pass, and to fade from within her thinking. And now, because there were the seven kilometers that Manolo must come on foot, lacking even the few centavos for the bus, and because there was no longer their private place near the whispering of the lake against the dock, she found them another amid tall pines that dropped their cones gently, and where the tarantulas were few. And she was fifteen, and it was time, and Manolo spoke of asking the permission soon too.

But it happened that Manolo did not ask the permission at once either, and then not for a long while. For next he was in the military for his two years, and after that, over a theft, in the prison at Mictlán for two more. But she was at work in the town herself again then, in the hacienda of some others who were wealthy, and since her one afternoon of freedom was the same as the midweek day for visiting she would take what food she had put aside from her own meager portion and go to him. And then, as was the custom with the wives, she commenced to bring a curtain for hanging at his corner as well. And by then her father was dead from the infirmity of the spine, and so there was only the aunt in Mictlán to speak badly of her. "We will marry," Petra said. "Will thee?" her aunt asked. "He is of much talk, but poor ambition, I think. Have there not been other suitors?"

And Petra said not. "It will be Manolo," she said.

And meanwhile the young señor was no longer in Chignahuapán either, because once, before the prison when he had gone there at rumor of some work that had turned mythical on his arrival, Manolo had sought out the very house of his father's friend to inquire, and even the friend was departed likewise. And yet something persisted after all. It was no conscious evocation, perhaps, nor any deliberate effort of recall. But at times, confronting the hillside upon which the elderly inglés Roderick now resided with his wife who was ill, or later still when she had become Manolo's wife in fact and their own home lay below it, pausing as she carried their water up the long hard slope from the zócalo, or in the feeding of such fowl as they might possess, she would see again if only fleetingly that troubled, estranged young face, or remember with curiosity still that moment in darkness when, lightly, at her shoulder, his hand had hovered. Or perhaps it was only because her own life bore so little mystery then, so little that might astonish her with all the passing of the days. She and Manolo did not own a bed, nor were there windows, nor even a door of wood. Yet it was good that Manolo was not one who depended upon the land, for many of the seasons were cruel, whereas in the town itself was carpentry, and the plumbing as well, especially in the domiciles of the rich. And it was good too that their marriage had been of her own choosing and not arranged by others, and that their house was grander by far than her father's had been, of adobe, and with a roof of tin. And there was even pride for her in that sometimes there were centavos enough so she might take their corn to the mill to be ground, instead of by hand, and contentment in that Manolo did not beat her so often as some, even when he was borracho, which was as often as any.

So it was only with a kind of wonder that she would remember yet again, on that afternoon when Manolo would arrive to clap her on the shoulder roughly, yet playfully, where she knelt at her stone mortar, to tell her, "Hear me, hear me! My old compadre, Steve, do you recall, from so long ago, whom I always proclaimed would one day return? So never let it occur that you mock Manolo Ortega as one who does not speak the truth, eh, woman? Can you believe?" But then there was something more that would come to her at once also, and with pain, even as she arose, the pestle still in her hand, to step past her husband and gaze up the fifty meters of rocky hillside toward the rear corner of the house at which she had glanced, idly, ten thousand times in the many years. It was not something of which she and Manolo spoke, but she had gone often to her aunt to elicit of the magic, and when she prepared the potions she had mixed them into his food as into her own. And once too, in the period of the Nativity of the Saviour, she had walked for the four long days with other pilgrims through the deep snows of the mountain road all the way to the miraculous shrine of Guadalupe in Mexico City itself, to beg upon her knees of the Virgin there. But the seasons of warm sun and then of the chill rains had lingered and died and been renewed again, and still it had not altered. So it was not of the past at all now that she thought, one wrist lifted to brush a strand of hair from her sweated forehead, as beside her Manolo said, "And with a woman, sí, a comely señorita of golden hair, but maimed, with a hand that is shrunken," thinking instead: *And he will ask how long it is that we are man and wife. And it will be a shameful thing to have to speak.* Then she turned to consider him, but for a moment only, not smiling herself though beautiful now and fully a woman, before bending to kneel at the stone bowl again, with that one sadness she did not voice, of seven years a wife without issue.

Then, with his presence, as memory became a part of daily thought, and more constant, what she would begin to recall most often was how little she had ever been able to comprehend. For now, too, there would be great oddness, and more that would escape her. "Because even when he speaks," she would say to Manolo, "is it not singular to your ear as well?"

"It is the Spanish, no?" Manolo said. "To have made no use of it for so many years, it would be difficult."

"There is more," she said. "Because the words are correct, and each I can fathom. But when he stops, always it is as if there remains some deep cavity into which many shovels of soil have not yet been replaced."

"Ah, woman, do not plague me with silliness, eh? If there seems more, it is your problem to listen attentively. I who can read and write now tell you this."

But she knew Manolo did not understand any better than she. As even on that night when he entered their home for the first time, perhaps two days after he had returned, when she offered him one of their two wood chairs of Toluca and he would not make use of it. "To sit with a wall of impacted earth at one's back," he said, "it is a thing I have not done for too long."

And with the pulque also, of which Manolo gave him to drink. "They do not have such beverage in los Estados Unidos?" she asked.

"Perhaps," he said. "But only at the frontier, in such areas as Texas where many Mexicans are, and with the maguey. But truly, it is the first time since as boys Manolo and I performed our disastrous experiments and became borracho together."

Watching him in the glow of their unmortared stone hearth she sat upon one of the chairs herself, although Manolo squatted only, upon his heels before him, and with such delight as she had not often detected in him before. But she knew it a thing of vast pride too, that he would be able to boast of his gringo friend once again. "Ah, compadre, it is too many years for too many things, in truth," he said now. "And in the beginning, when you were only those few kilometers across the lake, here I waited—"

"It was hard, Manolito. Often I thought to come, but—"

"Sí, sí, with all that had occurred. But let us forget, what matters is now, that you are here. Take of the jug, it will put steel in thy machete."

In the inconstant light she watched as he drank. But there was this too, to puzzle her, that malady she sensed in his cheeks that were hollow, and the manner in which his eyes had altered likewise, as if from some dread fever. Nor did they smile, even when he himself did so, as now when he turned to her with his cup.

"You do not indulge of the pulque, Petra?"

"Ah, at the fiestas, perhaps."

"She is as all women," Manolo said. "With sorry knowledge of what is pleasurable in this life. Satisfactory for being bedded and little more."

Embarrassed, she turned her head. Near her a chicken hunted for grain, and she waved it away. "Walk," she said. "In this house nothing of the table is discarded by chance."

"Times are ill?" he asked them.

"Never splendid enough to be generous with fowl," Manolo said. "But you should be informed that I have become one remarkable hombre at the manipulation of a wrench, amigo. Indeed, often it is declared that no wealthy in Mictlán might properly evacuate his bowels without the prior assistance of Manolo Ortega. We have sufficient."

"I am glad," he said. Then he had turned toward her again, scowling in a way she remembered also, as over the many books so long ago. "We will want someone at the house," he said. "For some few hours, perhaps three days each week. If you still do such work?"

"From time to time," she said.

"Speak of it together."

"She will come," Manolo said. "There is no monumental enterprise for her here."

"Perhaps Monday?"

"So be it."

He refilled his cup. "And have you been to the place since the old times? It is changed little."

"Sí," Manolo told him. "There is the heater making use of gas instead of wood, this I contrived to put in myself for the man Roderick. But it is a rare thing, do you not sense it?"

"Rare?"

"That you are come back. I do not mean to Mictlán, where I have always in some way known that you must return. But I am thinking of the house."

She watched him. Leaning forward now with his hands between his lifted knees, holding the drink, for a moment he seemed not to consider Manolo at all, but to look beyond him, into the fire. At last he said, "You feel it unwise?"

"Do you not yourself? To return to such a place?"

Finally he smiled. "This kind of thing, too, I seem to remember," he said, "from our discussions of long ago. I do not think I believe in spirits, Manolo. What remains of my father reposes beneath the concrete in the cemetery."

"There were other spirits also, perhaps," Petra said then, hesitantly.

He studied her. "Other?"

"It is not a matter I have forgotten. The demons to whom the señor spoke."

"You believed them that?"

"Did we not talk of it? Forgive me."

"No, it is my error. I do recall."

Thoughtfully, nodding, he looked to the fire again. Then, with abruptness, he laughed, and perhaps for the first time his voice was untroubled also. "Frail little Petra," he said. "And to have grown so lovely."

She giggled, lifting a hand in dismissal. "Sí," she said. "Very. Which purchases no rebozos for winter, however."

"It would. In another place than Mexico, where one must marry only another of one's class. In los Estados Unidos a girl need only be pretty to wed the most affluent of her choice."

"This is true?" Petra asked.

"As true as that Tlaloc lives upon his mountain and sends rain," he said. Smiling at her still, he clapped Manolo upon the knee. "In fact I should have married you myself, had I foreseen that your destiny lay in the hands of this unmentionable wretch—"

Laughing with him, Manolo arose, though it was at the not uncommon intrusion of a burro only, their neighbors' from below them on the slope, where it had snorted in the doorway. "And as we speak of unmentionables indeed," he said. "This pendejo that shall distract me all my days. Retreat, now! Go—"

But Petra arose now also, as had the other, while Manolo drove it off. Then, for the moment alone, for some reason she would not meet his gaze. Yet she was smiling, perhaps at Manolo's unserious ferocity without.

"You are happy with my old compadre, Petra?" the other asked.

"Ah, he is more of an hombre in his own vision, perhaps, than in final truth. But as has been told, there is the corn, an adequacy. And a roof against wind. Is there better than bread, anything?"

She had looked toward him at last, although Manolo was returning then also. "Monster," he said. "And to be awakened in the nights yet, thinking it my insatiable mate, only to discover that bastardo at my ear. But you do not depart so quickly, viejo?"

The other had set aside his cup, however, was crossing to the doorway. "There will be time, now," he said.

"Indeed, much. Let us be glad." As Petra watched they clasped one another, a hand at the other's shoulder each. And again, perhaps, the other's smile was his own as they held fast. "It is good, amigo," Manolo said.

"Sí," the other said. "Sí. I think it is good."

But then there would be this, too, to disconcert her, although it would not occur until many weeks thereafter, upon a morning when Manolo had already departed for some work at a great distance and there was still only the wakening cry of fowl amid the hills, only the cobalt intimation of dawn beyond the curtain at the doorway. Sweeping, with her broom of twigs, she had only then lifted aside the straw petate upon which they slept. And then for a long moment she would neither bend to it nor even move, staring dumbly, where it had rolled to lie before the hearth.

Nor did she braid her hair, but twisted it into a knot merely, as her eyes darted and flashed about the room, their poor home. All was familiar, unaltered, and yet was not—a sense of something furtive possessed her, ominous and unaccountable. At last she ran.

"But after so long, so many years?" her aunt insisted. "Yet you believe it the same, undeniably?"

"I cannot know," Petra said. "But there seems no difference at all, that I remember. The same feel upon my fingers, that same darkening circle within the larger."

"And you have no idea how it came to be where it was?"

† 209 †

"It was at the house upon the hilltop that I lost it. It would not have had an impossible way to be borne. The winds, perhaps the rains—?"

"Or some animal, sí," her aunt said. "Yet into your very home, upon the very hearth?"

"Could it not have rolled from without?"

"Sí, it would roll. But a sign then, assuredly—"

"Yet of what nature, tía? Of what meaning?"

"Ah, child, child, to have grown so distant from the old beliefs? Such fortune, and not to know?"

"Fortune—?"

"To lose a thing of such enchantment, and then to have los aires return it? For it was borne by no ordinary creature, child. Bury it now, though not deeply. Just within thy portals. Until—"

"Tía—?"

"As certain as that once each year the very dead must rise. Whatever is the great longing in thy life, or great desire, soon, soon, incontestably, it must come to pass—"

TEN

It might have been nine o'clock. There was a moon, although Manolo did not become aware of it immediately.

Then the darkness sidled away from him. Manolo realized that he had been sleeping, or anyway had come awake, directly below the hind end of a calf.

He commenced to raise himself. He collapsed. His head throbbed, and he seemed to ache in every fiber of his flesh. Manolo wondered why this should be.

Then he remembered. Remembering, he cursed. Or did he moan?

Only this was certain, that in indisputable misery he lay upon his back amid the cow droppings of some field.

But then not. Abruptly, sitting, smitten with panic, ignoring even his pains he grasped desperately at his various pockets. Nor did he even pause to question that his shirt should be torn to shreds. But already he knew, so that this time it was a moan undeniably, of immemorial hopelessness. "Yet thirty-seven pesos?" he said. "The complete and absolute thirty-seven? Can it be possible?"

At his left hip at last he discovered a single, crumpled bill. Wildly he fumbled for a match. *El Banco de México. Pagará Cinco Pesos a la Vista al Portador. 5.* Nor would it alter magically upon its reverse. *5. Cinco pesos. Banco de México.*

The match scorched Manolo's fingertips.

Five. Of the thirty-seven. Of the thirty-seven plus fifty centavos. Groaning now, stuffing away the bill, Manolo struggled to his feet. The notion to lift his heavy shoe to the calf's posterior he disregarded, since the ground beneath him swelled and receded like a sea.

But perhaps it was not the same calf anyhow, seeming far too docile now. Bitterly, he cursed it nonetheless, and then all calves and all cows indiscriminately.

But five pesos of the thirty-seven and one-half? Yet it was more than possible, it was achieved. Magnificently. And he alone, Manolo Ortega, had achieved it. To have had but three days of employment in these two weeks, and then within hours to have flung aside one's remuneration like so many rinds from rotted fruit? "Ay, pendejo. Presidente of the pendejos."

And the gift one had proposed to purchase for Petra, as the Señorita Fern had suggested one might do at such a time, this also? Sí, this also, since it was an obvious and apparent fact that even had one recollected, which one had not, one would scarcely have located such a gift in the cantinas. And had he been anywhere save the cantinas? Sí, he had been here, in this grand green arena of shit.

"I, Manolo, killer of bulls," he said. "A new Arruza in the plazas of Mexico, a Manolete reborn. May my member be sewn to my navel with black thread."

Near him, the calf responded by urinating.

"You also," he said. "Offspring of the whore cow of

the hemisphere, was it you who unbuttoned me? Or some similar illegitimacy of the same dam?"

The hammering in his head was fiendish. And had he been the only one so borracho to be left here to sleep?

"Armando? Ay, Paco? Who is alive, eh?"

Alone, Manolo sighed. Then he commenced to curse again, but with a finer, more deliberate precision now. "For it is only that gypsy of a Luis Procuna I mean," he said. "Since was he not the cause of it all?"

The argument he remembered well. They were in the cantina run by old Rosalio, with the name "Imposibilidad," and before them reposed a remarkable abundance of tequila and lemon and salt. Upon the walls were photographs of the racers of bicycles, and of the toreros as well. And it was Armando who declared that of those who still participated Arruza remained the superior.

"And are we to omit Procuna?" Manolo said. "Even to admit that he is erratic, a gypsy in truth. But when he is possessed of the cojones, is your Arruza half so distinguished with the muleta?"

"Procuna I have not observed," Armando said.

"And yet you rant? Listen, is it not but last winter that the gringo who is my compadre took me in his automobile to traverse all of that distance and then return in the same night? And one series alone, hombres, three with the right hand and then the high pass with the horns displacing the very sweat from his chin—such mastery as this your Arruza does not accomplish."

"And you have attended Arruza also, that you may compare?" Paco asked.

"Has he attended Arruza?" Armando said. "Three times in his delinquent life, perhaps, he has been to the plazas. As for the rest, he has watched sows giving birth in the muck."

"So must I prove myself with the cape in my hand,

then, before you will accept my judgment?" Manolo said.

And thus it had been determined. And thus too, because of Procuna, Manolo now stood agonized in every muscle. "As a torero you are a fine vendor of tacos, Luis," he said.

There was more, however. He was certain it had been no later than three o'clock when they had argued in the cantina of "Imposibilidad," for his money had remained veritable upon the bar then. And yet it had been almost dark when they had finally chosen their adversary. Ah, true, they had been occupied for some further period in the cantina of "Think on the Dead," and also there had been a time of sitting at a ditch in the street of Iturbide near where the aunt of Petra resided, during which there was additional passing of a bottle between them. Sí, sí, had not he himself visited the shop of the one-eyed Martínez to purchase it, and a tequila of Jalisco no less, for six pesos instead of the ordinary? "Ay, pendejo," Manolo said yet again.

He shuddered, his self-contempt viable truly now, for the remainder was but an imbecility of colossal proportions. For a cape he had made use of the very shirt which now rode about him in tatters, in an attempt at verónicas first, before the calf had been driven toward him. Even then he had several times dropped it. "If he makes but one respectable pass we shall bear him about the streets on our shoulders," Armando had announced.

Name of God! Once, upon his hands and knees, the shirt dangling between them from one of the innocuous horns, he had confronted the calf as a brother from the identical womb. Twice he had been dragged behind it, clinging to its tail. Ten or perhaps twenty times he had been battered to the ground. "Olé!" Armando had mocked.

And the children? Had there even been children, to scoff at this catastrophe?

But at least the pasture had ceased to reel now. With

infinite caution, his head a treacherous burden upon his shoulders still, Manolo departed the field of his disgrace.

Some few hundred tortuous steps beyond it he found the shop of the one-eyed Martínez still open. Discarding his final vestige of solvency upon the counter, as if in an ultimate capitulation, he said, "Mescal. The square bottle with the worm therein, at four pesos."

Perched upon a stool the old man grinned at him. "So it was a glory, this endeavor?"

"Sí, a glory. Sunday next I am to perform at the Plaza México, for twenty thousand silver pesos."

"As one of the mules who drag aside the bulls that have been dispatched, no doubt, from what I am told by Paco and Armando who passed here before."

"Better you save your wit for your wife in the night, old man," Manolo said. "Or is to seek out the hole with but one eye enough of a satire as it is? Do you sell me the beverage without further insult or not?"

In the street, pocketing the single token of his change, beneath a streetlamp he unscrewed the cap and drank deeply. The cantinas of "Imposibilidad" and "Think on the Dead" he assiduously avoided as he moved on.

At the zócalo, directly ahead of him along the street by which he entered, though past the farther corner, lights blazed in the clinic of the new doctor, and outside, curiously, at least a dozen persons waited. At the entrance a burro was hobbled.

"Hola, Manolo," someone called from a bench, Chico who delivered milk with his horse from door to door. "Defiler of bulls!"

"Enough of that, eh? What happens at the clínica?"

"Ah, some old seller of wood, it is said that his leg must be removed. But you, hombre? Accepting that you have become a matador of incomparable reputation, but has it occurred that you are a parent yet also?"

"Quién sabe?" Manolo shrugged. "The children are the work of the women."

"So too the caping of the calf, in that manner it is told you demonstrated this afternoon, no?"

"Chingado," Manolo said. The other's laughter followed as he crossed toward the bandstand, however. "*To-re-ro!*" Chico called.

Then there was yet another, from out of the nearer darkness. "Hola, Procuna! It is true that flowers were thrown? And the perfumed undergarments of the rich señoritas also?"

Manolo gestured obscenely without turning.

"*To-re-ro! To-re-ro!*"

"*Pro-cu-naaaa—*"

Beyond the square, in the callejón that would climb toward his home, he drank again, choking. "Chingados," he said. "May the progeny of all be conceived in cuckoldry." Then he lifted the bottle to the light, to gaze at the worm where it floated. "Gusanos," he said. "Maggots. Where at least I attempted. And as for my fatherhood indeed, should it be a son that Petra will bear for me, will they not perhaps one day see keener still?"

Manolo stood, thoughtful. And would they perhaps not? For what was to prohibit that he, Manolo Ortega, might sire a lad to confront the great beasts in an authentic suit of lights, to bestow honor upon his father in his advancing age, if not to say uncounted wealth? Granted, that to educate a youth as a torero was a costly proposition, and too, as any fool knew, all promoters and impresarios were pimps, and swallowers of bribes. Yet had not Procuna himself achieved fame despite the humblest of beginnings? And were it not possible that his compadre Steve might pay for such a thing?

"Pendejo," he said. "I, Ortega. I will have a son to become as Procuna, who cannot retain thirty pesos in my trousers for six hours." Again he drank, again dismayed over the gift for his woman with which he did not return, thinking of the pulque he might have purchased as well, that he might invite all for a fiesta in celebration. Manolo sighed. "Or shall I accomplish it still, with the isolated coin that remains? Surely," he said. "And then will be anointed by the Bishop of Toluca, at the miracle I have engendered."

But suddenly then, as if at some intrusion, Manolo spun about. Yet he had heard nothing, he knew. Instead he had commenced to brood, darkly. And his speculations were of that sort a man of wisdom knows to keep to himself.

"Or do you suspect that I might not perform such things after all, eh?" he said finally. "For the gift, and for the fiesta in addition?" Holding the bottle he began to nod, the nodding as if simultaneous with further ratiocination even though thinking was already terminated now, had raced ahead of slower speech. "Or do you still laugh?" he said. "Bueno. But be aware that Manolo laughs also. For if the talent with the cape is a thing one loses with drink, there remain other talents, perhaps, which one does not."

One more time, Manolo indulged of the mescal. Then he capped the bottle. "Eh, gusano?" he said. "So let us now demonstrate that mastery by which Manolo is still possessed."

He should have known better, should have at least sensed that to hold considerable experience in theft was one thing, but to have acquired several of one's most recent experiences at the expense of the same victim was something else. Later, obliquely, this would occur to him, at a moment when his wretchedness of earlier in the evening would seem as nothing. Now, however, already striding purposefully, adhering to the more secluded callejones so that he might avoid the zócalo, he thought only: The Señora Tinkle, the gringa Señora Tinkle. From whose accommodating province I removed first the mixer of foods which was operated by electricity, and subsequently the new third light of the automobile. Sí, the abode of the Señora Tinkle, who lives alone, and moreover is but a female.

The house stood in the high street of Tuxpam, with others of equal sumptuousness at its either side, but with its rear wall at the edge of a ravine that one might enter with ease some blocks away, to follow until one approached a suitable tree to be climbed. This Manolo did now, though on second thoughts pausing here and again to partake further of his bottle, or merely to savor his ever-increasing gratification at the redemptive brilliance of his decision, so that indeed he was finally humming as he went, a ballad of the women of Tehuantepec, of whom it was universally averred that none were more beautiful. Nor would he have been chagrined to perceive that he was becoming newly drunk, since in addition to all else his victim suffered a distinct lightness of the intellect. To reside in a cathedral of five rooms when one was utterly without family? And to possess no less than eight huge tanks in which one cultivated fish of a size indubitably too small to eat? In truth, the señora was loca.

The señora was also still awake. Manolo had forgotten the hour. Hoisting himself onto a low branch from which he could see across the well-tended expanse of lawn, he ceased to hum long enough to curse once, though mildly, at the light visible in several windows. He had secured what remained of his mescal below, at the outer base of the wall. Returning to it, settling himself there, he said, "Well, patience then, eh? Which to one who stealthily investigates the removable belongings of the wealthy is much the same as the rhythm for the torero." Conscious of the depths of the ravine beneath him, thinking absently of the spirits who dwelled therein, Manolo contrived the sign of the cross. Then he lifted the bottle to the moon. Not that many more swallows and he would obtain the ultimate delicacy of the corned worm.

The moon had crossed perhaps one hour overhead when he became sensible of it again, still through the bottle which, empty now, reposed somehow in miraculous balance upon his chest. With an indifferent flick of his hand he brushed it aside. Then, wincing as he endeavored to sit, he began to curse with new diligence, at a cacophony of banging in his skull which transcended even that of his awakening in the pasture. Worse, the branch above him seemed unquestionably higher than it had been.

Eventually he achieved it, to lie straddled there. The house was dark now, he had been granted that beneficence at least, even if the drop into the garden had lengthened intolerably too. With a jolt that revived all previous achings, Manolo thumped onto his hands and knees in the grass.

He remained in that attitude for some while, panting. He recalled a dog, but there was no sign of it now. "Perro?" he whispered.

Finally, cautiously, Manolo commenced to negotiate the lawn. He was halfway to the rear patio before it came to him that he was still on his hands and knees. "Idioto," he said. "So now instead of Procuna I am the bull."

But in either event, why Procuna? In truth, had it not been the incomparably greater Manolete of whom he had dreamed throughout boyhood? Si, bastante, enough of the other. Now Manolo would proceed in this thing with the inspiration of no less than the unparalleled Manolete himself. Rising, confronting the house with disdain, he commenced to hum anew.

Which in no wise salved the affliction in his head, however. Imbecile, not to have preserved some portion of the mescal. But perhaps he might discover a flagon of something equally medicinal inside?

Then he perceived that he would not have to enter the house to procure his remedy at all, since directly before him on the patio table, and in the moonlight appearing quite full, although he could not decipher its label, stood precisely what he sought. Delighted, Manolo drank. Rum, and of the most preeminent Yucatán quality. And surely, was it not a favorable omen likewise? Manolo felt exultantly less ill at once.

And then he was forced to question that anyone in all Mictlán might find cause to feel so elated. Not two steps away, contemplating him with nothing approaching animosity, in fact almost without interest, the dog stood. And where did the dog stand? Unbelievingly, Manolo bent to stroke it. Normally, on such occasions, Manolo would have secreted on his person certain judiciously selected tools of carpentry in advance of his arrival, whereas only now did it occur to him to wonder, lacking such devices tonight, through what method he might have achieved his proposed entry. But now here was the dog, this immaculately obliging dog, standing half within and half without—as if to remind Manolo that he might not even have thought to assay it otherwise—the unlatched door to the kitchen.

"Admirable, illustrious perro," Manolo said, and not even softly. "Ah, what a sublime animal." Still stroking the creature, he permitted himself the luxury of another drink before depositing the bottle in his shirt. "And into the arena with Manolete then, eh, perro?" he said.

Manolo had no idea what objects he might invest the house with the honor of supplying him. But immediately visible in the moonlight, once he had entered, were both a large pan of the sort heated by electricity rather than fire, and a pot of the style upon which the cover would fasten to contain an enormous pressure of steam. He recalled also that within one of the cabinets would be found a second mixer, less imposing than the one he had assisted in losing itself from here previously, and for which he had received sixty pesos in the market of thieves at Toluca, but electric likewise. So the sole difficulty lay in judging which of such items might convert itself into the most significant number of pesos this time.

Brooding over the matter, Manolo indulged in further of the rare rum. Above the sink, a clock informed him that it was after eleven, this in turn reminding him that he had not partaken of food in hours. There were mangoes in a bowl, but assuredly the larder of an affluent norte-americana would disgorge comestibles far less customary to the taste than mangoes? In the refrigerator, generously sliced, he found meat which had been roasted but which he could not identify, and cheese of a sort even less familiar. He gave the dog of the roasted meat also.

"And Manolete?" he said. "Did even the peerless Manolete earn finer for his table?"

It was the electric pan he decided upon. But when he stood once more at the wall beneath his tree, contemplating that and the bottle, he could not but wonder again if the pot that operated through steam might be more valuable. Undoubtedly it was larger. But was there greater worth in the fact of magnitude or in the fact of electricity? Pondering this, Manolo set down the pan and its cover. He drank. When he went back for the pot, the pan remained where it was.

Then, emerging anew, he did not return all the way to it,

but paused instead in the center of the lawn. Occupied yet again with the bottle, he had allowed the top of the steam cooker to rattle, and quite noisily. Yet it was with equal loudness that he spoke. "Let there be disturbance, then. She who has throttled no man between her sagging thighs in a decade, what if she hears but to burrow more deeply into her blankets? True, perro?"

But he did not see the dog now, either upon the lawn as he lay aside the cooker or when he was once again in the kitchen. It cost him a certain duration of time to unearth the mixer, since he was forced to strike innumerable matches in so doing, first locating these. Then, the bottle in his shirt of necessity now, he retrieved the steam pot from its place midway out, bearing it and the mixer, along with yet another utensil of wheels and a red handle, not electric evidently and the use for which eluded him entirely, to the spot beneath the wall where the first pan waited.

All of which left him with only one trivial obstacle, this being that even with the bottle retained in his shirt there would nonetheless remain some four separate objects to be transported. Or, should one take into account the covers of the pot and pan, as categorically one must, the total became six.

So he had to pass completely through the kitchen this time, and the living room as well, although he halted briefly in the latter to consider askance the numerous receptacles in which, below the absurdly inedible fish, tiny bulbs glowed. Here Manolo shook his head. "Loca," he pronounced.

From behind the bathroom door he removed a robe with which he anticipated he might devise a serviceable pack, and in the same room were towels that might sensibly be utilized to prevent the metal of one vessel from damaging that of another as they were carried. A sweater that had fallen from beneath the robe he flung indifferently upon one of the denuded hooks as inconvertible at the market. Crossing back through the kitchen he remembered the clock, however, which too was electric.

At the wall, drinking again as he considered pot, pan mixer, nameless utensil, pot cover, pan cover, clock, towels, and robe, Manolo at last sighed. The robe would have to be spread upon the ground, he established, then best be bound by its own sleeves. Taking it up, Manolo could not detect its color, although it may have been red.

Red? Sí, doubtless, it was red.

"Toro!" Manolo said.

Clasping the garment by its collar, its hem unfurled and trailing in a half-circle before him, with one foot extended and his shoulders thrust back, chin high, Manolo assumed the instinctive, the classic pose. "Toro," he called. "Aiii, toro! Mátame, bruto, try to kill Manolo, eh?" Stamping his foot, heedless, dashing, indomitable, he advanced. "Eh, toro? Come!"

Seven, ten, a dozen times then, the brave bull charged, thundering, and a dozen times in turn Manolo employed it so closely that when he concluded with the flourish of his media-verónica it was with his suit of lights drenched in the beast's attestant blood. The cheers were deafening, the olés without end. Indulgently, Manolo bowed and bowed.

"But thus in truth, never that gypsy Procuna at all," he said, "rather a Manolete reincarnated." Contemptuously, he knelt to his occupation.

He was humming once more as he completed it, perhaps aware of his song, perhaps not. Now there remained only the method of his encumbered departure, though it seemed a problem of no dimension. Regretting only that he had packed the bottle, he strolled casually to the patio for a chair on which to climb.

Then, momentarily, he scowled. Three chairs? Manolo might have sworn there had been four. Ah, well, an illusion of the moon, presumably.

So already he had crossed the lawn for what was to be the final time, and had set the chair at the wall below his branch, before he paused to scowl yet again. Or had the light gone on before he turned?

A light? For what purpose did Manolo require a light?

For a time he was able to blink merely, as he confronted it, an enormously powerful flash, until commencing gradually to discern what must indeed be the fourth chair just beyond. And how remarkable, could that now be the absent dog too, squatting innocently beneath?

A further moment was demanded for verification of the shotgun, as for the pale norteamericana face itself, emerging at last out of his blindness amid the graying hair in complicated devices for curling.

"Name of God," she said then. "A blender less than three days after you worked for me once, a spotlight the same evening I noticed you loafing next to the car downtown. All right, now and then, an allowance for charity. But this time—would you have left me anything except the bed you believed I might sleep through the Second Coming in?"

Perhaps ten minutes later he emerged, through the front gate, into the street before the house. There, baffled, he stood. "One week?" he said stupidly. "Six hundred pesos?"

Muttering, shaking his head, instinctively he lifted a hand to his shirt. But of course the rum was gone also, had been in the bundle. "Pay back?" he said. "The cost of the previously appropriated items when new?"

"Either that, or we march together to the oficina of police right now," he had been told. He had scarcely been in a position to argue. Nor had he even begun to comprehend why he had been offered the choice, writing hastily as he was commanded, a confession of the earlier thievings with his signature beneath. "One week?" he had said.

He said it yet again now, as, unthinkingly, he began to walk. And such a total as six hundred pesos? When only through a calamity of leaking pipes could he earn that much in months?

And in the chair? She had been sitting in the chair? Could such a night as this be possible?

He might murder her, of course, could return even tonight and silence her where she would sleep again. But doubtless she would have hidden the paper with care. And if in the morning it were discovered by the police?

He could not murder her. "Pendejo," he said. "Into the house, out of the house, into the house, out of the house. And a female, no less. First an unweaned calf, and then a female."

Manolo was ill. Six hundred pesos? And the ninety he had been paid for the saddle of the other gringo when he had salvaged it from the lake only a month ago, where now was that?

"Ah, thou unnamable Procuna," Manolo decided.

Yet it had not been Procuna, this at least Manolo knew. He alone, it was, not torero and not even estimable thief, but three times drunkard in one day. He, acclaimed toiler under sinks, who could scatter thirty-seven pesos about the cantinas between noon and the setting sun and still manage to become borracho twice more after that, upon mescal with the worm, yet, and a rum of Yucatán. "Desgraciado," he said.

He would flee, obviously. Witless harridan, did she sincerely expect that he would stand pissing into the wind until she led sour Curro Huerta to his door? By the

Friday to come he would be in Tehuantepec or some location equally removed. Tomorrow, on the earliest bus he would be gone.

Sí, tomorrow. With one peso of silver in his pocket. Yet another miracle he would institute.

Abruptly, startlingly, Manolo found himself in the callejón just below the house of Steve, at the start of the worn trail toward his own. How had he come here, could he truly be almost home? And with a shimmering fire upon his hearth, beyond the doorway where at this hour Petra must surely sleep?

Sick again, and weary, Manolo simply did not understand. Where? How? Only from his compadre, of course, of whom he had requested several times before, and by whom he had always been given. But ten, twenty pesos, and for food only, for Petra in truth, when there had been no work of any kind. Nor had Steve ever asked that it be returned. But so much, now? And for such a thing as to redeem a theft?

And then a vast, an immense sadness, pressed down upon Manolo where he paused, and a sorrow almost beyond bearing. It was not for today, for these embarrassments of stupidity alone, but for all of life as he had known it, here, upon these few rude meters of earth, with so many days of anguish, or despair, and eternally too, with the great, the unanswered longing. For what could it serve to be a man, to live, for such as he, who knew only that he must suffer and labor and die, and to taste of ashes forever, what good, what hope?

Manolo sighed. Well, in the morning he would gird himself up and would speak of it to Steve, he could do no other.

It was then that Manolo heard the fragile, distant cry. For a moment he did not understand this either, although he had lifted his face toward the house. Again it came, however, and something, some shadow, flitted across the hearth. The aunt of Petra, could it have been? And to have borne within her arms . . . ?

Dumbly, Manolo went up.

The aunt was kneeling now, beyond the fire at the woven petate where Petra lay with her head turned aside. Nor did she any longer carry what he had seen, rather it nestled beside his woman, where her sweated face, if she did not sleep, gazed beatifically upon it.

His pain forgotten, and his heart welling, Manolo executed anew the ritual sign of the blessing of Jesus.

"Tía?" he said.

"*Ah, Manolito, Manolito—*"

Arising, overcome, she rushed to him. "And art thou borracho on such a night? And thy shirt, so ragged? Ah, but no matter, after so long, so long, such joy for thee—"

"It is a boy also then, tía?"

"Sí, sí, that same torero of whom so often you have spoken. To gain this, and the money as well—"

Manolo confronted her dully. "Money?" he said. "Ah, sí, the money. So this, too, is talked about as quickly as the other of the calf, eh? Already, it is known how much I need?"

"Need? Need? What is this of need, with such a prosperity? With five, six—no, perhaps it is even eight hundred—more pesos than I have ever contained in my trembling hands at one time before, nor do I even possess the skill to reckon it. But in any case it was only now, after the midwife departed, that by sheerest chance I discovered it. While Petra herself has been in too much pain to speak of it at all—"

Scowling, wholly without comprehension, Manolo stared

as it was unfolded, at the notes of ten, twenty, of fifty pesos, that emerged from her ancient bosom. "Here?" he said at last. "Six? Eight hundred pesos?"

"Ah, such multiple fortune!"

His hand had lifted, hesitating. It fell away. Yet even as the infant whimpered, and then commenced to scream, he did not turn his gaze that way at once. And neither then was it the child at whom he looked, finally, but to Petra whose face lay toward him now, her damp tresses spilling black and unbraided upon the mat, her cheeks sunken and drawn. "Money?" he repeated. "Here?"

But he was not thinking yet. Or perhaps there remained too much in his head of the other, too much of imbecility, of mockery, of threat. So even when he did consider the infant at last, it was vacantly still, without awareness, as it screamed and screamed.

And then somehow he was thinking more clearly than he knew. Because he did not even seem to hear the new cry as it began then, louder than the child's, louder than the aunt's of protest as she rushed toward him where he had flung himself to his knees to jerk Petra by the scalp from earth, that drained and alien face toward his own, nor did he sense it his even as he struck, and then again, as his fist hammered and lifted and hammered anew, and as he roared, *"From whom? For what? Woman, for what were you given that money?"*

ELEVEN

The pains began at dusk. But they were only of the slightest, then. It was not until hours after dark that she labored to the hut of their neighbors below them on the slope, to seek a boy who might be sent for her aunt.

The house was clean, the dirt floor swept bare, their petate beaten against a tree. Some days earlier, too, she had scrubbed the garments in which the child would be swaddled. So she lacked only the cradle still, although Manolo had sworn to purchase one that very day, out of such money as was due him, a straw Moses basket of four or even six pesos. And perhaps tomorrow he would daub it with the slime and pitch to harden, that it might not be eaten through by rats.

Returning, for a time she was conscious of the smoke from her fire only, and of the sweat that broke upon her where she lay. So when she became aware of him it was as shadow first, and yet already kneeling, to waver and fall above stacked corn at the farther wall.

Nor, when she at last turned, the pain gathering and with her eyes filmed, did she see him well. For the moment she imagined him streaming with blood.

"It is now?"

"Soon," she said. "But thy shirt, what do I see—?"

"Nada." He carried his jacket in one hand, hair tumbled at his brow.

"But—?"

"Some occurrence at the new clínica merely. Petra, your aunt is informed?"

"Sí. She will come."

He looked about. "This smoke. Do you wish me to rebuild the fire?"

"The green wood is deliberate," she said. "To bring it forth more easily."

"Petra, that is a tale of old wives, not a—"

But she had turned, her jaws compressed at a new spasm, to see her own shadow leap above the corn. Then the fire faltered and snapped, and the image of a chicken sprang as from the hearth itself. Her hands were fists against the contraction.

In exertion still, she watched as the shadow of his jacket appeared now too, where he reached for something within.

"It is not of the subtlest that you are here," she said at last.

"Petra, to keep separate from Manolo, from the irresponsibility of the beverage . . . do you have somewhere that I might put—?"

"Go," she said.

She would not remember what place she had told him to use, remembering rather his hand, empty then, as it lifted to touch her once at the temple, or less than to touch, so gentle it was. And then the pains arose anew.

Nor was there any extremity of what followed that she would recall either. She could not say when he departed, when her aunt knelt in his stead. Once, crawling, as if to find succor in the frail constancy of her very shadow, she had tumbled headlong upon the corn, and then had snatched up a single ear to clamp between her teeth. And again, later, or perhaps this was before, she was clinging with both hands to the arm of her aunt though seeing fleetingly the broad, amused face of Esperanza the midwife also, and in an inchoate moment of calm could hear the soft bleating of a goat above her at the mat's edge, while beyond it past the doorway a distant star appeared to die and then to come alive again.

And then it was as if a small rain had fallen and ceased, when the earth gleams wet amid the stones, and the sun returns warm and sweet. Drained, and sweated, Petra endured curiously a vision of great birds with beating wings, and sensed the drift and surcease of blood.

And did someone sing without, some weary farmer who mounted past, the old lament about Veracruz, where miracles occur?

"Tell me of it, tía," she said.

"Ah, child, sleep. For what is to tell? Almost three kilos, perhaps. Shall I give you of water?"

"Sí, a sip, perhaps."

"Drink."

She tasted it at her lips, although she could not raise herself, could see nothing now but the glimmer of firelight upon the grooved dark metal of the roof.

"May I hold it, tía?"

"Impatient one, it will be at thy side soon enough. When I have done with him."

Perhaps she slept, although this too Petra could not have said with certainty. Nor if the child cried did she hear that either. And then it was as if hearing and seeing occurred through mist.

"*Money? There is so much of money?*"

"*Manolo! Manolito! A gift for the child, no doubt, since he is rich, your admirable friend—*"

"*Whore! Puta, whom for eight years I have called spouse—*"

Not struggling, she felt not the blows either, not truly, for there was only a massive numbness in her then, of the flesh as of the mind. And then as she fell back it seemed only his shadow that continued to strike, where she had watched the shadow of the other upon the same wall, that other arm, the jacket. Perhaps she understood that her aunt had seized the child, had fled. Perhaps she was conscious of act too, finally, but only when the blows ended and he was whirling from her, and only then in disregard of the blood that bubbled within her throat and with her hair flung and sweated across her eyes, her loins gushing, as she threw herself upward and cried him to stay, where his name sprang once from her lips before she crashed to her face at the fire:

"*Manolo! No!*"

Then it was after him still that she dragged herself, until she collapsed yet again, until she lay broken and feculent and without breath, and with all illusion disabused, perhaps all hope. "Dear Mother of Our Lord," Petra sobbed.

About her the fowl stirred, and from time to time also, gleaming and diminishing still, to the dark brink eastward again she saw that solitary star, beyond the low intermediate hills.

And beneath her even now did it lie, where she had buried it so many months before, the prodigious eye of the long dead bird that had turned to stone?

When he returned, it was to halt savagely for a moment

above her, his breath savage and torn, until the toe of his heavy shoe burst into her cheek and her head crashed back, but even in that terrible brightness to display the dripping, irremediable blood that bespoke it, that ran still upon his hands, his wrists.

"And let him bed you again now," he breathed. "Upon the very cot where in a sleep of pollution I perceived him. And where you may balance his head upon a stick when he does."

She awoke at dawn, in fever. Her right eye was swollen and sealed, her lips broken, each breath an agony. Hearing bare feet upon the earth, and then a sound of liquid being poured, for a long time she did not move.

Then her aunt was supporting her and was giving her to drink, although she could not master the cup. Where it arose beyond the entrance the sun burned in her skull.

At last she was placed upon the petate. A sarape was drawn about her, a damp poultice lifted to her face.

"And these accusations of the night, then?" her aunt said.

Dimly, she recalled Manolo's ultimate departure, the burning of his bloodied garments, the removal of tortillas and some bottle. Or had there been more?

"And this, then, is what was foretold—that for seven years Manolo was unable to present you ripe seed, and so you accepted of the other, who is now dead."

"He is dead? It is certain, tía?"

"As certain as that the police were seen there in the night, or that one remains beside the gate still. Perhaps I would climb the hill and inquire further, do you imagine?"

"It is known that it was Manolo?"

"Is the soreness in your brain also? How would it be known? He has abducted himself?"

"Sí."

"Bueno. But now you, as well. To my house. You must walk."

"I cannot. There is too much hurt."

"She cannot. Nor could she when the gringo came to partake of her, which is why she contains the hurt now. Listen, child, if it is learned that at such a time your husband beat you so grossly that you cannot possess the boy at your side, it will be a suspicious thing. It is too near the place of death, and the police might materialize for no reason other than that same proximity, to demand of food. Better it be thought that you gave birth elsewhere, that I could be ready and assist you."

"I cannot."

"Still. Bueno. But attend, then. Let it be said that I removed the child for the reason that Manolo was borracho. It is this that I will inform Ana Luisa, the wife of Marco Antonio the fisher in the house below."

"Where is the child?"

"Where? It is with Feliz, the daughter of my cousin Marta, who has an infant of her own and can nurse it."

"Bring him, tía."

"Bring him, sí. But first a mirror I will bring, that you may examine yourself. Time enough when we have heard more of this thing. Sleep again, that at least. And when you are able, walk."

"Tía?"

"Sí?"

"To dream of wings? Like a fury of great beating wings? And yet as if somehow it is a woman's form that hovers—?"

"More of signs she needs, who fabricates her own sorcery."

"I did not want this, tía. But the money—in my hurting, I forgot."

"Sleep, child—"

"Tía? Before Manolo, in our village, other boys there were. And here too, when he was in the military, and then in the jail. And yet they were as nothing, as the departing days that follow one upon each. But since we were married there was none, until this of the birth. Tía—"

"I am here."

"Is all of life so sorrowful? I did not take into my mind that Manolo should kill him. I do not understand. I wanted only—"

"She does not understand. Listen, child, hear me well. It is a simple thing and an ancient thing. You have donated horns to your husband, and he has slain the man with whom you did so. But this will pass. He will be more drunk than before, and he will beat you more than before, and the child too. But even this will be noble, in that it will remind you that such must not occur again. And that is all that is to be understood. Now I go. The broth I brought is near you. In the evening if needed I will bring additional."

"But the rising wings, tía? The great birds?"

"The great birds. Who is to solve what riddles you have dreamed? Perhaps nearby in the night came the xopilotes, the vultures, since they are arranged even now upon the roof where the body still lies. Sleep, Petra—"

"Vultures?" she said.

But her aunt was gone. Near her was only the burro, nuzzling at something upon the petate, and with that marking upon its spine where years and years ago, doubtless before even the mother of Petra's mother's mother was born, one such lowly beast had brought succor to the Lord Jesus.

And he was dead, truly?

He? With whom for the only time in her life, as never

even with Manolo, she had shed all of her clothing, and with whom she had not been ashamed?

So it was not to be until evening, twilight, that she would learn. She had awakened several times before this, once to be fed from the bowl by Ana Luisa, who lived below, but if there was talk then in her indisposition and in the continued sweat she lost it, or did not comprehend.

And then it was the boy, the son of Ana Luisa called Juan, who told her, squatting where he had come to reconstruct her fire at the dying of the light. Yet it would escape her still, or seem beyond all possibility. "But the woman?" she said. "The tall señorita of the dark hair and the name of Lee?"

"Sí," the boy repeated. "The same."

"And it is not the gringo, the Señor Steve, who was killed? But he is in jail for this thing?"

"This is as I have heard it, Petra, and told you once earlier too, in truth, although I could see you had the fever still, and did not follow. And that it is undeniable I know from my schoolmate Jorge, who is a nephew one time withdrawn of Curro Huerta himself."

Turning, the boy unloosed fagots, piling them upon the hearth. Disbelieving, confused, Petra gazed toward him.

"He is not dead?" she repeated at last. "He is not? But she? And he has said that it was he who killed her? He, himself, has said this?"

"Sí. And the funeral has been held already also, in that place where only the unbeloved spirits are. With some few gringos only, and no padre. At noon, it was."

"They have buried her where?"

"In the cemetery which is abandoned, where no one any longer brings food for the dead on even that hallowed day when surely they must awaken. Indeed, where the other gringa, she of the golden hair, was found by the doctor when she wandered last night. But no, you would not have heard of this either—how the second señorita awoke to discover the deceased one, and then fled. Ah, Petra, such a time you select, to be chastised by your man, to miss all that is exciting. For there is even another gringo arrived now too, in only this hour, whom Carlota from the oficina of telephones has declared she was awakened long before day to contact at some obscure place in los Estados Unidos. And so it is assumed that a fabled mordida will be paid soon as well, and that the original gringo will be free."

The sun was hidden, the new fire wavered and flared. For all her pain, Petra had thrust herself to her elbows. Yet how could it seem as if she were returning from some far market, and with infinitely more burden of merchandise than she might sustain, or even though while much of it was rotted and spoiled, she could not determine which portions to set aside?

Because a mistake, Manolo made? And already, it is the other who is buried?

So that he who was dead is alive again?

And yet he, he of himself, has said that he has done this thing?

She fell back. Perhaps it was only at the weight of her very breasts, ripened and replete and unsuckled. Or was it at the pressing of the stone upon her heart?

"I do not understand," Petra said.

So it is morning, yet another dawn, before she is able. And even then, when she attempts to arise, it is to falter for some moments upon her hands and knees before she can lift herself at one of the chairs, where she will sway and almost stumble.

She possesses two rebozos, which hang from a nail, and into both of these she wraps herself. With an agony of bending she retrieves stale tortillas, to tuck within a fold.

In the doorway she pauses, breathing heavily. There is nothing more for her here, nothing she requires. At her side, where caulked mud has sifted and fallen, a once gaudy representation of the Annunciation hangs, framed meticulously long ago by her own hand in the crushed tinfoil of discarded cigarette packages, that too now worn and lusterless. Confronting it, with renewed aching Petra makes the sign of the cross.

In this early hour the town is quiet, and still, although already the sabbath rings slowly from the churches far below as she commences her descent. Each step is torment, and she rests often. Skirting the hovel of Ana Luisa and Marco Antonio, she will avoid the more traveled callejones also, pursuing odd byways past fields plotted and pieced, or the trails of burros, and of goats. One arm she clasps beneath her breasts, the other is at her waist. She passes almost no one. When she does, even in that forsaken gray light, she averts her discolored, swollen face.

Long before she has achieved the street of Iturbide there is a taste of blood in her mouth, and she must halt twice also to secure leaves and dry grass that will restrain the flow at her loins. Nonetheless, when she is among the level, swept streets with the houses of two and three rooms and some of concrete floors, she is striding even more rapidly, although with her head flung back where she struggles for air. Passing the home of Feliz, the cousin of her aunt, she hears an infant whimper, perhaps her own, but she does not stop, or cannot. Only in her aunt's doorway will she stagger and then catch herself up, to lean beneath the lintel gasping.

So it is a moment, or more, before her aunt will speak, where she stands before the iron stove at which she has been occupied.

"Finally, then," the aunt says.

Petra must have another moment, however. Then she is able to nod. "So the child, tía? You will obtain him for me, please?"

"Sí, sí. But he will suffer no tragic dereliction at five minutes further of a stranger's breast. If indeed you are prepared to nurse him anyway. You have eaten?"

"Sufficient." The aunt has wiped her hands upon a cloth, gesturing toward a stool, but Petra does not sit. As her breath settles she gazes at the beaten earth of the entry. Then, swallowing, again she says, "Tía, por favor? The child?"

Considering her, at last the aunt shrugs her shoulders. "As you desire. But you will remain these next days here."

"I am going to our village," Petra says.

Now the aunt considers her more intently. "More of magic," she says, though without mockery. "It is an exercise of remarkable proportion that you have arrived even here, I think. But you will go to our village." Brushing aside the rebozos to draw toward her the upper portion of Petra's befouled and sweated dress, she says, "And about this I am right, as well. With such bruises the pain will be too great to feed."

"I will be at the village by nightfall," Petra says. "If it is true of the nursing, I will find some burro or goat along the roadside."

The aunt's hand lifts to raise Petra's chin. Petra allows this also, and the searching of her face. Then the aunt nods. "Sí," she says. "I believe you will go."

There is a board across the ditch before the house, and upon this the aunt stops and looks back. She would appear pensive only, now. And yet perhaps she sighs. "It is the house, most probably," she says. "First the father so long ago, and then the woman of Friday night."

"Tía?" Petra says.

"Or is it perhaps the cemetery? For surely, it cannot

be a salutary thing, so many dead from olden times, and none to honor them. Sí, perhaps the spirits there, demanding propitiation, to have achieved it. Ah, well, I will fetch the boy."

"Tía?" Petra says again.

Already within the street the aunt turns. "Sí?"

"The cemetery?" Petra says. "In the night now past, since the killing of the woman—something came to pass in the old cemetery?"

"Thou art not aware? Truly?"

"Tía. Last night, Saturday, there was more that came to pass?"

"More?" her aunt says. "What more, but that which we had mistakenly believed beforehand? The gringo, who was in the prison throughout the day, and was then released. You have not heard that this time he is truly dead?"

TWELVE

*A*nd Ferrin was here? Here? After all the unaneled
and euchred years, he too, thrust back?
And Lee, already now, had been . . . ?
Standing just without the flickering aura of a
streetlamp in the anguished callejón below the house, he
struggled to cope with the illusive recitation. "A little before noon," she went on. "In the old cemetery."
Fumbling for cigarettes, he found none. Vaguely, he
recalled giving them away at the prison. Her cheeks
seemed drawn, her face pallid.
"And you weren't—?"
"I was asleep. Finally. But June Quigley says there
were only six people. Dear heaven, it must have been so
grim, without even a—"
Without?
"But Ferrin, then? It was he, the mordida—?"
"He had traveler's checks—evidently he had been getting
ready to go to Europe. Joe and June were able to scrape

up enough cash to change them. I've just heard most of it myself, Steve, it's all so new—"

His head ached. It had commenced in late afternoon, a dull throbbing, from confinement perhaps, or from the heat, in the roofless walled pen he had just quitted, where it had been soaked up as if into some vast well of earth. Now the pain had settled at the base of his skull. "Give me a cigarette," he said. "Have you—?"

He watched her remove them from a pocket in a blouse he had never seen her wear before, the brand not hers either. *Talisman*, the matchbox said: *Scorpio. Your fortune.* The match failed to strike at first, and then sputtered. "Are you all right, Fern? That doctor, last night, he told me you—?"

Forlorn, or perhaps only weary, she nodded. His hand had lifted to deposit the cigarettes into his jacket, until he realized he had left that with someone also. Jesus, he thought, and practically every cent in my pocket too, as if I . . . divestment? Divestiture? He put the package into his shirt, surprised as several times earlier by the stiffness, the caked and indurate blood.

"But then you haven't seen Ferrin either, Steve—?"

"Seen? Jesus, did not even know he was . . . anyway, it's not ten minutes ago that Huerta let me out. I was going up to the house, for—"

"Steve, are you . . . is there anything else that has to be done, legally, I mean illegally, whatever you'd call it, with the police? Or can we—?"

"We—?"

"Can we go quickly, Steve? Leave this place? Since we have to anyway? We could pack in no time, there's so little, nothing, that I need—"

"Fern, good Christ, you—"

Before him she waited, only her golden hair touched by light, seeming smaller than he knew, more frail. And last evening, in that immense, rife darkness to which the doctor had said she fled? Yet there would have been a candle burning too, he knew. Holding the Del Prado his hand wavered between them. "Fern, listen. You . . . we—"

"Steve—?"

"Damn it." He became aware that he had broken the cigarette, had crushed it between his thumb and forefinger until the lighted end had fallen. "Damn it," he repeated. "How would you . . . could you believe that we, now—?" He flung aside the stub. "I'll drive you to Mexico City, to . . . some hotel. Then . . . Monday, when the banks open, you can get a plane. Jesus, it's—"

Her breath had caught, although she was standing absolutely still where she stared at him. Inhaling deeply he was forced to clasp the back of his neck. There was an odor upon the air of meal, a sound from nearby of poultry at roost.

Still she had not moved. "And as if we have lived through an almost identical moment before," he said. "Haven't we? When I told you not to come with me to start with. A year, is it? Or isn't it? Is time, too, just an—"

"But—?"

"—Just one more illusion? Standing in that . . . ossuary I lived in, the night Lee had appeared. But could not convince you even then that I was not capable of—" He confronted her. "Fern, listen to me now, reasonably. It is finished. *Ite missa est.* Even back then, yes, probably I still half-believed in it myself, a chance for . . . at least escape. But now, after . . . or have I even . . . debauched you more than I knew? After all this . . . to think that there could still be a—?"

Torn, she had averted her face. Beyond her the cobblestones began, only to fall away tragically, heaped and broken, yet finally bleeding smooth also, into shadow like wetness toward the zócalo. And beyond that too, he thought, where they might be followed to yet another darkness where Lee lay in a place neither of them had yet visited. And Eric? Art there still, truepenny? Moonlight softened the clashings, however, the guise of hideous trees. Then he became aware that she was trembling.

"Fern? Dear God—now? Still? When it develops that even I myself had no idea how . . . of the depths to which it—?"

"Steve, we have to talk, cannot just—"

"Talk? More? Consuming our lives away with—?" He sucked in air, the pain crashing against the root of his brain. His eyes were closed. At last it diminished. "I have to find Ferrin," he said. "About midnight, though. We can be there by three. And that will be . . . must, the—"

Had she sobbed? Slowly, as if in some eternal charade of damnation, an Indian labored toward them beneath a staggering weight of grain. And midnight? When hell itself breathes out contagion to this world? Or were they no longer here even now, his mind so suddenly full of an inference of New York, of a sound of rain, a year since? Braced ponderously athwart his own shadow the Indian mounted past.

"Buenas noches—"

"Buenas—"

In spite of his burden the Indian managed to cross himself. Gazing after the man, unconsciously he touched his shirt, then scowled down upon it.

"Steve—?"

"Fern—?"

"Will you answer one question? Only one, for all that you think it banal, or absurd, or—?"

Now it was he who would not face her. "Fern, I do not . . . love you, if that is what you mean? Or not in the ways of that very banality, that might pretend to . . . redeem, salvage—"

Her breath had been audible, and he saw that her withered hand had been raised. Again his own hand was at his neck, those constricted muscles. Benares, had it been? Off the road south, toward Hyderabad? That yogi seated for so long with one arm upthrust against a stump that the arm had shrunken like something vestigial? But Jesus, I should have learned that trick of breathing, at least, he thought. Sensing her torment, impotent before it, he waited only.

"All right," she said at last. "I'll . . . decide if I want the ride. On the other hand I might just stick around. Indefinitely, since the place is so full of endearing memories—"

"Fern, damn it. Can't you realize that Lee is—?"

"Don't you think *I* know that? Oh, my God, don't you think I know? And if I still want . . . still need—?"

Her voice broke. The light attained her face too then, though for an instant only, and only faintly, within its silken tossed halo where it lifted, like some worn, monochrome angel's upon old paneling. And if there were any way at all? Any? Yet even as his hand again arose, reached toward her now, with a new sob she had turned, in flight, was stumbling away from him in the direction of the zócalo.

"Fern?" he said quietly.

Yet he did not call out, would not let himself think to follow. At last he lighted a new cigarette.

And on the ghats, long after Yama and the relinquishment of wish . . . at Samadhi, would it be—and the death of consciousness itself?

He noticed the dog only when he turned, though it was quite close to him, gaunt and terrier-like, watching with one forepaw arrested. Amid distended shadows its yellow eyes glinted balefully, gleamed and died. "No," he said sharply, about to walk. "Don't you try."

When he glanced behind himself, entering another cal-lejón where the going was level, it was following, though it halted as he himself, the same paw lifted. Then he understood that it was injured. He laughed, gravely, without sound. "But what, then?" he said. "Not only the passing fellahin executing signs to ward off demons, but even outcast beasts thinking I can perform . . . can cure . . . well, get over here, then—"

He was kneeling, a hand extended. In a ditch beside him, its odor rank, stagnant water lay deep. But the dog refused to approach farther.

"No?" he said. "Smarter than the rest, are you? The blood, can it still be? Or something more? A stench from the Pale, maybe, or . . . no. Stop that, now. Stop—"

But the animal continued its abrupt snarling, savagely even, its teeth visible now within the curling mouth. Nor was that paw any longer raised either, rather it scraped tentatively at stone. "Well, the devil," he said. "Be cursed instead, then, mendicant fool—"

But he had no more than started to arise when it sprang, terrifyingly, so that he fell to his knees again as it did, as he flung out a hand, an arm. Viciously, the jaws snapped, missing and yet not, that sleeve jerking and then shredding loudly although he was already turning with it too, lung-ing himself, to grasp instinctively at the injured foreleg and feel what he had not yet seen, the raw wetness of the wound at which the animal itself must have been tearing. His other hand was fast at once also, jammed beneath the working jaws while the first, his right, twisted desperately there, at the leg, until the growl became a scream of pain. Again he crashed down, however, the writhing weight greater than he had expected, the teeth gnashing only inches from his throat as they went.

Then he rolled, actually flinging the dog across himself past the ditch's edge, jolting to his elbows yet again though with both hands still fixed as he plunged it under, as he drove it elbow-deep into the poisonous sewage.

There he held it, choking it even, though prone himself and gasping, and frightened now too, finally having time for that. But the exploding bubbles at last became fewer, his own breath too was slowing. Then he could smell the foulness again, that and his own sweat.

When he released it, it was without drawing back at all, though it endeavored to struggle anew, sprang pitifully once and then again, before it collapsed with its head upon his very arm, to lie throed and wet and heaving upon him.

At last he built himself to his feet. Brushing at himself, drawing the tattered sleeve across his brow, he said, "Jesus. Now, Jesus." Absently, he touched his throat.

He had lost his cigarette. When he took another, the match trembled in his hand. He discarded both.

Some steps away, he halted. He looked back, frowning. After a moment, he said, "Or which one are you, then?"

He returned. "But Christ, who else? Name of God backwards, is it supposed to be?" Even when he nudged it with a shoe the dog continued to pant merely. "So—what are you reading these days, Eric, eh? Halevi? Saadyah Gaon? Anselm on the primacy of faith? Or dreaming still of your squandered youth, maybe, when you meant to take that pilgrimage to Tel Aviv and meet Bialik? Listen, old mole, did you ever finish that sestina on the death of Pascal?"

He began to laugh. "Damn, and I never did tell you I've been doing a little myself again too, did I? A whole schoolboy's notebook full, in fact. More unladed shit, to clutter the mind and crucify the hours—old crud?"

Neither did the dog move when he knelt to pry loose the heavy stone from beside it. He raised the stone in both hands.

† 247 †

"Stop following me, damn you," he said, hammering it down.

"Good Lord, but a dog? In the street—?"
"Nothing, it's—"
"But your shirt—?"
"No. From yesterday. I—"
"You—?"
"A drink. Here, this place is as good as—"
" 'Impossibility—'?"
Ferrin released his tattered sleeve, looking from the cantina's sign back to him. "A . . . yes, all right, I could use something too, perhaps—"
"Beer?"
"Fine—"
He rubbed the sleeve across his face, conscious of filth still, and then ordered two bottles. Familiar rotogravure pictures caught his glance beyond the narrow zinc bar, tacked there. He had stepped amid four or five Indians, their conversation at once halting. One, not entirely a stranger, contemplated his disarray with a frown, though curious only, and he remembered that he had once won fifty centavos from the man at a cockfight. "A dog," he explained, in Nahuatl. "There was but a single bone for the two of us—"
"And astutely you surrendered it," the Indian said. Several laughed, talk commenced anew.
"But there is always that moment," he said, turning with the cerveza. "I suspect you could encamp here for as long as the Babylonian captivity, and still, when you came into a place like this, they . . . Jesus, that face, do you know it? It's—"
"Face—?"
"That photograph, the torero. It's Manolete, dead since . . . not long after Eric, in fact, though they still . . .

revere. But if there is anything that should draw you to all that, make you see how it can truly approach . . . tragic ritual, Eleusinian, if you cannot discern it in that one martyred, ravaged expression—"

"Yours—"

"Goat song. Though of course it was the bull in truer antiquity, too . . . *what did you say?*"

"Lee, one night. Asking what you looked like, and the only snapshot I had was . . . but a day or two later, just browsing, and I came upon—"

"Well now, Christ, he—"

"Anyway, I decided it was foolish. And you are finally far too—"

"Not—?"

"No. It's strange, but I never think of you as . . . but are you sure you're all right, Steve? Would you rather sit? You still look shaken—"

"Jesus. You yourself, do you mean? Without stopping since . . . five o'clock this morning, would it have been—?"

"Yet somehow I am not even tired. Or combating a kind of unreality, I suppose, after so long, to be back—"

But they had crossed to one of the two tables. Jacketed, seeming sweated although it was cool now, Ferrin accepted one of the misted bottles. "Listen, do you want a glass? I can—"

"No, it's . . . I don't actually want this either—" Ferrin sat. When he withdrew cigarettes, jiggling the crushed pack, he lost several to the wet tabletop.

"Will you drink some, for Christ's sake? You can't just cut yourself off like—"

"Yes. I mean, I haven't been, in fact, since . . . these three months, now. Out of . . . simple necessity of survival, perhaps. Frying eggs. But when did they let you—?"

"An hour ago. Less. They waited until dark. But . . . listen, that mordida, they told me you—?"

Not looking at him Ferrin nodded. He had produced matches now also, the American paper sort, and struck one. But then he held it merely, at the table's edge where the cigarettes still lay. "That fellow who telephoned—Twintrees?—he arranged the details." He shook the match without result, finally dropping it into the tin tray. At last their eyes met. "Having enough cash was just . . . fortuitous. But then, to . . . intrude, was a decision I—"

"Intrude? When I—?"

"I knew Lee was here. Could tell, after you came and went, even those many months later—"

"Ferrin—"

"She had no life with me—"

"Good Christ. But she is—"

"Yes."

"And still, you—?"

His head throbbed still. Above them, the glare of a shadeless bulb was barbaric. "Ferrin, I confessed, officially, to—"

"Absurd. For what? To make some kind of spurious restitution, charged with a crime you did not commit, for those others you imagine you did—?"

"Damn it, what do you know about what I—?"

"Don't I?"

"*What? You think you—?*"

"Have always suspected, yes. Understood it would have to be something like—"

"But—"

"Yet you have . . . endured that long enough, hardly had to assume a new burden now—"

"Endured? Good Christ, do you truly believe that I . . . or if you know that, do you also know the extent to which I . . . hated him, even? Do you know that he killed my mother? Drunk then too, in a car? Went off the road—"

"In fact that too, yes. He told me more than once—"

"Told—?"

"And was perhaps a better man than you knew—or at least than he was capable of being with you, after that. But knew precisely how you felt—"

"Damn it, he—"

Deliberately, he struggled against vertigo, snatching up one of the wet cigarettes, flinging it aside, lighting one of his own. "Ferrin, what has this got to do with . . . us, right now, sitting here, with you paying for . . . when by all local standards you should have come down with a gun in your luggage, or—"

"Because I might have been of some . . . help, long ago, perhaps. And obviously was not, which—"

"God damn it, Ferrin, I never asked for . . . all this . . . charity, when I do not . . . don't give a damn about Eric and two months from now will not feel anything about . . . Lee either, yes. Luxuriating in all your . . . capacious assumption of other people's problems, when it can only—"

"Only—?"

"Disgust me. Damn it, why can't people simply let me . . . or at least see, understand, that I myself am empty of everything except . . . the basest sort of desire, maybe. Good God, to have gone to Vermont that time, and then to have found that with even the wife of the one human being I have ever known who . . . that even the morality of that did not exist for me—"

"Steve, no. If not with you, she would have been driven off eventually anyway. I have as much guilt over that, the drink, as—"

"Guilt? Guilt? Ferrin, merciful Allah, if I could once in my recusant life feel guilt it would be . . . exultant. Listen, is it only me, have I become totally inarticulate, finally, if even you do not understand what I . . . ? *Credo quia absurdam*, is that what I am supposed to avow? Some synthetic contemporary equivalent of Tertullian's sad joke . . . to believe if only *because* it is impossible? Ferrin, when there is nothing with any meaning, dear Christ, how can there be guilt? Or even now, here, with Lee dead, after all this . . . when even the essential *horror* eludes me? Mistah Kurtz, my ass. Listen, that . . . confession of mine, all right, spurious or otherwise, but do you literally think it was gesture only, something like . . . poetry, God forbid? When it was almost an . . . acceptance, finally? Into that jail where there is not even a roof, where the prisoners sleep under the eaves in an open court . . . and to get out of time, there, to stop . . . pacing it off by those intransitive moments in which we endure our . . . fugitive small passions, puny griefs . . . I am talking about freedom, believe it or not. Of a sort where, in a certain period, Peter would even be allowed to forget the bastard who—"

"Yes. Perhaps. As would Judas—"

"*As—?*"

Again their eyes met. Yet Ferrin's were only innocently pained, or despairing, while he himself had arisen. Why was he standing? Directly before him, in full sight of the cantina's entrance, the open urinal loomed, an uncloseted excusado as well, lacking paper, with leaves heaped upon a shelf adjacent. But true: if tragedy could occur in a context of restrictive time only, six months after the fact would Hamlet waste a second thought on any of it? He flicked his cigarette into the infested bowl, above him pipes sweated and trickled. By the rivers of Babylon, there we emptied our bladders, yea, we wept . . .

Ferrin was at last drinking when he returned, the tracings of broken veins visible upon his cheeks, the once handsome face. "Islero," he said, sitting again.

"What?"

"A Miura. I just remembered, the bull that killed Manolete. Already deified itself, and enshrined like Mithra's own, or some sacred beast of—"

"What will you do now, Steve—?"

"—Memphis, or . . . *what will I—?*"

With reasonableness and concern Ferrin's questioning gaze forced his own to fall. Somehow he felt almost giddy. "Do?" he said ultimately. "What? Go wander again in the land of the forest sages, out of the southerly Ganges, hand in hand with Mahavira? Prove the Trinity in such a way that no rational intellect might thereafter deny it exists, like Raymond Lully? Seek out the grave of Tulsi Das? Or Kabir? *Quo vadis, Stephanos—?*"

"Steve—?"

"Whither I go, thou canst not follow me now, but thou shalt—"

"Steven—?"

"Or why am I thinking of Maimonides? Old Rambam? Those nine years in Fez, maybe, pretending to be a Moslem? How shall we sing the Lord's song in a strange land? Listen, there's . . . Kierkegaard's father, do you know the story—?"

"What on earth has Kierkegaard to do with—?"

"His father, this was. At the age of twelve, hungry, or something . . . and he cursed God. Which for the next seventy years he claimed he could not cease to agonize over. But which simultaneously prevented him not at all from becoming one of the shadiest businessmen in Denmark, or from . . . raping a servant girl. Damn it, Ferrin, all I mean is . . . man can endure anything, which only proves he endures nothing at all. But that one revelation, perhaps, is the very suffering he cannot abide. Which—"

"Steve, there has got to be . . . man, the fundamental human potential for—"

"You would say something like that, of course. Jesus, I do curse you sometimes, do you know? It's why the Mohammedans stoned poor Lully to death, too, incidentally, butting in down there with that same sort of—"

"Life itself, something, there must—"

"Though . . . Ibn Latif, didn't he steal everything from? And the Cabbala? Like your . . . cherished Aquinas, who couldn't have written forty percent of that drivel, without Maimonides himself beforehand. Which only reaffirms the—"

"Steve, are you drunk, or—?"

"And that dog. Tearing at its own guts . . . simply trying to . . . survive, until I started to . . . what better symbol, for—?"

"Yet a person like Renoir, Steve, when he had to have the very brush tied into his hand—?"

"Ferrin, Ferrin, will you please hear me? Once? When all other is . . . all vestige of hope, or—?"

"Then this other girl? She alone, even—?"

"What—?"

"I don't know her name. Living with you—"

"Oh, that simple-minded son of a bitch, he even told you about—?"

"And crippled too, did he say? And if she has suffered all of this, accepted—?"

"Ferrin, are you suggesting that I . . . ? Dear God, I just . . . deliberately, drove her off. And that probably the first . . . exercise of decency, that . . . listen, she has undergone enough—"

"Is that yours to judge? Steve? Especially if she . . . in spite of all, to have sought you out again now, my God, it's incredible—"

"No more so than—"

"Than—?"

"This very conversation. You, telling me to—"

"And can you repudiate it, then?"

"Ferrin, I don't . . . *want* this from you. Can only go on as—"

"Or if only to . . . get outside of yourself, for a change? If only for her, her own need? Because she is evidently in a precarious mental state also, they said, so that any further shock might—"

"You are telling me this? *You? After—?*"

"Steve, yes. And yet another notion, an implementation, perhaps. I was going . . . in a few days, Italy, trying to get back to . . . at least to start by seeing a few things again, Piero, Masaccio's chapel in . . . but won't, now. So why not—from Veracruz, say—a freighter, to New York, if for no more than . . . time to taste the sea, to think—?"

"Oh, Christ, Christ, Christ—" Again he was standing, but fatigued now, someway spent. And stinking too, he thought, like . . . Michelangelo, at best. Had he touched his beer? "Ferrin, listen, theoretically I'm supposed to scram, now, tonight. Are you . . . do you have a place to—?"

"Twintrees'. He gave me a key, if I can remember the address—"

"Calle Benito Juárez. Look, I'll . . . see you later. Sometime before I leave. We'll—"

"But what are you—?"

"My head is splitting. And that damned dog, I'm still . . . Jesus, this gaudy, babbling, and remorseful day. I just don't—"

He was at the entrance. "All these . . . words. Or have I said that before? But I am suddenly just so tired of . . . being a stranger in a strange land, can it be that simple? That profound—?"

"Steven—?"

"Later," he said.

Cur Deus homo—was that it? The problem is: how can God forgive man's sin?

But why Anselm? Why anyone at all, for that matter, when . . . ?

I wish to declare that I entered my home at approximately midnight last evening and killed Mrs. Leonore Priest with a machete. I alone condemn myself and have no accuser.

Fool. Bloody fool . . .

Halted just within the ancient chapel, between the indrawn shattered doors, he pressed at his temples where the pain had shifted now, unrelenting. His face contorted, he scowled into the familiar abandonment, that gutted sanctuary. There was moonlight, transilient, falling in disjunct patches across the slabbed floor, the enormous mutilated cross, and into what he thought of as his own corner as well, where cached behind a removable stone his candles reposed. He did not seek one, however. Was the notebook there also? In a jacket at the house? "My genizah," he muttered, smelling orchid, the rank jungle without, hearing locust. "But here, though?" he said. "Last night, she . . . and upon her knees, before the—?"

Fern . . . ?

And yet how strange, since he would have been willing to bet that Manolo himself would have chosen . . . or had he, perhaps? "Manolo?" he said. Peering now, rear regardant, he pursed his lips. "Hola, compadre?" he called. Then he laughed. "Though I suppose you would still think me dead, not? Mano? Old brother?"

Laughing still, he said, "Well, come anyway, then. Come, let us sit upon the ground and tell sad stories of the deaths of . . . or a new reading lesson, better? *The Coming Forth by Day*, shall we? Composed by Thoth, in the very handwriting of the divinity? The *Sefer Yezira*, inscribed by Abraham and God? Or bring the dog too, since I don't imagine you can exorcise a demon simply by bashing out its . . . art about, dog? Eric? Isaac—?"

The insects persisted, in infernal diapason. Conscious of the stiffened cloth of his shirt, though with the stains invisible here, abruptly with both hands at the collar he tore it asunder, shredding it downward and hearing a single button strike the floor. Drawing it from off his shoulders he toweled himself, at the back of his neck, beneath his arms.

"Or would it harrow you with fear and wonder to discover that los aires can sweat, eh, Manolo?" he said. "Or, Jesus, did you even get a look at that funeral today, maybe, and think that that, too, was . . . ? Reality, shall we discuss instead?"

Unconsciously, he was knotting the remnant, twisting it into a rope. He flung it aside indifferently, toward the altar's base, losing sight of it as it fell. "Tlaltechli? And the flayed one, did I say? And all of that . . . insanity, with the machete itself, not an hour before she—?"

Lee . . . ?

Turning, he had scraped the wall with his upraised hand, and so halted, thoughtful now, where it lingered at the cool worn stone. His lips were compressed. "But to . . . Firenze?" he said. "The Cappella Brancacci, where even . . . Leonardo, Raphael, once came to stand and stare?" He let fall his hand. "Except no, New York. But a boat still? From Veracruz? To . . . work out one's salvation with diligence, perhaps—?"

Again he tested the coolness. "And then what? 'Ah, but stay, thou art so fair'—?"

Yet his hand was at his mouth, it hovered, and almost feverishly then, anew, his eyes roamed the dark scarred walls, the archaic pietà, the shadowed high beams. How long had he been coming here, was it eight, nine months? And to have been writing after all? That itself, almost as an act of . . . ?

But why was he here now, what was he doing in this place?

Raising it to the light he considered his watch. The

crystal had been smashed, and when he listened he heard
no sound either. "Damn you, perro," he said. "Fern? So
I need you in spite of myself. What hour, Fern?"

But it could have been no more than thirty minutes since
he had left Ferrin. Without reason he crossed to retrieve
the shirt, then stood holding it. "Fern?" he repeated.
"Oh, Christ, if it were possible? After all this, to . . . even
out of . . . need, did he suggest? Except—"

Standing at the cross, beneath the shattered arm which
even as he stretched a hand toward it soared just beyond
reach, he looped the knotted garment about it, then stepped
away. It hung swaying, ghostly. "Your broken line of
Yin," he said. "Change, does it mean? Flux? Take it in
offering anyway, maimed clown, a rag for your brow."

Once more he stood as if listening, in that solitude, the
darkness fecund and strange. The *Kol Nidre*, was he thinking of? Some forgotten strain of . . . Corelli? Vivaldi?
Where had he last heard either?

Domine Deus? An oboe solo, with a soprano, with bass
strings? The *Gloria?* When?

Something caught his glance in a corner, beyond one
of the askew doors. Crossing, he found it a bottle. Then
he discovered tortillas also, stale and brittle upon the
stones. "So you truly are about, eh?" he said.

Uncapping the bottle he determined it tequila. Holding
that, taking up one of the hardened wafers also, he laughed
again. "But the blood and the body both, then?" he said.
"And this . . . unleavened host, if I prick it, will it not
bleed?"

Drinking, after a moment he bit into the tortilla also,
though it crumbled, disintegrating in his hand as he savored
the eternal grained substance of meal. "Verily I say unto
thee, this day shalt thou be with me in—"

Or . . . Eleusis, did he still have in mind? The sacred
dancing and song, torchlight on sweaty faces, all meaning

so zealously preserved? Before the descent into Hades and the revelation of the ear of corn? The king of Thebes deposed, Isis dismayed?

Io non mori,' e non rimasi vivo . . .

Fool again, rote fool.

"Dante, fuck you," he said. "And, dear Jesus, fuck all the . . . unnecessary books—"

And lay hands upon the man, the blinded, dreaming man . . .

The tequila was raw in his throat. In the doorway now, confronting the ferns silvered and primeval beneath the pines, he said, "Manolo? Show yourself, why not? At least let me advise you how I have verified the Trinity beyond any reasonable doubt—"

Laughing anew, he said, "Jesus, and did I not, in my fashion?" Only the dregs remained, and he cast the bottle into the matted undergrowth. Then, abruptly, he turned quite still, his voice became almost a whisper. "Oh, damn it . . . Mano? Listen, it was not . . . deliberate, my . . . ultimate betrayal. And do you think I understand, even begin to? Because if it was only . . . compulsion, then I have . . . no will at all, am only—"

Petra? He is absent, thy borracho wielder of miraculous wrenches—?

In Chignahuapán, an unforeseen employment. These three days. He will sleep at the house of a cousin.

Petra . . . ?

"And my other two . . . sanctified whores?" he said. "One gone already, alas, into the desert fastness? But, Christ, I did not mean it to be either of—"

Again he touched stone, finding it warmer here, outside, the day's sun retained. Or was it he himself, perspiring still, for all that it was chilly?

And . . . decay, violation, did he smell, more rife than all that proliferated?

"Manolo, you dismal, botching bastard," he said.

With a sigh, though calm, he struck flame to a cigarette. "And you too, old randy bones?" he said. "Thy canonized relics, over which no *Kaddish* was ever spoke?" Beyond a grisaille of laurel the grave lay out of sight, however. "Though I could manage a *Kyrie*, more sure. Or a *Dies Irae*, probably. Yet only because of . . . Mother, if that mitigates anything—the music? Old Ananias—?"

From somewhere nearby a cock crew, at which he lifted his face, poised, the cry hideous and protracted. And the bird of dawning, he thought, after which no spirit might walk abroad? But had it been only last night that she quoted it? Could it be? And when he had taken up the Anselm, Eric's own, from the arm of the chair?

The problem is: how can God forgive . . . ?

And then he had gone out, was standing before both, finally, Lee's for the first time, that earth fresh turned and damp, the other all but indistinguishable in its sunken collapse, below the listing stone. "And how indeed shall we sing it?" he said.

He discarded the cigarette. "Or would you rather talk, after all?" he said. "Old cantor? Go ahead, speak, I charge thee, bring thee airs from heaven or blasts from . . . never mind. My head is . . . adders and serpents, let me breathe awhile, I just want, need—"

Eric? But . . . back, must I keep going? And were there, truly, truly, paved avenues and glittering street-lamps below the Hanging Gardens two full thousand years before the birth of . . . ?

Before . . . Gethsemane?

Again within the chapel, inexplicably weary, or more, as if somehow near exhaustion, he sensed himself fevered as well, his lips parched. There was dirt on his fingertips also, although he did not remember kneeling, touching the ground at all.

Or like . . . those tales your own father told, of Judah Halevi, one more who might have died on the road to . . . or was it . . . Jerusalem, at the very gates, where—?

Now he felt ill, drained utterly, and for a time stood entirely without movement, or breath, while it seemed that from some incalculable remove, and yet discernible as from within an abyss, incursive there, he could hear a sound of flow, as of something at the ebb, in seepage upon earth.

"Father?" he said. "Grandfather? I just want . . . just need—"

But it amused him too, began to, then, as at last he turned deeper within, as he said, "Now? Jesus, what can I want, what need, now?" Perhaps he heard the footfall, or a rustling of leaf, but the laughter was mounting at the same time, private and evisceral, even as he achieved the base of the altar, and he could not halt it. Beautiful and desolate, her withered hand uplifted in protest, or in supplication, she was staring at him where she had entered along the sandalworn path to make her visitation at Lee's grave. He lost purchase even as he attained it, but the shirt was fixed.

THIRTEEN

"I lifted him down," she said absently.

"Sure, kid. Sure."

"I did not believe I would be able, and yet I was. Do you know?"

Now the man did not reply. Seated with his chair tilted and his sandaled feet propped at the window ledge, in undershorts, perhaps twice her age and fleshy, ill-shaven, he was reading, in Spanish, a bullfight newspaper that he held high to shield his face from the brilliant afternoon glare. Beneath the second window, where she sat cross-legged, naked, at the foot of the unkempt bed, even more directly the light bathed her. Sketching, from time to time she paused, the pad uplifted, to frown, less in dissatisfaction than in a kind of childish, puckered uncertainty. She worked in chalk, though there were paints beside her, five or six colors smeared upon a shard of glass, brushes upright in a jar. A pungent odor of turpentine pervaded the stillness, the heat.

"Then the terrible birds came, too," she said. "Did I tell you of the birds, Paul? The beating wings?"

"You told me."

"They begin at the eyes, most often. As if to blind the very dead."

"That's gruesome stuff, kid."

"Paul?"

"What?"

"Were there carrion birds at Golgotha, do you think?"

"Huh?"

"Or do I mean Calvary? Is there a difference, Paul?"

"Sweet Jesus, would I remember? What do you want to keep on talking about that stuff for?"

Rising, Paul discarded his newspaper. Despite the sunlight, that deceiving radiance, the room was bleak, cloacal, sparely and shabbily furnished. Heaped upon an unpainted table tortillas lay, and from a paper sack other foodstuffs had spilled, cartons indifferently torn open, a broken cheese, several cans. There was wine. With a yawn he crossed to watch her sketch.

"You still doing them same pictures, huh?"

"I find them difficult."

"You sure don't change them much. What's that word again?"

"Pietà."

"That means them women and Him? Holding Him, like that?"

"Many have done them."

"Sure, in museums and all. That's sure you on the end there, though. With the yellow hair. Real nice."

"Thank you."

"But who're them other two, then? That dark-haired one, and the one looks like an Indian?"

"They are there," she said.

"Sure, sure. But they got to be somebody, what with

you always make them the same, that way. I'd recognize that first one if I passed her on the street here."

"She is from del Sarto, actually."

"Huh? Is that the name of the place you—?"

"It is not a place, Paul. And you will not see her, I don't think."

"But you still ain't about to tell me where all this goes on, huh?"

"In the chapel."

"Well now, hell, kid, anybody could see that. That big cross, and such. But what I mean, what chapel? Del—?"

"You ask me so much, Paul. Sometimes I—"

"I know, I know. Them headaches. Listen, I'm just trying to help—"

"I carried him down. And then shielded him, that the great birds would not come—"

"And then some Mex gave you a lift in a truck, and when you got off the truck you was here. That part you told me ten times."

"There were goats. And Juan Diego, the driver was called. He would take me to his home, he said, but first he had to bring the goats to market. And then I did not wait."

Paul studied his knuckles. "Swell," he said. "Just swell. Me with outdated papers, trying to keep my nose clean, and now . . . well, Jesus, nobody could say I didn't try. You hungry or anything, kid?"

"Thank you, no."

"Just going to keep drawing them things, are you?"

"I would like to get it right. Thank you for buying the paint, Paul."

"Hell, don't thank me. I mean, it's me, went out and picked up the stuff, but it's you got us the money, you know? What I mean, it's only fair."

"All right, Paul."

Stepping into wrinkled khaki pants, he watched her still, her renewed scowl as again she extended the sketch-pad in her deformed hand, her tongue between her lips. Upon the wall near her a tiny lizard darted rapidly downward, hung for an instant alert, disappeared. He removed a shirt from amid the bedclothes.

"Listen, kid—?"

"Yes?"

"Last night. You sure it was okay?"

"Okay?"

"I mean, you sure you don't mind that sort of thing? What I'm saying, we can really use the dough, you know?"

"I do not mind."

"I mean, not that it will be every night, or nothing. Anyhow, it's a pain, me waiting around like that. Maybe we could work out a signal or something—like, say you could fix the shade a certain way, so's I'd know when it was clear to come back up?"

"Whatever you want me to do, Paul."

"Anyway, since you said there was lots of other times—?"

"There were multitudes, yes. And a shade then too, though it was always drawn down."

"I mean, I wouldn't never of suggested it, if you didn't tell me about all them others, you know?"

Working, she did not respond.

"Normally, I got dough anyways. From picking up them old stone statues and junk, and peddling them to dumb tourists down near the docks. Except the damned spics are touchy all of a sudden, even that fake pre-Columbus stuff ain't supposed to leave the country."

Still she concentrated, her lips pursed.

"But that's what I figured you was up to right at the start, you know? I mean last week, when I ran into you just standing around near that church, that way."

"It is a lovely church."

"Oh, yeah, sure. But what I mean, that same day you got off that truck from . . . where'd you say it was?"

Again, preoccupied, she said nothing. At last Paul sighed. "I guess I'll take off for a spell, you don't mind?"

"All right."

"Anyway, that turpentine you spilled before. It makes my eyes sting, like crying. You going out yourself?"

"For a little while, perhaps."

"You won't go no farther than down the block?"

"It is the only place I go."

"You pray, or something?"

"Pray?"

"That church—being there all the time?"

"I wanted to paint one once, I think. Only the silence. Or that filtered, secret light, alone in the afternoons."

"Yeah, must be nice. You got another headache too, huh?"

"It has not ceased. Since that night, and he went up on the windy tree. It is like a sound I hear."

"Like a sound?"

"Can it be whispering, do you think? Or yet . . . as beneath the sea, almost. A current under sea, so very like, that picks his bones in whispers? The pearls that were his eyes?"

"Hey, now, sweet Jesus, I just thought. You don't get to talking like this when they . . . I mean, like last night, them two spics who took turns? I mean, like, they might get some idea . . . well, you know—?"

"I listen to the whispering. Or else I am not here at all, but watching. Paul?"

"Sweet Jesus. What?"

"I am the one who dies when he is not loved. Did you say we have money, Paul?"

"Well, sure. Like I told you, from last night— from them other couple of times, too. You need some more painting stuff, do you?"

"Once I had many, long ago. But they always wished me to play with the other children, instead."

"They, who? You had what?"

"Just a doll. Please?"

"Huh? Like kids, you mean?"

"A Raggedy Ann, if you can find one. Paul?"

Questioning, bathed innocently there still, she had turned to gaze upward at him. Again Paul sighed. "A kid's doll. Yeah, I guess you might want one at that."

"Will you buy one for me, please?"

"Sure. Sure, kid. This afternoon."

"Thank you. And . . . Paul—?"

"Kid?"

"To think they would lay her in the cold ground. You won't stay away until after it's dark?"

"Don't I come back and turn them on for you every night? It's just that stink, Jesus. A few cervezas, is all."

He was at the door. "Paul, what time is it?"

"Jesus, quién sabe? What difference does it make? Forty times a day, asking me the time. Just listen for the bells, why not?"

"All right, Paul."

And bells did strike then, even as he departed, twice, remote yet limpid, windborne, perhaps from the harbor, or beyond. Long after they ceased her face remained lifted, attentive. Then, to herself, as if in astonishment still, although it had been a week, or more, softly she said, "Veracruz? And is there more beautiful a word?"

"I lifted him down, Father," she said.

† 267 †

With curiosity the friar considered her, a Dominican, white-robed, and cinctured, a darkly rubbed wood cross suspended low amid his skirts, from a step above her before the arched entrance. Towering upon the sun-bleached facade, niched saints gazed blindly seaward, in that shimmering glare that washed the wide, swept pavement, fell luminous and cruel upon the ragged women who importuned daily there. "You did what, my child?"

"Lifted him down. The gallows man."

"Poor child, you have suffered a loss of that sort? May I ask whom?"

"He who went upon the rood."

"But hanged himself? And without the sacrament, was it, then?"

"His were all sacraments," she said. "And brave, translunary things, all air and fire."

"My child? But do you live here, perhaps?"

"With Paul, sí."

"Paul? Your father, he would be?"

"Full fathom five, my father lies. Amid the secret whisperings, upon a shelving off Cádiz."

"Cádiz? I do not comprehend. You have been in Spain also, so you say?"

"El Greco, I have known," she said.

"But . . . and yet your husband, then, this other—?"

"I wished to be his bride, in truth. But he has outsoared the shadow of our night."

"Con permiso—" Apologetic, the friar extended a hand. "It is English, is it not, with which you would be more comfortable?"

"And she, too, who loved him, nevermore."

"She—?"

"My sister, perhaps. Or was she I? And yet I only am escaped alone to tell thee."

"My daughter, will you do something for me?"

"What might I do, Padre?"

"Your Spanish. Forgive me. And my failing as well, that I cannot use your own tongue. In the rectory is a brother who does speak it, however. Will you wait, that I might ask him to talk with you?"

"I come here often," she said.

"As I have seen—"

"Father? Is it possible that I might wear a cross? One such as yours?"

"You do not possess one? The crucifix?"

"No one ever gave me one, I do not think. But perhaps because it would not fit."

"Fit—?"

Glancing automatically at her withered wrist the friar stood discomforted. "And yet I sense him often, nonetheless," she said.

"Señorita—?"

"But as if in darkness always, where I must start at his touch. Or . . . how odd, can he be standing between me and the fire?"

"Ah, but sí, sí," the friar said. "For is that not where He stands eternally? For the salvation of us all?"

"Yet why cannot I even remember—?"

"Remember—?"

"Some holy candle's flame, perhaps, and one whose flesh was seared therein? An agony, in gardens—?"

"And would you like to be instructed in such things? Here? To commence with catechism itself?"

"Within the church? And with the infant Jesus watching, upon the high glass where the sun breaks through?"

"There are places set aside for study. And with many books."

"He, too, read many."

"Your father?"

"Adam—?"

"The Father of us all—?"

"And yet if I am she, who then is my—?"

"Dear child—?"

"Padre—?"

"Will you wait as I ask? These few moments only? And that peculiar odor, as well. To please me—?"

"Go, Father—"

Idly, then, she watched him climb, his palm upraised to stay her despite her compliance, and his cassock trailing, until he paused beneath the lanceted arch to smile reassuringly yet again before he disappeared. And then it was the women she confronted instead, when she turned, some dozen at least and many less old than she, but with infants shielded by their rebozos all. At once they were supplicant each. "Tomorrow," she told the nearest. "Forgive me, that I have forgotten today. You will be here tomorrow?"

"Might I do otherwise? My days are this."

"Vaya con Dios—"

Distantly, beyond sere palms, twin spires arose of yet another church that she looked to now, with a campanile, and against the raw, flawless sky above, flecks merely, upon dread wings vultures rode motionless, or drifted inland from the bay. Passing slowly, as if without direction, a man considered her momentarily, or her deformity perhaps, which out of old instinct she drew aside, and then studied her face also, the thin lines of broken veins evident upon his own in the glare, not Mexican, before contemplating the church in turn and then mounting to enter as had the other, the priest. At her back another beggar approached. "For the child, señorita? That suffers so?"

The infant lay inert, although at its cheek, amid woeful dishevelment, the woman's breast was bared to nurse.

"And how old is the young one, then?"

"One year, it has."

"Ah, and I know of one having but one week. And I listened for its cry, although it was lost to the winds below the hillside, perhaps—"

"Señorita—?"

"And thine? It is ill?"

"It does not see, alas. But view for thyself—"

Adjusting her cradled arm, and loosening her rebozo further, the woman drew her free hand across the child's face. Open, in appalling blankness the eyes did not follow.

"It is God's will," the woman said.

"Ah, but how sad, how sad. Can it not be medicined?"

"Who can say? With money doubtless all things are possible."

"Money—?"

"With infinite counters of silver, such as one may indulge a lifetime in dreaming of."

"Yet I have money—"

"Ah, señorita—?"

"Attend me. As from last night, when there was one and then another, and for which Paul said it was fifty pesos."

"I do not understand, señorita—?"

"And it is as nothing. As if to hear a fall of gentle rain, no more, or seeping sands. And sometimes, too, it is he that I remember."

"He—?"

"And he has salved many, as even the padre, now, has said is so."

"Which I have heard, and do in part believe it—"

"The poor child—"

"But the money, señorita? You would perform this thing that you know, and then would give of it? Truly?"

"Why, with diligence—"

Others were about them now, compelled by the golden

hair, perhaps, sedulously clustering. "And may I hold the child?" she said.

Possibly, then, it was she herself who noticed most immediately, where she had reached upward, although it was one of the others who cried out. Her hand fled back, it wavered. And then the mother had seen also.

"Name of God—?"

As if from incredulity, or in refutation, again she endeavored to take it. And yet again, undeniably, it occurred, at once the infant's eyes responded, they darted toward her.

"Mother of Our Lord—"

"Holy, holy, holy—"

"But—?"

Backward she stumbled. But the mother had sobbed, or moaned, in a kind of ecstasy, and yet another, snatching first at her sleeve, had abruptly whirled and was dashing up the gleaming steps. *"Father! Ah, Father, come—"*

Before her then, still others had flung themselves down, were clinging to her garments, while more backed off, they crossed themselves. Her hand, that hand, was at her lips, and baffled she turned and turned, as at the valuted entrance the friar finally reappeared, though it was another at whose robes the woman pulled.

"Señorita—?"

When she fled, in that heat, it was as if through a mist, or beneath some sea, and she lost footing more than once again, but did not fall, before she achieved the corner. Behind her one of the voices came in English now also:

"Miss! Miss! If you will kindly wait—"

"Mother of Jesus—"

"No more than when she lay hands upon—"

In the disreputable hallway, behind the door she had fortuitously found open, gasping, she heard them press past. She had cut her heel, although not severely, and when she touched it finally, and then paused to taste the warm blood upon her fingertips, she tasted the astringent turpentine also, even as the wound itself began to smart from it, and her eyes to tear. Then she would be occupied at the windows for some thirty minutes or more, though no longer weeping, before Paul would appear to find her squatting beneath them, which with the most opaque of her available pigments she had rendered as if permanently drawn down.

FOURTEEN

Behind a screening of brush, disconcerted, he hesitated, amid the tumbled wood crosses, the sunken mounds. Languishing and remote, the light that gave him pause may have been that of a solitary candle, deep within the ancient vault.

Nor had the quickened breath of his flight yet diminished when she too intruded, apparition-like, unreal, to gaze at first upon the light herself, the shadow of the huge, shattered cross where misshapen it flickered and fell. For some seconds an acute apprehension gripped him. To be here? Now? When so few moments before he had heard her in the very house, that interrogation from beyond the archway where at the cot he had spun with the blade still amok and streaming in his fist?

Yet his head was clear now, of tequila, of mescal, of rum, only the outrage filled it any longer. Her own machete would be easily wrested away. Perhaps he saw the blood that defined it, sensed it the same. Perhaps he finally sensed her distraction too, as her sarape fell aside, as she knelt pale and vulnerable there, and he arose.

Later, bitterly, again he would think it: Sí, as it should have been, initially his life, and then the partaking of his woman. So he would not even quite understand, as he sprang back, whether he had truly heard the other, the doctor, or whether some rare instinct had stayed him.

When they departed, the candle extinguished now and the doctor talking steadily, persuasively, as he led her out, after a period of debate he deposited his tequila and his tortillas within. Then, squatting at the outer wall from where he might flee in any of several directions, he brooded upon justice, upon dispensation, and the soul.

"Chingado, my compadre Huck," he muttered.

Then again he had to doubt that he had chosen with wit, since newly there was intrusion, although too, in an instant, he realized this to be upon the roadway only, peons in drunkenness, passing. "—Sadness," he heard. "And yet so gracious an hombre, to purchase the bottle for us—"

Still it was with caution, however, that he crept out in reconnaissance.

"Emiliano? You will not sleep? When disgracefully we have been so tardy in these few meters from the zócalo alone—?"

From behind the dismantled gate in dappled moonlight he discerned them, at the road's farther side, one who stood swaying, sombrero in hand, the other who upon a small hillock lay prone.

"Emiliano? And the burro, its burden—?"

The beast, too, he perceived then, cresting a rise in the near distance where, a sack upon its back, it plodded inexorably onward. Beside the other the second peon now sat also, and drank.

"Emiliano?" the man repeated. He thumped the other upon the shoulder. "Walk, then, burro," he called.

When the man lay back himself, his head cushioned at the other's hip and the sombrero slanted across his face, Manolo at last stepped fully into the moonlight, the road.

In the pocket of his shirt he possessed the inconceivable, the unimaginable total, of seven hundred and seventy pesos, that currency snatched from the hands of the tía of Petra. Three times, even in flight, he had paused disbelieving to certify the amount. And yet in the house of the gringa, the Señora Tinkle, somewhere remained the confession, the debt of six hundred. Nor, even should there develop no subsequent harassment from this thing of the vengeance, would it of some ingenious dreaming miraculously disappear.

Inevitably then, though with rather more sagacity than he had demonstrated at such pursuits but an hour or two earlier, Manolo commandeered both beast and its burden, by following at a considerable remove merely, as undeviatingly along the unpaved road the animal paced a familiar passage about the lake, toward Chignahuapán and the nameless villages beyond.

It was perhaps an hour after dawn when, its halter for the first time in hand, he led it to the stall of the seller of beef in a dusty hillside marketplace. "A side, I believe," he announced. "I am disposing of it for a friend. And the burro, likewise—"

Beside him, women awaited their turn, and from behind the makeshift kiosk in khaki a policeman emerged, yawning, though Manolo no more than licked his lips at his appearance. "Aid me, eh?" the butcher requested.

Scratching himself, the officer looked on drowsily, although it was he, surprisingly, when it commenced to slip once the merchant had unloosed it, and then to fall, who bounded forward to ease the carcass to the ground. Then he stared, insipidly, once it thudded down despite his efforts, to lie between them sheeted still, save for the portion that had come away in his hands. Manolo stared also, even as the butcher at last spoke, and quite rationally too, as if at some commonest of misconceptions. "And am I expected to carve delicacies of a human leg, hombre?" he asked. By then Manolo was running, however.

Absolutely, irrefutably, categorically, he had resolved to set aside a sum sufficient to repay the gringa. By all the saints, he had. By those same saints he had scarcely anticipated the drunkenness of the ensuing days either, in Chignahuapán or elsewhere. Had he been in Toluca as well? Perhaps he had been in Toluca.

Even time, the calendar, became ultimately evasive, so that only this at the end was incontrovertible: that he had been back in Mictlán some few moments at most, when not steps from the inviting asylum of the cantina "Imposibilidad" the dismally ubiquitous vehicle of Curro Huerta braked sharply beside him. With lidded eyes, implacable, though speculative, the jefe scowled. Manolo sighed.

"Of the pots and pans?"

The jefe nodded, reaching to unlatch the nearer rear door. "The warrant exists," he said. "It will be six months, more or less."

Yet extraordinarily then, once Manolo had entered, across his shoulder for a long moment the jefe stared and stared.

"My chieftain?" Manolo said.

"Of the pots and pans. And we have nothing additional to discuss?"

"My jefe?" Manolo said again.

In bafflement and consternation for several days he paced ceaselessly, about that vast walled enclosure, and took to muttering to himself also, at what he was able to put together of it from the talk of the other prisoners.

"But killed himself?" he said. "The night thereafter?"

Yet he would not speak of it to Petra, when she appeared on the first of the appointed days for visiting. Still displaying evidences of her beating, she brought food, and a curtain to be hung in domesticity at some corner beneath the eaves as well. He beat her again, soundlessly, behind it, not really hard, perhaps believing he knew why. On her next visit he did the same. After that he stopped.

She did not mention the child, which he presumed with her aunt on such occasions. She had been to the house on the hill one final time, as it occurred, at the request of the Señor Talltrees who was to seek tenants as in the past, in behalf of the long departed Señor Roderick. From the belongings of the deceased sundry had been presented her, although only one object did she make use of, which, remarkably, she had never before noticed, discovering it upon the hearth when she cleaned, and not so severely charred that it might not be salvaged for the infant. The remaining Manolo would vend at the market of thieves when he was able.

Then one day Manolo informed her that it was chilly in the nights, and she brought him one of the garments from the residue after all, a jacket of the rich that had been worn by the other. "If needed, I can stitch it to fit more approximately," she said.

"It will be adequate for sleeping," he told her. In harsh sunlight they were seated at a wall, and from an inner pocket, incuriously, she withdrew something flimsy, a notebook of the kind possessed by children at school. There was writing, in pencil, on many of the pages. "Ah, that also can I utilize," Manolo said. "Never is there sufficient, for when one excuses himself."

"Sí. I had meant to bring you some leaves," Petra said, offering it across.

Printed in the United States
by Baker & Taylor Publisher Services